Love for Beginners

ALSO BY JILL SHALVIS

Wildstone Novels

Mistletoe in Paradise (novella)

The Forever Girl

The Summer Deal

Almost Just Friends

The Lemon Sisters

Rainy Day Friends

The Good Luck Sister (novella)

Lost and Found Sisters

Heartbreaker Bay Novels

Wrapped Up in You

Playing for Keeps

Hot Winter Nights

About That Kiss

Chasing Christmas Eve

Accidentally on Purpose

The Trouble with Mistletoe

Sweet Little Lies

Lucky Harbor Novels

One in a Million

He's So Fine

It's in His Kiss

Once in a Lifetime

Always on My Mind

It Had to Be You

Forever and a Day

At Last

Lucky in Love

Head Over Heels

The Sweetest Thing

Simply Irresistible

Animal Magnetism Novels

Still the One

All I Want

Then Came You

Rumor Has It

Rescue My Heart

Animal Attraction

Animal Magnetism

Love
for
Beginners

A Novel

Jill Shalvis

HARPER LARGE PRINT

An Imprint of HarperCollinsPublishers

HarperCollins books may be purchased for educational, business, or sales promotional use. For information, please e-mail the Special Markets Department at SPsales@harpercollins.com.

FIRST HARPER LARGE PRINT EDITION

ISBN: 978-0-06-309039-2

Library of Congress Cataloging-in-Publication Data is available upon request.

21 22 23 24 25 LSC 10 9 8 7 6 5 4 3 2 1

I wrote this book in the early days of quarantining for COVID. My house had swelled to hold all nine members of my immediate family. Remember those days? The logistics of feeding that many people three meals a day, plus keeping enough toilet paper in the house, was a huge challenge. BUT . . . while I anticipated it being a really hard time, it somehow turned into the opposite. We hung out together as a family for the first time in years. We played games and cards until late into the night. We reconnected. Looking back, as hard as the times were (and they WERE hard, some of us lost jobs and other things, I don't want to minimize that), it was also one of my favorite times as a family. So . . . to family, both blood and the kind you make.

Love for Beginners

Chapter 1

Step 1: Get over yourself, the fear is all in your head.

A live was better than dead.

Or so the rumor went. But damn, Emma hurt from head to toe. Even her hair hurt. But the funny thing about spending two months in a coma and then the rest of the year in a rehab facility reacquainting herself with where her limbs lived was that it'd given her some hard-earned perspective.

Yes, she felt like ninety instead of thirty. And yes, half the time her left arm thought it was a useless club that hung from her shoulder. Not to mention the rest of her body pretending it didn't have to listen to her brain.

Alive was still better than dead.

Her physical therapist had taught her that mantra. The man was diabolical with what he'd put her body through. She'd lost track of how many meltdowns she'd had on his table. He'd been extraordinarily kind, taking each one in stride with a sympathetic but steady professional touch, patiently waiting her out, letting her calm down before going at her again—which he always did. But she hadn't privately nicknamed him Hard-Ass PT because of his hard ass. Okay, so he had a hard—and fantastic—ass, but he didn't know the meaning of Give Up. Emma couldn't argue with his results, though. She was now doing things the doctors said she'd *never* do. Like walk.

But she still hated him with a passion of a thousand suns.

And yet, turned out there was something she hated even more. *Stairs.* "Seven," she said out loud, teeth gritted, jaw locked. "Eight . . ." The exhaustion was insidious, running in her veins instead of blood, but the stairs were part of her penance for surviving the accident, when not everyone had. "Nine." She gasped for air. "Ten."

There were fourteen in total, so silver lining—she was in the home stretch. Each step brought her closer to adulting on her own for the first time in a year. A year of having everything she did, every single thing, supervised.

"Ten."

"You already said ten, hon," her ex-BFF, Cindy, said in a very gentle voice, the kind that insinuated Emma was a child. "Which makes it eleven. *E-lev-en . . .*" she repeated slowly.

Emma sent her a long look. Yes, sometimes her brain and mouth couldn't find each other and she got her words mixed up. The docs had said it was normal. BC—Before Coma—she'd been a runner and a PE teacher, and because she loved dogs more than people on most days, also a dog trainer. Having grown up here in the small adventurous town of Wildstone, a mid-California coastal spot marked by gorgeous green rolling hills dotted with ancient old oak trees, her whole existence had been defined by activity. But she'd lost the ability to do anything she'd done before.

She had no idea who she was now.

"Should you really be taking the stairs?" Cindy again, sounding genuinely worried.

"Yes." Because Emma refused to go back to their old apartment. She swiped the sweat out of her eyes. Hard to believe that she used to run 5Ks for fun.

"Careful. You're really pale." This not helpful statement came from her other side—Ned, her ex-fiancé.

Emma took another step. *Twelve.*

"Emma." Ned put a hand to her elbow. "You shouldn't be moving out so soon after getting out of the rehab facility. It's only been a few days."

Emma had gone from the hospital to the rehab center to the apartment she and Cindy had shared for four years, the one that Ned now lived in, so she *literally* hadn't been alone in a year. At the moment, she was holding on by a bare, ragged thread. So it took every ounce of control she had not to throw Ned's hand off. "I'm doing this."

A soft whine came from just behind her, and then a cool, wet dog nose nudged into her palm. Hog was her emotional support dog, because yeah, that was a thing for her now. After one too many nightmares in rehab, one of her occupational therapists had given her a two-year-old 110-pound St. Bernard/Chewbacca mix. Historically, the breed had been used to help find and save travelers. The gentle giants were calm, patient, relaxed, and sensible.

Hog's job was to watch out for Emma's emotional well-being and protect her as needed, but as it turned out, he was named Hog—short for Groundhog—for a very good reason. He'd flunked out of service dog school for being afraid of his own shadow. Didn't matter to Emma. He drooled, he ate anything not tied down, and he had gas that would kill an elephant. She loved him ridiculously anyway, even if, as it turned out, *she* was *his* emotional support. "Good boy."

He licked her hand.

"This is ridiculous," Ned said. "Just come back to our place. I'll even stop complaining about Hog's . . . intestinal issues. It's not necessary for you to move out, Emmie."

Oh but it was. Deathly necessary. And not her death, but his. And possibly Cindy's too. "Hog only has gas issues because you make him anxious."

Ned looked at Cindy. "Tell her. Tell her she shouldn't leave."

"She shouldn't leave." Cindy's eyes were filled with what seemed like genuine guilt and remorse as she looked at Emma. "Roomies forever, remember?"

More than most, Emma understood how guilt and remorse could screw a person up. She was living proof. But Cindy had been her best friend for *twenty* years, right up until Emma had been hit by a car, punted fifty feet straight into a coma.

Then, later, at some point sitting in the hospital waiting room, Ned and Cindy had decided that it'd be a good idea to sleep together. Granted, they'd been told Emma's chances of survival weren't good, but she'd proved the doctors wrong.

Her mom said it was because she was too stubborn to die. Undoubtedly accurate.

In either case, apparently Ned and Cindy's relationship had only strengthened while Emma had spent the rest of the year in the rehab facility. And now, a year later, the two of them were still going strong. In fact, Ned had moved into Cindy's bed—in the apartment Emma and Cindy had shared for years. Romantic, right?

"And our place has an elevator," Cindy said.

Like Emma didn't know this. She might be foggy on a lot of things—her memory was still shoddy at best— but she remembered the basics of her life. Well, mostly. And yeah, an elevator right about now would be even better than the nap she desperately wanted. But she'd live in hell before going back to her old apartment. Actually, scratch that. After losing her fiancé, her best friend, her jobs, she was *already* in hell.

It wasn't that she was heartbroken anymore. Months ago she'd come to terms with the fact that Ned and Cindy had done her a favor. And maybe she'd forgive them someday, but forget? Doubtful.

Clearly Ned hadn't been the right one for her, and honestly, she could no longer remember why she'd ever thought he was. But Cindy . . . that hurt. "Let me save you some time," she said. "I appreciate the help these past two weeks after I was finally sprung from the rehab facility. But there's no way I'm going to keep staying where my ex-fiancé and ex-BFF are sleeping together. Loudly, by the way. You guys do realize how thin the walls are, right?"

Cindy smacked Ned in the gut and glared at him. "Oh my God, I told you!"

Emma tackled another step. *Thirteen.* Hog was right with her, panting hotly on the backs of her legs. "You think I want to know that Cindy howls like a banshee, or that you do her up against a wall?" She whipped around and glared at Ned. "And you do remember telling me you couldn't do it that way because it hurt your back, right?"

He opened his mouth, but Emma turned away, staggering up the last step, breathing like a lunatic. The good news was that she'd done it. The bad news was that she'd just come face-to-face with a man leaning against the wall, feet casually crossed, a set of keys in his hand.

She might've yelped in surprise, but frankly, she was too tired. Besides, she knew him. All six feet of lean muscles and unruly hair the color of a doe's fur, which, was to say, every color under the sun: all shades of brown, mahogany, even some red and blond. Clearly only finger tousled, like he didn't have time to be bothered.

Hard-Ass PT, aka Simon Armstrong.

Why did she know exactly how many strands were blond and red and brown? They'd spent *hundreds* of hours together over the past year. In each other's space, his hands on her body. For most of those hours, she'd been in so much pain she doubted he'd ever noticed her spiked heart rate for what it was.

A reluctant reawakening of her body.

Not that he'd given her any indication of a return interest. Nope, he'd been nothing but professional. She was good at reading people, but Simon had a poker face she'd kill for—not to mention dark lashes over eyes that were as hard to name as the color of his hair. Greens and browns and golds swirled together in what was technically hazel, but seemed too tame of a word. Those see-all eyes of his could express a wide gamut of emotions from a quiet patience to an intensity that burned. At the moment, though, he seemed amused as he stood there, clearly having heard the conversation coming up the stairs.

"Sounds like you three need a moment," he said.

The old Emma would've died of embarrassment. But Emma 2.0 didn't do embarrassment. She no longer gave a shit what people thought. Or so she reminded herself as she lifted her chin. Pride before the fall and all that.

The exes squared came up behind her with their faux worry. Or maybe it was real worry. That was the beauty of her new attitude—she didn't care.

"How did you find this place anyway?" Ned asked, not yet seeing Simon. "Thought you couldn't find an apartment anywhere in Wildstone that would take you with your yearlong income lapse."

"I got lucky." It'd been much more than luck. Simon had told her about the available apartment and said that he could help facilitate her approval. Which meant he wasn't all hard-ass . . .

She'd gratefully jumped on it.

The building had once been a single Victorian home, but being in such close proximity to the beach had made it crazy valuable. Somewhere in the 1950s it'd been separated into four apartments, two up, two down. Emma was moving into apartment 2A, because unfortunately, nothing had been available on the bottom floor. It didn't matter, she was beyond grateful for it because, as it turned out, Ned was right—nobody wanted to rent to a woman with no current source of income other than a few part-time hours at Paw Pals, the local doggy day care where she gave dog training classes.

Luckily, she'd received an insurance settlement from the accident, which she'd vowed not to touch unless it was for a life-changing reason, but in the end, she'd decided not having a roof over her head was a life-changing reason, so she'd used some of it to pay first and last and security deposit on this place.

Simon smiled at Hog. "Hey, big guy."

Hog was afraid of most men. Emma had tried to get his history, but it was sketchy at best. Her guess was that he'd been abused, most likely by a male. Now there was only one man Hog automatically melted for, and that was Simon.

Emma understood the melting on a core level, though after all these months she was so good at ignoring it that Simon had never even noticed.

He didn't notice now either as he crouched to Hog's level. Her big doofus of a dog let his legs slide out from beneath him, hitting the floor, making the foundation shake like an earthquake.

Simon just laughed and used both hands to rub up and down Hog's belly, promptly melting him into a puddle of goo. Emma understood that too. Those big, warm hands of Simon's had melted her too, plenty of times. Not that he'd noticed that either. Which was when she realized what felt weird—she'd never seen him outside of a PT session, or in anything other than what she considered his PT uniform of a form-fitted performance long-sleeved T-shirt and basketball shorts or sweats. Today he was in Levi's with a hole across one knee, an army-green Henley, and battered sneakers. He had a few days of scruff going and she could see a few tats sticking out from where he had his sleeves shoved up to his elbows.

He looked . . . real.

And disarmingly handsome, which wasn't good. He had a way of making her feel things she had no business feeling—not for her PT and not for men in general. All it did was make her want something she couldn't have, leaving her with one more ache in her body she didn't need.

Simon was still loving up on Hog, clearly clueless to her thoughts. After all, theirs was a strictly professional relationship, even if after all these months they also felt like friends. Which they weren't, because she wasn't on the friend train. Or any train that involved a relationship thanks to a myriad of reasons like her cheating ex, the accident . . . her physical limitations.

Ned eyed Simon carefully before turning to Emma. "You're dating already?"

She nearly laughed. Dating? She was barely breathing. And besides, as already noted, she wasn't on the relationship train, thank you very much. "No longer your concern," she said. "Simon, this is Ted."

"*Ned,*" her ex corrected.

Emma shrugged and pointed at her head, like *sorry, coma* . . .

Simon rose to his full height and smiled at her, clearly enjoying her using her temporary disability to her benefit. Ignoring the very slight flutter in her belly at the unexpected smile—*very slight!*—she rolled her eyes.

Ned held a hand out to Simon. "I'm Emma's fiancé."

"*Ex*-fiancé," Cindy said very quietly, without a single hint of how she felt about the slip, Freudian or otherwise. "And I'm Cindy, Emma's best friend."

"Also an ex," Emma said.

Cindy winced.

Emma reached out for the keys, belatedly realizing her fingers were trembling from getting up the stairs on her own steam.

Simon looked at those fingers, then into her eyes and . . . didn't hand over the keys.

And here was the thing. He was perceptive. Too perceptive. She turned away.

"I don't see you being able to handle those stairs every single day," Ned said. "It's too much for you."

"Agreed." Cindy nodded. "You should come back home, Emmie."

That place was no more home to her now than the hospital or rehab had been. And if one more person called her "Emmie" she was going to lose it entirely. She turned again and found Simon watching her, amusement gone. "You okay?"

At his question, Ned looked at her and frowned. "You really are pale, Emmie. *Are* you okay?"

"Great, actually," Emma said. "Think you guys could go down to Ned's car and unload my boxes while I finish up the paperwork?"

Simon lifted a brow. He knew there was no further paperwork, but thankfully he didn't contradict her, and her exes squared went back down the stairs.

Hog lumbered to his paws and shook. Fur flew around him like a halo. So did drool. Both were all over Simon's jeans. She knew he'd told her that Hog wouldn't be a problem, but . . . "I'm sorry. He doesn't usually shed so badly."

"Another fib." Simon sounded amused again as he brushed Hog's fur from his jeans. "Don't worry, four-legged fur babies are always welcome here. Even the giant ones."

Emma let out a relieved breath. "Appreciate that. I *really* needed to get out of my old place."

"I can see that. Nice one on calling him the wrong name on purpose."

She grimaced.

"Hey, I'm all for self-preservation," he said.

Grateful for Simon's nonjudgment, Emma leaned on the wall for support. "Damn. I hate that I'm still breathing as if I just ran a 5K, like I did BC."

He smiled because he knew all about "BC." She'd told him lots of things about her life Before Coma during their PT torture sessions. "So . . . the key?"

He inserted it into the lock for her and opened the door. "Do you need help with your boxes?"

"Nope, I've got it. Or rather the exes squared got it. There's no way they're going to leave me in peace until I'm settled. Or dead. Whichever comes second."

His mouth curved slightly. "Nice to see your attitude is the same in or out of PT."

"Don't you mean my *bad* attitude?"

That bought her a smile, but he was smart enough not to comment. "I'll leave you to it then, if that's what you really want."

"It is." Hog pushed the top of his head against Emma's palm again with a soft whine. Comforted by the touch, she leaned into him.

"Emma. You sure?"

Hell no. She wasn't sure about anything. But the old Emma had lived to please others. Emma 2.0 didn't want to do that. She was making changes. Up until now, her life had been about perceptions and keeping up with the Joneses. She'd worked several jobs, none of them paying well, but all of them adding to the image of a young woman at the top of her game: fit, able, and social media worthy.

But at the end of the day, when she'd been out of sight for a year, it hadn't mattered, and every one of her wide circle of friends and acquaintances was gone.

Or boinking each other.

She'd been given a reset, a second chance that she'd crawled out of hell for, and she was going to do things right this time.

Simon was still waiting calmly for her to respond. She already knew he had patience in spades. He was gentle steel, always pushing her to the very ends of her endurance and beyond, waiting as long as it took for her to get it back together—which she always did. He'd proved that to her time and time again. He knew her limits better than she did. Resistance was futile.

"I'm sure," Emma said. "I've only got the four boxes anyway, and one of them is a case of Girl Scout cookies."

His approval of her toughness was in his smile. "I'm right downstairs if you change your mind." He turned to the stairs and her gaze slid down his body. She might be off relationships, all of them, but she wasn't dead. Good to know. "Wait. Why are you going to be downstairs?"

"Taking care of my dad, who lives in 1A. I had to move in with him for a bit after his strokes."

"Right." He'd told her this already. "Sorry."

"Don't be. I forget shit all the time and I have no excuse."

Emma shook her head. "You forget nothing, including exactly how many reps I'm supposed to do, even when I try to cheat."

Simon shrugged. "I was born with a cheat radar."

She wished she'd been born with a cheat radar. That would have been handy before getting involved with Ned for nearly a year. "Thanks for getting me into this apartment."

"Happy to help."

Oh, how she hated to be helped, and given that he just laughed softly at the look on her face, he knew it too. When he left, she blew out a sigh. Simon *thought* he understood, but he didn't. Couldn't. No one could. After all she'd been through, after watching her parents give up a year of their lives to sit at her bedside and worry, her biggest fear now was to be a burden. To that end, she'd just last month finally gotten her parents to fly back to Florida, where they'd retired right after Emma had graduated from high school. A dream come true for them.

Not for her. She'd been to Florida to visit. She wasn't a fan of the heat, the humidity, or the flatness of the landscape. Nope, she was a California girl through and through. Once upon a time, Emma's biggest dream had been to run a half marathon. That seemed like a lifetime ago now.

Her new plan? She had no clue, other than it had to be bigger than her old one. Maybe it should be to appreciate surviving, learning to live her life to the fullest.

She stepped into her new apartment. Other than the pics Simon had on his phone, she'd signed the lease place unseen, so she was relieved to find it was even roomier than she'd thought. The kitchen, living room, and bedroom were filled with nooks and crannies typical of an old Victorian. It was furnished, which was a bonus because she hadn't wanted anything from her previous life. Comfy-looking leather couch and chair, a huge TV, an oak table and chairs, and a king-size bed with navy-and-white bedding that looked so inviting she almost crawled into it on the spot. All of it looked well loved and well lived in, and Emma sent a silent thank-you to whoever had furnished the place. It was clean, definitely masculine, but also warm and cozy. It felt . . . perfect.

Shutting the door behind her and Hog, she was immediately drawn to the big picture window and the view of the Pacific Ocean. Turquoise water, dotted with whitecaps and sailboats, stole her breath.

Still sweating and trembly, Emma made it to the couch, collapsing onto the cushions. Hog plopped heavily to the floor at her feet, both of them thrilled with the glorious view but even more glorious silence. Some of her tension started to drain away.

Until someone knocked on her door.

Hog jumped up and hid behind the couch.

"It's open," Emma said wearily to the exes squared, wishing she could hide behind the couch too.

The door opened, but it wasn't the exes squared. It was two high-school-aged boys, both tall, gangling, and clearly twins, wearing matching T-shirts that said RJ MOWING SERVICE.

And they were carrying her entire life in four boxes.

Hog peeked out from behind the couch, his hangdog face creased in worry.

Emma managed to sit up. "Um, hi?"

"Hi," one of them said. "We take care of the yard of this property. I'm R." He jabbed a thumb at the other kid. "He's J. Simon gave us twenty bucks to carry these boxes up here for you. Uh . . . is that a bear behind the couch?"

"Nope, just an anxious dog named Hog. What do R and J stand for?"

"Robert," the first kid said, patting his chest with his hand. He pointed at his twin. "Jeremy. We hate our names so we go by R and J."

Jeremy nodded, but didn't speak.

They were so identical it was almost spooky, but then Emma realized that while R had two green eyes, J had one light brown, one green. He nudged R, whispering something in his brother's ear.

R nodded. "Right." He looked at Emma. "So does Hog eat people? Cuz he's drooling like maybe he needs lunch."

They all eyed Hog. The classic-looking St. Bernard was massive, heavy, and potentially powerful, with a thick furry coat. Emma could see how he'd been mistaken for a bear because only his huge head was peeking out from behind the couch. He was panting slightly, his big milk chocolate eyes filled with deep concern.

"He eats everything *but* people," Emma said fondly. "Also, he's a very large scaredy-cat. I'm . . . kind of his emotional support person." Then she said to Hog, "It's okay. They're friendlies."

Hog, always good-natured even when scared, gave a tentative wag of his tail and came out, waiting to receive all the love. Both guys were happy to give him what he wanted. In two seconds, Hog was on his back again, tongue lolling in happiness while he received all the pets.

"What happened to the couple who was supposed to carry my boxes up?" Emma asked.

"Simon told them we had this," R said. "And that they should go because the sprinklers were going to come on and ruin the new wash job on their Lexus. The guy said he could move the car and park on the street instead, but Simon said the street cleaners would be coming through soon so it was best if they just left. The woman had to talk the guy into it."

Not sure how she felt about Simon being her own personal superhero for the day, Emma searched her pockets, hoping she had some money to tip the teens. "Thanks so much for the assist. I really appreciate it." She went to stand up. "Let me just find my wallet—"

"Simon told us if we took a tip from you, he'd fire us," R said.

And then they were gone, and she was blessedly alone. If she could've done a happy dance, she would've. Instead, she settled for flopping onto the couch again. She was on her own. *Yay!* She looked around and her smile faded some.

Alone meant she didn't have anyone to open a jar when her shaky fingers couldn't grasp it tight enough. No one to sit on the bathroom counter while she showered to make sure if she fell, she had a quick rescue.

No one to be there when she woke up from the nightmares of being back in the coma, trapped in her own mind.

As if he sensed her worry, Hog joined Emma and they both tried to watch the beautiful scenery, the water, the puffy clouds lazily crossing a bright sky . . . but they promptly caved to the exhaustion and took a nap. And for those few hours, Hog wasn't the only drooler.

Chapter 2

Step 2: Listen.

B eing in a coma was a funny thing. One minute you were jogging and singing along to Pink in your headphones as you hopped off the curb to cross the street, and in the next beat you were . . . nowhere, just floating somewhere above reality, but below the after-life.

For Emma, it'd been like sinking underwater, terri-fied and unable to move, not even to open her eyes, at the complete mercy of the tide. She could hear things going on around her, all of it warped, as if going through a filter.

Later she'd learned that had been the heavy drugs they'd had her on, but at the time, all she'd known was that she couldn't open her eyes or move as real life went on around her. The snippets of conversations she'd caught had come to life vividly behind her eyelids, like dreams.

She could still remember two women talking about one of them hooking up in a supply closet with an ER doc the night before. She'd gotten pregnant and had given birth to a litter of healthy puppies. Ten of them.

Obviously she'd been given *really* good drugs.

She'd heard Ned and Cindy talking quietly to themselves about a cruise to the moon.

Her parents promising her that if she would only wake up, they'd help her learn to fly.

Then two more female voices; one of them had just broken up with her boyfriend who was on fire, racing through flames, carrying his dad on his back everywhere he went. She'd dumped him for leaving her behind.

Emma had to laugh at those dreams or she'd get anxious again, the kind of anxiousness she'd suffered during her coma, where she'd felt like she was drowning but couldn't wake up and get out of the deep water.

She'd never been a fan of swimming, especially in the often rough and choppy water off the coast, but being stuck in her own mind in the ocean had been hell.

Later she'd found out that after a postsurgery infection and a dangerously high fever, and then a subsequent seizure, they'd put ice packs all around her. Which demystified the horrifying dreams about trying to swim in the ocean but feeling too weighed down to move.

It'd demystified everything, because postcoma, she'd realized that everything she'd overheard had some level of truth to it.

The worst part of all of it had been the insidious pain.

Not surprisingly, it'd been Simon, during those first PT sessions, who told her something that had stuck with her.

They'd been in Emma's hospital room, her still hooked up to all sorts of things, weeks before she'd been released to the rehab facility. The lights had been on low because she'd had a migraine, probably brought on by the pain and her inability to manage it effectively.

The anticipation of pain is worse than the pain itself, he'd told her, a lean hip perched on the edge of her bed as he worked the muscles in her left leg. *Close your eyes.*

She'd spent way too much time with her eyes closed, but there'd been something so compelling in the gentle steel of his demand that she had done what he said.

Now go to another place. A happy place.

She had strained to remember one. But she was practically humming with anxiety. No job, no prospects.

Her left arm had seceded from the United States of Emma. And yet none of that was first in line. She didn't need a shrink to tell her what *was* first in line, what her constant low level of anxiety *really* came from. She'd always known the root of it.

Survivor's guilt.

Go to your happy place, Emma. She smiled now because she could still hear Simon speak to her as he had that day, clear as a bell, like he was right there with her.

Where's your happy place today? Dream Simon asked.

Same as always. *Avila Beach.* Where the bright sand and the pretty ocean melded together like heaven on earth. It took her a minute, but finally she could hear the water lapping against the beach. Birds squawking at each other. The salty scent of the ocean air all around them, a warm breeze on her face. She was on the warm sand with the heated, hard body of a man lying with her, spreading sunscreen over every inch of her body . . .

Wow. Okay, so this really was a happy place today, and she smiled, liking Dream Simon a whole lot. She hadn't dreamed of or yearned for physical intimacy in . . . a long time. She'd actually thought that part of her womanhood might be lost to her forever—

"Turn onto your belly," came Dream Simon's low, gruff command.

Mmm. She liked his sex-on-a-stick voice.

"Emma."

Her eyes flew open. Not Dream Simon.

Real Simon.

She wasn't at the beach. She was at physical therapy, and she'd dozed off.

"Turn over," Not Dream Simon said.

"'K, but I usually get dinner first . . ."

"Funny." He nudged her over with his big, strong, warm hands and she had to swallow her moan.

"Am I hurting you?"

"No." She squeezed her eyes shut and buried her head in the crook of her right arm, wondering if her ears were on fire.

Or if he could read minds.

No. If he could, he'd be running for the hills. The man was hot, but he'd never, not once, given her a hint of having any lust for her bod.

Just as well. Her mind might be suddenly ready for a physical relationship, but her body didn't exactly seem ready for prime time. A mental inventory proved that to be true: aching limbs, aching ribs and back. Aching *everything*. Which made it official. *Still not ready.*

Well, except for maybe her traitorous nipples . . .

"Lift up."

She snorted a little to herself because now everything in this session was going to sound dirty to her. But she knew what he wanted, and unfortunately it wasn't dirty at all.

"Emma."

"Right." She took a deep and shaky breath because damn, he was particularly evil today. She held her arms straight out in front of her and her legs behind her and arched her back. Theoretically, every part of her should lift off the table, except her belly and hips. It was a good stretch for an able-bodied person, which she wasn't. Her left arm raised about an inch, before dropping heavily back to the table.

"Again."

She could feel a fine sheen of perspiration on her skin and her every muscle trembled with effort—

"Hey." Simon bent and put his face level with hers. "You with me?"

Yep. Yep, she'd just been with him. On a beach. Naked . . . Which was incredibly eye-opening for her as her lady bits twitched for the first time in a year. Not trusting her voice, she nodded up into those hazel eyes. Green and light brown swirled, surrounded by a ring of milk chocolate brown. Mesmerizing.

"Where did you go?" He'd taken his hands off her. "You okay?"

"Nowhere," she said quickly. "I'm good."

"So you can do it again then."

Damn. And note to self: *never* tell Hard-Ass PT you're good.

"Or," she said, "we could go have one of the juices you guys sell out front."

"After. This first."

Damn. "So where's your *happy* place?"

Simon arched his brows.

"Come on," Emma said coaxingly. "I know you must have one."

"Oh, I do." He smiled. "It's just under lock and key."

She put her hand on her left calf, rubbing it before it could cramp. "Seriously? You're not going to share?"

"Not right now. Right now we're concentrating on your recovery."

"I'm recovered enough."

He nudged her hand away from her calf and began to knead it for her. "'Enough' isn't the same as your long-term goal of working your way back up to a 5K."

"That was BC."

"Stretch your legs like I showed you." He waited for her to start doing that before speaking. "So your standards have changed then?"

"Well, yeah. Life changed."

"Emma." His voice was quiet, concerned. "Doesn't have to be that way. You can get back there."

She looked away, not sure how to tell him she no longer coveted her old life. Problem was, she didn't know what her new life looked like. "Maybe I don't need to be the same as before."

He was quiet a moment, watching her stretch the way he wanted, occasionally adjusting her posture to suit himself. "Here," he said.

"What?"

"My happy place is here. Helping people."

That gave her a warm fuzzy, something she didn't often feel here in the torture chamber. "Thanks," she whispered.

He nodded and she kept working. Sweating. And occasionally swearing. "It never gets easier," she gasped.

He was quiet a moment. "We've been working this program, facilitating your healing, rebuilding muscle mass for months and you've come so far. But there's still a lot of work ahead."

She blew out a breath, not sure she was up for it. "Awesome."

Ignoring her sarcasm, he adjusted her again. His hands warm and firm, pressing her into place, holding her there a beat, signaling how he wanted her.

"What work?" she finally caved and asked.

"We've been working on your body, but not your spirit."

"Not your job," she managed, breathless from holding the position. And maybe a little bit from having his hands on her.

"It is my job, Emma. And I'm good at it. When you let me be."

She couldn't see his face. Probably for the best. "What's that supposed to mean?"

"You already know."

She flopped over onto her back to look up at him. "Humor me."

"It's whatever's in your head telling you that you don't deserve to be all the way healed."

Their gazes locked and her heart started pounding. "Why would I feel that way?"

"Because you lived. When someone else didn't."

Her throat closed. Just shut off both her air and her ability to speak. She sat up, curled her legs beneath her, and dropped her head to the tops of her knees. How did he know? Was she that transparent?

"Emma." Simon gentled his voice. "I know how much you loved running. And I know what the doctors told you about not expecting to ever get that back. But I've told you that I believe otherwise. I *still* believe it."

She lifted her head. "You do?"

"Yes. You've been working on the weight machine. You've even been on the treadmill—"

"At a crawl."

"Which is faster than you were last month. You've been climbing stairs to get in and out of your apartment the past few days. It's all working. I'll have to check with your doctor, but we can try pushing harder now that you're weight bearing. How does that sound?"

She chewed on her lower lip, not sure. "I don't know."

He studied her for a moment. "You do realize you're in the driver's seat here, right? No one can dictate the path of your life except you."

"Not true. A car dictated my life. Detonated it, actually."

His eyes went very serious. "Yeah, okay, and that was bad. But you're standing on your own two legs. You're doing better every day."

Maybe. Emma slipped off the table, winced at her aches, and made her way to the mats in front of the windows with a beautiful view of the water in its glorious summer glory. She sat down, exhausted and distressed over how quickly she tired. She looked down at her body, which she sometimes didn't recognize. Once, she'd been all lean, toned muscles. Now there was no tone, no muscles. "It's hard." Fighting for every inch of mobility all the time. Fighting through the brain fog. Dealing with her new reality.

Simon dropped to his knees at her side. "Life is hard."

He wasn't going to let her feel sorry for herself. Which, she supposed, she should be grateful for. She thought about apologizing for her bad attitude, but knew he didn't want an apology. He wanted her to try harder, to get full recovery.

"What's wrong?" he asked. "You're off today."

She shrugged, but he knew her. He understood her. Which currently made him the only one in her life who did. "I'm . . . feeling things," she admitted.

"Pain?"

"No."

His eyes held hers and she had the feeling that maybe he *could* read her mind, which was a bit horrifying, so she closed hers.

"Emma—"

"We about done here?" she asked.

"Nope." He pointed to . . . She sighed. The lat pull-down machine.

"Goodie."

He smiled but didn't back down. He did adjust it to no resistance. Just movement for today. She'd take it. She watched him counting her lifts. He was right.

She'd gained strength, more and more each day. Her body had been wasting away when he'd come into her life. She was still limited by internal healing and her own mental health, but she really was doing better.

"It's Friday," he said. "I imagine you've got somewhere to get to."

Did Netflix count? "Sure," she said instead of admitting her social life meant sharing a bowl of popcorn with Hog. "You?"

Kelly, the owner of the rehab facility, had just walked into the room and laughed. "Simon the workaholic? Doubtful."

"There's nothing wrong with working hard," Simon said.

"Even when it gets you dumped by your last girlfriend because your life's too crazy for a relationship?"

The two of them exchanged a long look, then Kelly laughed and turned to a machine.

Simon looked at Emma. "Five more."

"You put work before a relationship?"

"Make it ten."

"You did," she said, finding a smile at his bullshit blank face. He wanted her to move on, but no way. He knew *everything* about her. It was her turn. "Why?"

"Because he thinks he's too busy to have a life," Kelly said.

Simon ignored this, but Emma was fascinated and needed more. Still, she started moving before he changed the count to fifteen. "*Ouch.*"

"What kind of ouch?" he asked. "The 'I don't want to do PT today' ouch? Or 'I need a nap' ouch?"

"A nap sounds gr—" Emma gritted her teeth on the last word as her calf muscles suddenly seized, making her curl into herself. She tried to straighten her leg to ward it off, also knowing she couldn't, and sure enough the cramp gripped her like a vise, sending searing pain through her whole body. She cried out as she scrambled up, putting weight on the foot, trying to relieve the pressure.

Hands caught her. Simon, of course. He dropped down to massage her leg, working his magic until the unbearable tightness was gone and so was the pain. "Breathe," he said quietly and waited for her to do so, to mimic his slow, steady breathing.

But it was hard to draw air in slowly and steadily when she felt betrayed by her body. It'd been almost a year, a whole damn year, and she hated the helplessness of knowing that her body still couldn't be trusted.

"It's okay to be angry," Simon said while his hands continued to work on her calf.

Emma opened her eyes and found him watching her carefully. He did that, always assessing what he was doing, how she was taking it, and there was comfort in that. Much as she teased him about being a hard-ass, he was actually the opposite.

"You're not doing your stretching at night," he said.

"Not as much as I should," she admitted through clenched teeth. "I know, not exactly the sharpest knife in the drawer, right?"

"You're plenty sharp, Emma. You've just got a couple of blind spots. We all have them."

"Yeah, right. Name one blind spot of yours."

Those fascinating gold and green eyes of his held hers, a slight raise to his brow, and her insides got a little squishy. *She* was his blind spot?

His hand, on her leg, squeezed a little as his eyes lit with amusement and affection, which had her gaping at him like a fish out of water. "Um . . ."

His low chuckle didn't help. He pointed at her, gesturing her back to the stretching she wasn't doing.

Right. And clearly he could find his professionalism in a single heartbeat, but she sure couldn't.

"Do your stretching at night, before you get into bed."

"I've been using nighttime to stress about getting work. People ask about my huge gap in employment, which means explaining I was in a coma, which then changes how they look at me."

"And how do they look at you?"

She gestured to herself. "No one wants someone this damaged. I come with implied problems."

"Any implied problems are their own. You're not damaged, Emma."

"You might want to get your eyes checked."

"My eyes are fine."

Her breath caught in her throat. He was hunkered before her, close, *very* close. They'd been in this position many times before, but they'd never stared at each other while her heart thundered in her ears.

Kelly moved past them.

Flustered, Emma jerked to her feet and backed away.

Simon didn't move. Nor did he seem flustered in the slightest. Just got quietly to his feet and waited for her to look at him.

"We done now?" she asked.

He gave a slow nod. "For now."

They stared at each other and she wondered if there really was something there or she was just imagining it. And why that thought came with a little fear. Fear she wouldn't be ready, that she'd never be ready again. "Okay, then," she said. "Gotta go." And like she did with just about everything, she ran off like the hounds of hell were on her heels. Well, okay, *walked*, because her legs hurt and running was no longer in her repertoire.

Chapter 3

Step 3: Be aware of your RBF—resting bitch face.

Alison Pratt was used to shit days, but today took the cake. Work sucked. Life sucked. At least five times today she'd gone to call her boyfriend, Ryan, who always, *always*, knew how to make her feel better, but when she pulled up her favorites, his contact was no longer there.

Because oh yeah, he'd broken up with her. Heartbroken, she'd deleted him out of her favorites *and*—because she was weak—changed his contact to *DO NOT CALL!*

Leaving work, she headed down Wildstone's Commercial Row, the fun, quaint four-block-long "downtown." The Old West–style buildings had been there since the early 1900s and were filled with an eclectic, quirky mix of touristy, artsy galleries, ski and bike shops, cafés, and B&Bs.

Alison stopped at Caro's Diner rather than go home to her empty town house. Empty because, though Ryan hadn't officially been living with her, he'd kept stuff there. A toothbrush. Clothes. His Xbox . . .

All gone now.

Sick of thinking about it, Alison walked through the postdinner crowd. Not much of a people fan, she typically headed straight to the back booth, which was almost always open since apparently she was the only introvert in the area. She slid into the booth, and two minutes later Louise, her favorite waitress, showed up. She was at least seventy, possibly a hundred, and wore her usual uniform of a hot pink button-up dress, white apron, and sassy expression. "Hey, doll. Your usual?"

"Yes, please, but double the fries and add a beer as well?"

Louise eyed the empty seat across from her, winked, and walked away. She hadn't bothered to write anything down on her pad. She wasn't going to charge Alison. She never did. Alison managed this building. She actually managed a bunch of buildings in the area for Armstrong Properties. That was her job, and it was a good one. She couldn't take full credit for it, as she'd gotten it via nepotism. But the salary was good and she was better than good at the job. Plus she loved no longer being poorer than dirt.

Her boss favored this place because it was a short walk from where he lived. Alison favored this place because the diner made the best french fries on the planet, and her favorite comfort food happened to be french fries and wine.

Five minutes later, Alison was sipping her wine and working her way through the french fries when Simon came in and sank onto the bench across from her. Her cousin—and reluctant boss—smiled in gratitude when she pushed the beer she'd ordered toward him. He dug into the french fries as well.

There were other people at tables near them. Any of the female persuasion were eyeing Simon. This had been happening since puberty, when he'd shot straight up to six feet and, thanks to his athleticism, had the build to go with it. And then there was his laid-back attitude, the one that effectively hid a sharp intellect and a low tolerance for BS. All of which added up to an attractiveness that drew women to him like bees to honey.

He never reacted to this. Either he didn't notice or didn't care. Alison knew it to be the latter. Simon was *always* aware of his surroundings.

He took a long pull on the bottle before wearily setting it back down, as if maybe his day had been as rough as hers. "So. What's the big 911?"

She doused a french fry in the bowl of ranch dressing Louise knew to always bring her.

"Ali."

"*Alison*," she corrected. "You know I haven't been Ali since high school. And how do you always know when something's wrong?"

"One, because you literally texted me 911 to get me here. And two, you've got on your power suit, kick-ass heels, and your hair's practically sizzling. You're clearly in pissed-off mode. Something happen on the job today I need to know about?"

"Mr. Barnes yelled at me for the sluggish plumbing still being sluggish." She dragged yet another fry through the dressing.

"We were held up by yesterday's surprise hailstorm."

Yeah, hail in June. Welcome to the midcoast of California, where the only guarantees were unpredictable weather. Last year in June they'd gotten snow. The June before that the temps had climbed into the nineties. There was no telling what could happen. "He didn't give a shit about the hailstorm. A direct quote, by the way."

Simon shook his head. "We still came through within twenty-four hours of his call. Which is twelve hours faster than our contract states we have to be." He ate some more. "I swear, I've got no idea how my dad handled all the crazy. I told you months ago you should cut Barnes loose as a client. With all his demands and complaints, he makes far more work for us than money."

Simon had the patience of a saint—except when it came to dealing with assholes, which Mr. Barnes definitely qualified as. The problem was owning and operating a property management firm had never been Simon's dream. Not even close. Nope, his passion was physical therapy. But when his dad had a stroke two years ago now, and then a second one a month later, all of Armstrong Properties had fallen to Simon to keep running, forcing him to give up full-time PT. Now he could only keep a few select PT patients for the two half days a week he could get home care for his dad.

It was slowly killing him.

"Barnes is just a blowhard," Alison said. "But his money's good. I can handle him. Now tell me why you put someone in your building and skipped all the vetting process. Plus I still don't have a copy of the lease and they've been in it for three days."

"I handled it."

She gave him a long look, because one of the most annoying things about Simon was that if he didn't want you to know what he was thinking, you didn't get to know what he was thinking. "You *voluntarily* dealt with a new renter? Since when?"

"Since I live in the building too. It's a friend. Don't worry about it. I'll get you the lease. It's all signed, she's good to go."

"*She?*" Alison made the one-syllable word about a thousand syllables. "Who is this *she?*"

"Let it go."

She smiled. "I'm not good at that."

"No kidding."

She studied him.

He just kept eating french fries.

"You doing her or something?"

Simon paused for a sip of his beer. "Keep asking your boss personal questions like that and you can forget next quarter's bonus."

"You *are*," Alison said with a laugh. Sure, she was going down a dangerous road because Simon never made idle threats, but nothing was more fun than teasing him when she was miserable. And misery loved company. That was just a fact. "You're *totally* doing her."

"Drop it." He pointed at her. "Stop deflecting. It's not Barnes or my new neighbor upsetting you."

Damn his perceptive ass, because just like that, she was suddenly struggling with tears. He leaned forward, putting a hand over hers. "What aren't you telling me?"

"I don't tell you everything."

"I wish that was true. Tell me what's wrong."

"Nothing." But dammit, her eyes filled. "It's Ryan." She sniffed and struggled for composure. Knowing it was really over between her and the man she'd loved for close to a year, the only man she'd ever fallen for, was a direct hit to her heart, a pain that resonated so deeply she knew she'd never be rid of it. "He . . . broke up with me."

"Because?" Simon asked with careful neutrality.

He and Ryan were tight. Several years older than Alison, they'd gone to high school together before she'd gotten there, and even now they played on the same softball rec league team. "Because . . . much as we try, it's never been as good as it was in the beginning."

"You mean when you two were stuck together, alone, for a week? No distractions from the real world?"

She'd gone on a rare Tahoe trip with the local ski club, and because the weather had gone bad at the last minute, only four people had gone. When the storm warnings went from mild to dire, two had left early, leaving just her and Ryan in the rental cabin. "It was twelve days." And eight hours, but who was counting? "And no distractions? Are you kidding me? I didn't know him at all and there he was, a total stranger who was about to find out what I look like without makeup, and how I sing ABBA's songs to myself in the dark because I get nervous, and that the only thing I can cook is spaghetti and toast . . ."

But from the start, there'd been an ease between them. Ryan was an engineer and good at . . . well, everything, making her feel safe and secure in the cabin. Her sarcastic humor had made him laugh, and he'd told her he'd desperately needed that. Laughs.

And then there'd been their physical chemistry . . . Her hair started smoking just remembering how good they were together alone.

It'd been long after, when they were no longer alone, that their problems had set in.

Simon smiled. "I remember your panicked texts, which of course didn't come through until after you'd gotten off the mountain, and then they all came in one big rush. 'Simon! I'm stuck here with a guy named Ryan who says he's your friend, but I don't know him and we have no power, which means no blow dryer. He's going to see my hair au naturel! No one sees my hair au naturel, Simon!'" He laughed. "Then the texts slowly shifted to things like 'wow, he's actually nice' and 'did you know he's smart as hell' and 'I hope you don't mind if I kiss him, because I already did . . .'"

Alison lost herself in those memories—going out into the blizzard to load up on more firewood, foraging in the pantry for things they could eat, sitting side by side in front of the fire they had to maintain or freeze, talking until dawn about anything and everything, feeling like it was just the two of them in the entire world, forging an intimacy that had felt like they'd been together forever.

She'd fallen hard, and her only solace had been that she knew he'd fallen just as hard.

"You and Ryan are very different," Simon said quietly. "But different can be good."

"Not in this case."

"That's because once you got back from Tahoe, and reality crept into your relationship, you didn't know how to deal with it."

She nodded at the truth of that. "I guess I'd hoped it could be just the two of us forever."

"Yes, you mean you wish he didn't have such a full life because it meant that you needed to fit into that and you weren't interested."

"It's not that I wasn't interested," she protested. "It's that I don't know how. I'm . . . shy."

Simon laughed.

She pointed at him. "Okay, fine. Not shy. But I don't . . . like people."

He laughed again.

"Okay, fine. The truth is, he's got family and a tight-knit group of friends, and they've all been together forever, and I was new, and it was all so intimidating to me that instead of trying to fit in, I just . . . didn't."

Simon nodded, eyes solemn, well aware of her past and just how unused to being loved she was. Alison exhaled a rough breath, hating that Ryan had wanted only one thing from her: for her to integrate herself into his life. And she'd been too self-conscious, too worried that she wouldn't measure up to even try.

"It was important to him," Simon said.

Because like Simon, Ryan remained close to anyone who'd ever been in his life. His friends went as far back as his childhood. And then there was his family. He'd lost his dad early and had stepped up to be the man of the family, taking care of his mom and sister, which meant he was involved in their lives in a big way.

Unfortunately, they were also deeply invested in *his* life, and besides being nosy as hell, neither of them approved of Alison as a good fit. This had made every gathering—of which there were many for the very social family—difficult for Alison. "I hate that I blew it," she said softly, the fries not sitting so well.

Simon pulled the plate closer to him. He'd always been a bottomless pit. Her too, which sucked. She'd have to work the fries off in the gym. So would he, but he'd enjoy it. "Knowing the problem is half the battle," he said. "Fix it."

She sighed. She was the first one to be annoyed when people used their shitty childhoods to excuse their adult behavior, and yet . . . she did exactly that on the daily. "I don't try to push people away, you know."

"I know. But for the record, you're good at it."

"You seem to stick just fine."

"Because you're my person, and you've never let me down."

He had no idea how thankful she was that he wouldn't let her push him away. "Thanks," she murmured, sincerely moved. "And same." Then she stole the last french fry. She scooped up an obscene amount of ranch dressing with it and ate it blissfully. "Ryan said he wants the woman in his life to be his best friend. But I'm much better at the other parts of being his girlfriend. The easy parts."

"There are easy parts to a relationship?" Simon asked.

"The in-bed parts."

He grimaced. "Look, just be the real you."

"And who's the real me?"

"The girl with a nonexistent dad and a mom who treated her more like a servant than a daughter. The girl who grew up hard and fast all alone to make her own way in the world."

"I wasn't all alone. You and your dad helped me out."

"Not soon enough," he said with regret. "You were good at hiding your situation, and we were good at not looking deeper. Which to this day still makes me feel like shit."

Alison shook her head. She didn't want Simon to blame himself. He and her uncle Dale had given her a future with Armstrong Properties, and she loved them for that. Yes, sometimes she still yearned for something that she'd gotten herself on her own, but she'd work on that. "None of it was your fault. I'm fine."

"And yet you still keep everyone at arm's length, never trusting anyone. On the rare occasion someone does get past your defenses, like Ryan, soon as you realize it, you sabotage yourself."

She stared at him, knowing it was all true. "Why do I put up with you again?"

He sipped his beer. "Because we're cut from the same cloth. Plus, you love me, and you know I'm right."

"About . . . ?"

"Everything."

She had to laugh. He'd been at her back for as long as she could remember. He was her closest friend. Maybe even her only *true* friend. Whether Simon believed it or not, he'd gotten Alison through that shitty childhood, her rocky teenage years, and even now was *still* standing up for her, even when she didn't deserve it. "We're both pretty screwed up, aren't we."

Ignoring this, he lifted a hand in Louise's direction, winked at her, and their waitress blushed like a young girl and brought another plate of fries. Simon dug right in. "Speak for yourself. So how exactly did Ryan break up with you?"

"Why?"

"I'm surprised is all. I know how much he cares about you."

She felt her throat burn, because in the end, that hadn't mattered, had it? "He talked me into one of their group dinners. The one last week that you had to skip cuz you couldn't get coverage for your dad. Afterward, I guess someone told him I was stuck-up, and not as invested in him as he was in me."

"They did not call you stuck-up," Simon said, looking angry on her behalf.

"I don't know what words they used. And does it matter? My point is that he took their opinions to heart and gave them more weight than how we feel about each other."

"So . . . you finally actually let him know that you love him then?"

"Well . . ." Okay, maybe she wasn't done with the french fries after all. She took another. And another, until Simon stopped her.

"Fine. I didn't say the actual words, but we're beyond words."

Simon did not look impressed by this. Plus it was a lie. She and Ryan *hadn't* been beyond words. She *loved* his words. She just hadn't been able to give them back to him because, again, she was a big chickenshit.

"In my experience, most people actually need the words, Ali."

"*Alison*," she corrected. "'Ali' was the bitchy mean girl from our growing-up years. I'm trying to evolve." She sighed. "*Trying* being the operative word, anyway."

"Look at that, you *can* use your words." He toasted her with a french fry. "See how easy that was?"

"Ha ha." Alison finished her wine. "Do you want another?" She tipped her glass toward his empty beer.

"Can't. Dad had a bad day and I have to get back."

She really felt for Simon. He'd literally given up his life to take care of his dad, and it wasn't as if Simon had had it easy before Uncle Dale's strokes either. Yes, she'd had a shitty childhood, but Simon? His mom had died after a long, drawn-out battle with cancer when he'd been a freshman in high school, catapulting him into adulthood far before he should've been. It was a miracle he'd made it through and kept his easygoing temperament and that way about him that inspired trust and loyalty. He was everything to a lot of people, including her, and he deserved far better.

"I'm sorry." She put her hand over his. "This is his third bad day in a row."

"Actually, it's been more like a week since his last good day."

Alison could see how tired Simon looked and felt sick for him, but also mad at herself for not seeing it. She'd been too wrapped up in her own world and breakup with Ryan, which made her selfish. Maybe she should let him call her Ali after all.

Or . . . you could stop your behavior, swallow the fear, grow up, and turn over a new leaf right now.

She drew a deep breath. "I'm coming over after work tomorrow anyway. I'll bring dinner."

"Thanks. But whatever you do, don't turn on the news."

"Why?"

"Because every time you come over, you two start arguing about politics. You get him all riled up, and then he keeps me awake until three in the morning yelling about millennials destroying the world, and I've got an early PT patient the morning after."

"I thought you were only doing PT two half days a week now."

"It's fine. I've got a few patients who still need to see me at least two times a week. I can't just cut them loose without jeopardizing their recovery."

"Give them to Kelly."

"I've got it all under control," Simon said.

Control being the operative word. Simon liked his control. "Hmm. Is this early patient the woman you refuse to talk about?"

Instead of answering, he pulled out his wallet, and she found a laugh on this shitastic day. "Okay, so that's a yes. She must be cute. What's her name?"

"I don't date patients," he said. "It's unethical."

"It's not like you're a counselor or a doctor, Simon. You . . . limber people up." She smiled to let him know she was teasing. He worked his ass off and she knew exactly how hard and demanding his work was.

He gave a slow shake of his head and let out a reluctant smile. "You're a nut."

"And you're deflecting. Means she must be much more than just cute."

He stood and tossed down enough money to cover the tab and a tip. Louise wouldn't charge them, but Simon insisted on paying anyway. "I don't have the bandwidth for this conversation. Need a ride?"

"No thanks." And as she watched him go, hands shoved in his pockets, broad shoulders set like maybe they carried the weight of the world, she wondered for the first time if their way of adulting—which for Alison was to never be dependent on others again, and for Simon was to keep his promise to his dead mom to take care of his dad no matter what—was shortsighted.

Because surely there was more to life than just trying to survive it. But if there was a better route, she had no idea how to get on it.

Chapter 4

Step 4: Put yourself out there.

S imon jerked awake when someone hit the wall
switch and his room lit up like day. "What the—"

"I made food."

His dad's stroke-thickened voice could sometimes
be hard to understand, but not for Simon. He sat up
to find the man standing in the doorway wearing . . .
Hell. *Nothing.* "Dad—"

His dad waved a piece of bread triumphantly. "Toast!"

Simon swiped a hand down his face. "Where are
your pants?"

His father shrugged.

It was still dark outside. Simon glanced at the clock.
Four. In the morning. "It's not even light outside yet."

"Which is why you're still not rich."

Oh, good. The age-old argument about how Simon was a slacker. He only worked Armstrong Properties, PT shifts, *and* took care of his dad, but he refused to get drawn into an argument, at least not before caffeine. "Okay, tell you what. You find some pants and I'll make breakfast."

"Already made it." His dad waved the piece of bread again, bread that was most definitely not toasted. "Took out the trash too. I'm no slacker."

His dad had pulled himself out of the gutter by his bootstraps, and as a result, he tended to push Simon hard. Not that it mattered now since his dad didn't seem to remember the tough, impenetrable man he'd been prestroke.

Simon asked, "How did you get outside? I set an alarm on the doors."

"I unset them."

Jesus. "You do remember you're no longer allowed to take out the trash, right?"

"And you weren't *allowed* to be an idiot when you were a teen. Didn't stop you."

True story.

"And that's a stupid rule anyway, about the trash." His dad shifted his weight, a little guiltily. "It's not my fault that the last time I took it out, I scared a raccoon and it ran across the lawn and into the building next door, where the demented thing demo'd the entryway."

"That's not what got you into trouble. You weren't wearing pants that night either. Someone called the cops and said there was a vagrant disturbing the peace. You got a ticket for indecent exposure."

"Bah. People are too sensitive. Can't even live my life in my own home."

There was no arguing with the man, so Simon got out of bed. "I'll make us breakfast. Clothes, Dad."

"You're not wearing anything."

Simon bent for the jeans he'd left on the floor and pulled them up. "There. Now you."

"I don't like pants."

"*No one* likes pants. They're just one of life's fun burdens." Simon headed toward the bathroom. "I'm going to shower real quick, then I'll feed you. And then since I'm up, I may as well get some paperwork done. Ed's your nurse today."

His dad went hands on hips. "Ed's mean."

"He's a good guy."

"Last week he wouldn't let me make a grilled cheese sandwich."

"Because last time you caught the pan on fire and set off the fire alarm." Simon realized he was hands on hips now too, same as his dad. He dropped his hands to his sides.

His dad did a pretty decent eye roll. "Where's Jodie? I want her today. She makes me cookies."

"She'll be back the day after tomorrow. And I make you cookies too."

His dad huffed out a sigh. "You chintz on the chocolate chips."

"You're supposed to be cutting back on sugar and trans fats; your doctor said your diet was killing you."

"My diet *is* killing me."

"Your *old* diet."

His dad sighed. "I miss sugar and trans fats."

Simon put a hand on his dad's shoulder. "And I'd miss you if they killed you."

His dad sighed, but patted Simon on the head, like *good boy*. He had to reach up to do it too, but it was what he'd been doing for just about all of Simon's life and it made Simon's chest tighten and gave him a smile at the same time. Until his dad spoke again.

"And I thought you gave up your patients."

Simon nodded. "A lot of them, yes."

"So what's the problem? Armstrong Properties is a great place to work."

Simon reminded himself that his dad had worked himself up from a broke kid to a real estate mogul. It never occurred to him that his dreams weren't Simon's.

"It is, Dad. You did good."

"You could do good there too. That's why I built the company, as a legacy to you."

"I like being a physical therapist."

"Yeah? And what has that ever got you? Do you own the clinic? No. Are you your own boss? No. Someone could take it away from you at any time."

Yeah, and Simon was looking right at him. Not that it was his dad's fault. But his dad thought of Armstrong Properties as his baby, and being a control freak, he'd asked Simon to take over running it himself until he could get back to work. It was a full-time job. They had thirty employees who handled everything from seeking new available real estate to marketing long- and short-term rentals, to collecting rent, to maintenance and repair, to responding to tenant issues. They were the best of the best in the area, his dad had seen to that.

Now it was all on Simon to keep his dad's only source of income strong and profitable. His own life was taking a hit because of it. But every time he thought about walking away from the responsibility, he remembered his mom at the end of her cancer battle.

Promise me, baby, promise me you'll be there for your dad no matter what.

Those had been her exact words, and they haunted him to this very day. Because he *had* promised. To his shame, it hadn't happened. Instead he'd continued to steep himself in resentment over how his dad had been after his mom's death. Demanding. Grumpy. Angry. Simon had gone into survival mode for middle and high school with the man, and then, needing out, he'd gone off to college in San Diego, six hours south of Wildstone. He'd stayed after graduation . . . in spite of his promise to his mom.

For months leading up to the stroke, Alison had been calling and texting that something was off, that Simon needed to come home.

He hadn't.

He'd stayed gone until his dad's first stroke.

Dale Armstrong was a different man now, milder for sure, but also . . . mellowed, even kind. Funny. People loved the guy. As for Simon . . . well, he'd worked his way through the built-up resentment. Mostly. But still feeling haunted by the promise he'd broken to his mom and the fact that he hadn't been in Wildstone when his dad had suffered the strokes, he was doing his damnedest to make things right.

"Pants," he said to his dad now. "Then kitchen."

"You're as mean as Ed."

"Uh-huh," Simon said and gestured between him and his dad. "Apple. Tree."

His dad laughed gruffly.

A few hours later, Simon was at Armstrong Properties. The place was housed in a building just a few blocks off Commercial Row. Wildstone had been experiencing growth and was considered a hidden treasure off Highway 1, down a narrow two-lane highway between wineries and ranches.

The day was a long one. He had to give out a handful of eviction notices due to nonpayment of rents and attend three meetings that could have been emails. And one of their properties had a pipe burst. His dad would say that was the job. But the job was slowly sucking the soul out of Simon.

At the end of the day, he'd normally rush home to relieve his dad's day nurse. But tonight Alison was on deck, thank God. So Simon changed into running gear and used up some pent-up energy to jog to Synergy PT Clinic. Three miles later, he entered the building, his tension drained. Drawing a deep breath, he headed straight to the juice bar in the reception area with a bone weariness that made Kelly laugh at him.

"Aren't you supposed to be in your prime?" she teased.

"I am in my prime."

"Two years ago, when we were dating, maybe."

He arched a brow. "Maybe?"

She chuckled. "Okay, so you were definitely in your prime while we were together. Thanks for giving me the best year of your life, blah blah. Now hush because I've got something to help you. Hold please." Kelly turned to her workstation. She specialized in creating unique juice concoctions geared toward each individual patient's needs. Simon had no idea how she did it, but her mysterious potions were better than any medicine.

He watched her at work, thinking about how much better they were at being friends than romantically involved. For one thing, he didn't have to worry about making time for two in his crazy life. For another, there were no expectations on him.

"You just missed Emma Harris, by the way," she said. "She came in to use the treadmill."

His heart gave a little kick at her name. "How did she do?"

"Great. One mph for ten minutes."

Considering the first time he'd seen Emma, she'd gotten winded just sitting up in bed, she'd come a long way. Not that she'd agree. "Did you remind her she's up from last week?"

"Of course. But she wants to be running like she used to." Kelly was chopping up fruits and veggies. "I also told her she's lucky to be upright and breathing, but she wants more. I mean, most would've given up after having their doctors tell them they were going to be in a wheelchair for the rest of their life."

Emma wasn't the type to accept anything. She'd come so far, and was resilient as hell, and Simon loved that about her. Loved being a part of her recovery, and as he watched Kelly work, he thought about how much he missed being here full-time. But until either his dad got back on his feet or he agreed to trust Simon enough to find someone else to run Armstrong Properties, this was his life for now, and lonely as he sometimes got, it was why he couldn't entertain the thought of a relationship right now. If he'd learned one thing from his past relationships, it was that he didn't have enough of himself to give. "That fat sparkling diamond that's wearing you is blinding."

Kelly sent him a dreamy grin and flashed the ring. "I know, right? Scott's got great taste."

"Well, he asked you to marry him, so yeah he does."

Kelly's grin widened. "Thanks. It's ridiculous how giddy I am, but I can't seem to stop smiling."

He smiled at her, genuinely thrilled she'd found the love of her life. She deserved it. "If I was marrying the girl of my dreams, I'd be smiling too."

"Hey, you could've chased after me when I dumped you," she said.

Simon shook his head, knowing she'd been right. He hadn't been the one for Kelly. He adored her, maybe even loved her, but he was not *in* love with her. Never would be. "You did the right thing, breaking my heart."

Kelly's look at Simon was more than a little regretful. "I didn't break your heart. I did think mine was broken for a bit, but for what it's worth, I'm sorry for how it went down."

"Don't be." And he meant it. She'd been unable to handle him taking care of his dad twenty-four, seven; they'd literally never seen each other, and he'd never blamed her. She deserved better. "I'm happy for you, Kel."

"And I want to be happy for you too. But you haven't even made time to meet anyone, much less date since—"

"Don't start."

"You deserve love too, Simon."

Maybe. But not right now with his dad needing him as much as he did. It wasn't fair to a woman, and he wouldn't put someone else through it only to possibly hurt her in the end too. Even as Simon thought this, his brain flashed him a picture of Emma smiling at him, eyes shining. Yes, he wanted her. More than he'd like to admit. But she'd been through enough, he wouldn't add to it. "It's just a busy time—"

Kelly turned on the blender and drowned him out, and he laughed. He got it. She didn't want to hear the excuses anymore. Hell, he was tired of making them.

She turned off the blender, poured the frothy, peachy concoction into a large glass, and handed it to him. "Drink. And you do realize you've been saying you're too busy for a life through two relationships now. Me, and then Maggie. And now you've given me half your patients so you can work your fingers to the bone keeping your dad's business afloat—even though being in an office is slowly killing you."

All true. But there was nothing he could do about it at the moment. He was just starting to come around to the realization that his dad might not get any better than he was right now. Which meant Simon needed to plan for that and make some hard changes. Not ready to talk about it, he sipped from the glass, then looked at it. "Why does this taste like magic and rainbows?"

"Because *I'm* magic and rainbows." She turned to the counter, where she also prepared and served on-the-go healthy bites. Two minutes later he had a plate of food in front of him as well. He didn't even realize that he was hungry until he'd practically licked his plate.

Kelly watched him solemnly. "You're a good guy, Simon. You make sure your employees are taken care of. Your friends. Your dad. Your cousin. You make sure *all* of us are okay, but you forget the most important person—*yourself*."

Not wanting to get into it, Simon stood. He took care of his own dishes, then hugged her. "Thank you."

"You mean 'thank you, now butt the hell out.'"

"Yes," he said, making her laugh as he left to hit the gym in the back for twenty minutes. It was the only "me" time he was going to get today. Maybe tomorrow too.

After a quick shower, Simon finally headed home. It was eight o'clock at night and he was already dreaming about bed.

But once inside the building, he hesitated and pressed an ear to his front door. No yelling. That was good. He could hear the TV. Also good. Alison had things under control. So he kept going, drawn up the stairs by a woman he shouldn't be thinking about, much less want. On the second floor, he paused in front of Emma's door, but he had no business fraternizing with a patient, even if they had become friends. He knew she'd been busy the past few days interviewing for jobs. He hoped she'd had some luck. She deserved some good luck for a change, though he'd never met anyone who could take the bad hand she'd been dealt and come out swinging as she had. She was a fighter, and damn, that was attractive.

Too attractive. That wasn't his professional opinion, it was his very human one. But he was good at pushing aside unproductive thoughts, and thinking about Emma Harris in a not-professional way was *extremely* unproductive.

So he kept climbing, taking the nearly hidden back set of stairs to the third floor, the attic that spanned the length of the entire building. At the very far end of the attic, in a deep, dark corner that few even knew existed, was another set of stairs, steeper and more than a bit rickety. He'd long ago put up a sign to keep people safe.

Or to keep the roof access private and for him only.

Having to move in with his dad had been . . . difficult. Simon had needed somewhere to escape to, a place that was all his, where he could just be. He'd found it on the roof, specifically the widow's walk above the back half of the attic, hidden from the front of the house.

His own personal hideaway.

As far as he knew, no one else ever came up here, so he'd claimed it as his own, a hidden pocket of space away from his dad, away from everything and everyone.

In a world gone crazy, it was his safe haven, his quiet place. And the view of the sparkling ocean didn't hurt. The days were long in June and today was still making a decision between light and dark. The entire world was cast in glorious blues and purples as the day slowly gave way to night.

He'd grown up in this building, which originally had belonged to his grandparents. They'd renovated the house into four apartments, and his dad had skipped college to manage the building, slowly collecting more and more properties, expanding to property management. His dad loved people, loved connections, and had made it work for him in a big way.

Until two years ago, of course.

Now Simon was in charge, waiting for his dad to recover and heal and express even an ounce of interest in his old life. He hadn't. The doctor had told Simon to give it time.

At the top of the stairs, the door to the hidden widow's walk was open and he stilled, immediately knowing he wasn't alone.

Chapter 5

Step 5: Don't give in to the fear.

Simon stepped onto the roof, not knowing what to expect. It couldn't be his dad. No way could he manage the stairs, and Alison was unlikely to let him try. Plus, thanks to his cousin's fear of heights, she'd never ever make it up here. That left 1B, which was currently empty, 2B with Mrs. Bessler, who wouldn't spare the energy to get up here, or . . . 2A with Emma—who wasn't exactly a fan of stairs.

Which, damn, left Alison after all. His dad must've fallen asleep early and she'd gone exploring. He loved Alison, but the last thing he wanted was to be around someone and talk. After a shit day, silence worked for him in a big way. Alison *loved* to fill a silence.

Only . . . it wasn't his cousin.

It was Emma. All five feet five inches of lithe, willowy body that at first glimpse might seem fragile, but that was an illusion. She sat on the love seat Simon had dragged up here a couple of years ago now. Hog was next to her, his soft snores drifting on the wind. Emma was head back, watching the day turn to night. It was a gorgeous sunset, the sky streaked from purple to red across the sky, but Emma's mouth pinched, a sheen of sweat on her forehead. Everything about her pose screamed exhaustion and pain. Guess he wasn't the only one who'd needed an escape from life tonight.

She'd been through hell, but she was made of tough stuff. Tough enough to survive eight surgeries to repair her myriad injuries after being hit by a car. She'd coded twice on the way to the hospital and had received twelve pints of blood. She'd had an intracranial bleed and a multitude of fractures; the most serious had been in her humerus, ulna, and radius—which now all sported new internal hardware.

She was a walking, talking miracle.

When Simon had first been brought in to help facilitate Emma's recovery, the two of them had talked, coming up with daily, weekly, monthly, and long-term goals. This had given her something to work toward. Her long-term goal had been to get her life back, the way it was when she'd been happy and healthy enough to run a 5K and be working toward her real goal—a half marathon. Her daily goal was simpler—to be pain free. Through sheer grit and determination, she'd come further than the doctors had ever thought she could. But she had her limits, and the way she was carefully holding herself had him worried.

Though Simon hadn't made a single sound, Emma turned her head toward him and, even in the near dark, unerringly found him.

"Go away."

He smiled. "I think you mean hi."

"Nope. And stop right there," she said, pointing at him as he came closer. "I can already feel your assessing PT gaze. Knock it off. I'm fine."

Her dark brown hair had been shaved off a year ago during the brain surgery for the intracranial bleed. The strands had grown back, falling to her chin like soft silk, loose and a little bit wild since, he assumed, with her left hand still not back on its game, she had trouble with it. Her eyes were the exact same color as her hair, mahogany brown, and had a way of drawing a person in.

Even when said person didn't want to be drawn in.

He'd never seen her in a lick of makeup, and for some reason, that drew him in too. But it also meant he could see exactly how pale she looked. "You're not fine."

She looked at him.

He looked right back.

She raised a brow. "Oh, was that a question?"

"No, because I know you. You pushed yourself too hard and you're in pain, but hell will freeze over before you admit it."

Emma didn't respond, which she had a habit of doing when she didn't want to lie. When he'd first started working on her, she could hardly handle any touch at all. Her surgical scars had healed, but they had left her skin so tight it hurt. He'd started with deep-tissue massage to help break up scar tissue, which was incredibly painful, but effective in regaining mobility. She'd spent their first three weeks together alternately swearing at Simon and crying while pretending not to.

"How about the leg cramps where you had the crushed nerve. You still getting those?"

"Is this Hard-Ass PT talking? Cuz I don't want to talk to that guy until my next torture session."

He smiled. "Hard-Ass PT?"

"I've called you that before."

"No, you haven't."

"Okay, correction. I've called you that before, just not to your face." She drew a deep breath, let it out slowly. "I'm sorry," she said. "I'm okay, really. Just . . . stressed." She closed her eyes. "I've been meaning to thank you for lending me R and J on moving day. I'll pay you back."

"Not necessary." She wore leggings with a strappy workout tank, both hugging her body. Her feet were bare.

He already knew every inch of her body. Professionally, he'd had his hands on most of it. He'd never allowed himself to catalog any of it. But she was right. Tonight she wasn't his patient. She was just a beautiful woman on his rooftop. And she was sexy as hell. "For the record, I was asking how you are as your friend."

Turning just her head, Emma assessed Simon with that dark gaze of hers before letting out a sigh and dropping her head to the back of the love seat. "I'm dealing. Somehow, I decided it'd be a great idea to push myself with the stairs, but then I found the second, hidden staircase, and decided to push even more—and then I was too tired to get back down. I live here now, right on the roof. I plan to die here. There are worse places, right?"

Simon gave a low laugh, but something in his chest tightened at her admission, making him want to reach for her and pull her in. Problem was, Emma hated being coddled even more than she hated needing help, so he simply nodded.

"Not a bad place to live," he said. "And great job getting up here, by the way. Two additional staircases, and that last one's a bitch. I'm impressed."

"Don't be. It took me an hour and nearly an Uber, but I'm too broke to call one."

She had to get a ride wherever she wanted to go now, since after her accident last year, and during her third surgery, she'd had a seizure. Protocol had necessitated putting her on a seizure med for one full year—which prohibited her from driving during that time.

She had three weeks left on that sentence.

"You know you can call me anytime, right?"

She shrugged.

"Emma."

"Okay, I know. But I don't want to have to."

"Everyone needs an assist every once in a while."

"Yeah?" She swiveled her gaze to him again. "When do you need an assist ever?"

He laughed. "All the damn time."

She seemed intrigued by this. "Name one."

"Whenever I need to do anything outside regular business hours, which means outside of my dad's day care, when my cousin steps in for me. I'm here right now because of that help."

She thought about that and nodded. "Okay, I stand corrected." She lay back. "It's nice up here. I was enjoying being alone and watching the water before you came in and looked at me all worried and concerned, like I'm broken."

He snorted. "You're not even close to broken. As for being alone up here, hate to break it to you, but I've been coming up here my whole life to be alone, especially this past year while you've been slacking."

Emma gave an unexpected laugh that just about stopped Simon's heart as she sent him a side-eye. "Do you know you're still the only one who'll joke about my life with me?"

"You gotta joke the bad away, or what's the point, right?" He thought of his dad, who'd once been so intense and unbending, but poststroke had mellowed into a guy who didn't have the capacity to hold on to bad shit. "What's happened is a part of you now. Doesn't mean you have to take it seriously all the time. Joking is healthier than not dealing."

"Oh, I think I've done enough *dealing* for a lifetime."

He chuckled in agreement as she slowly scooted over to make room for him. He opened the icebox that was his coffee table, the one he'd dragged up here from the attic. He'd run a cord back inside it for electricity. He took out a beer, opened it, and offered it to Emma.

Though he sat on her left, she used her right arm to reach for it. If they'd been in PT, he'd have called her out on it and made her work her left arm. She actually gave him a measured, expectant look, *daring* him to say something.

He just smiled as he grabbed another beer for himself.

Emma rolled her eyes. After a sip, she sighed and relaxed. "Thanks," she said, her voice softer. Warmer. "I mean, I wanted chocolate, but this'll do. So. You've lived in this building your whole life?"

Mirroring her position, Simon leaned his head back and closed his eyes. God, he was tired. "On and off. My grandparents handed the property down to my dad. I grew up in 1A."

"Where you're now living with your dad."

"Yeah. A newish development. He needed the assist, so I moved back in. I come up here to clear my head."

"It's a good head-clearing space," she agreed, and then she did something he loved.

She just sat still and let him be. The silence was glorious. He'd been bummed to have his space invaded, but turned out he didn't mind her company at all.

Crickets sang. Wind rustled the old gorgeous oaks lining the yard. After a while, Emma turned her head to him, and he felt her taking him in. "You look almost as bad as I feel. Rough one?"

"Yeah."

"Want to talk about it?"

"Just work shit."

"Wow," she said dryly. "You're really good at sharing."

He had to laugh. "Not my strong suit. How's the job hunt going?"

"You know, you'd think a woman with a numb left arm and a habit of mixing up her words and forgetting . . . well, *everything* would be in more demand."

"I'm sorry."

"Me too. I've had a lot of interviews, but no bites." She shrugged. "It's not like I'm being picky either. I offered to pick up additional shifts at Paw Pals, but my boss doesn't need more hours from me, and the dog training isn't going to pay the bills. I even interviewed for phone sales the other morning, and I hate sales."

"What do you want to do? What are you good at?"

"That's the thing. I don't know anymore."

"Emma—"

"No, I don't need empty platitudes, honest. I'm just grateful you were able to get me into the apartment.

Without you, I'd be stuck with the exes squared or moving to Florida to live on my parents' couch." She shuddered dramatically.

"Speaking of the exes squared . . ." He'd known she'd had a fiancé. She'd been wearing a ring in the hospital, but then when he'd seen her in rehab, the ring had vanished. "So while you were fighting for your life, the guy who'd asked you to marry him slept with your best friend?"

"*Ex*–best friend. But yes."

Jesus. At least he'd been dumped while able-bodied, not completely helpless. "Want to talk about it?" Simon asked, trying to keep his anger for her out of his voice.

"Not even a little bit."

He nodded his understanding of that. Hog deserted Emma and climbed on top of Simon for a cuddle. He wrapped his arms around the big guy, who set his heavy head on Simon's shoulder.

"Traitor," Emma murmured with no heat and possibly even a smile in her voice. "He likes it up here too. So why do *you* need a hideaway, Simon Armstrong?"

"Work. Life." He shrugged. "Up here I don't have to think about anything hard. It's my safe-space bubble from the real world."

"Sorry I broke into it."

"I'm not."

"Thanks," she whispered, her gaze locked on his for a long beat before she turned back to watching the stars now twinkling down on them. A slow-moving cluster of clouds began to streak the sky.

"That one looks like two dragons doing it," she said out of the blue.

It really did, and he laughed, then gestured to two puffy round clouds just barely touching. "What about those?"

She snorted. "If you say boobs . . ."

He laughed again. "Oh, so you can point out dragons getting down, but I can't point out boobs?"

"Just sayin', it's a very guy thing to see."

"Well, I am a guy, so . . ."

"Hmmm." She took another sip of beer, staring up at the sky. "I mean, yeah, okay, they do look like boobs, but they're *definitely* store bought."

"And?"

She sidled him a look. "Do guys really like that sort of thing?"

"To be honest, I'm not sure we're that picky."

She smiled and sat up slowly, unsuccessfully hiding her wince. She stretched her arms and her neck and winced again. When she caught him watching her, she shook her head at him. "I've just been doing more than I should. Unpacking and stuff."

"I'm surprised that your ex didn't offer to unpack you."

"Oh, he was done unpacking my stuff the day of the accident."

"He clearly wanted to stick around and do something for you."

"Yeah, well, the last thing he did was my best friend so I think he's done enough. And it's not like I can really blame him. A year's a long time to wait."

"Not if it's the right person."

She looked at him again, and something happened to the air between them. It crackled with a new energy. Not much surprised Simon anymore, but Emma had from the very beginning, and now was no different. Before this past week, she'd never looked at him in a way to suggest she might be interested in him as something other than her PT. But he was pretty sure she was looking at him that way now.

It stole his breath.

"I need to tell you something," she said quietly.

"Anything."

"I'm off men."

The words made sense, but completely contrasted with the way she'd shifted closer. He'd done the same, which was stupid and dangerous on his part. She'd been hurt enough, and he moved back.

"I'm sorry," she said. "I don't know why I said that, why I thought you should know."

Simon was torn between the urge to touch her and trying to ignore the way her eyes drank him up. But then she made a soft sound that went right through him in the very best of ways and closed her eyes for a single breath before meeting his gaze again. "It's just that there's something here, isn't there?"

He gave a slow nod. "Yeah, there is." And while Emma might be surprised by it, he wasn't because he'd been doing his best to pretend it didn't exist for a long time now.

"But I really am off . . . everything," she whispered.

"It's okay," he whispered back.

She shifted her weight to straighten out her left leg, which he knew still cramped up on her. She needed at least one more surgery to fix what was suspected to be a slipped screw from her tib-fib fracture, but could also be damaged nerves. "Did you get the date of your next surgery yet?"

She looked relieved at the subject change. "I'm still working it out with insurance."

Unfortunately, she had crap insurance coverage. As a PE teacher at a local private high school, she'd been an independent contractor. The self-employed coverage options were appalling, and as far as he was concerned, also a crime. She'd gotten a settlement, not nearly enough in his mind, and certainly not enough to pay for an out-of-pocket surgery. "Need me to help you stretch that out?"

"What I need is chocolate. Or more alcohol. Or some combo of the two."

He opened the icebox and produced a bag of chocolate candies. "Leftovers from Valentine's Day," he said when she raised a brow.

"It's June."

He shrugged. "And?"

She snatched the bag. "And what kind of a monster lets candy sit around for months uneaten?"

He laughed and feigned trying to take the bag back.

"Touch it and die." She looked at the bag more closely, reading the slogans on each individually wrapped chocolate. Love you, or love you not. "A girlfriend?"

"An ex."

Emma's brows went up. "Do you have an ex-squared too?"

He gave her an amused look. "No."

"Lucky you." She opened the bag. "It feels a little like we're in high school sharing a bottle of booze you stole from your dad's stash."

"My dad's stash also included an old stack of *Penthouses*. If you want me to go grab those, just say the word."

She smiled and tipped his heart over.

"How did your mom feel about the *Penthouses*?" she asked.

"Hard to say. She died a long time ago."

She met his gaze, her pretty dark eyes warm and sorrowful. "That sucks."

If she'd given him an empty platitude, he'd have done what he always did when it came up. Nodded and moved on. Because he never talked about it with anyone. "It was cancer. When I was a freshman in high school."

"Oh my God. How devastating."

"Yeah. Neither me nor my dad dealt with it well." Apparently now that he'd started playing the sharing game, he couldn't seem to shut the hell up. "Another beer?"

"Not unless you plan to carry me down. And nice subject change."

Simon laughed, and so did she, and it was a beautiful sound. He wasn't sure he'd ever heard it sound so easy and carefree before. And if he wanted her to remain a patient, he'd have to make sure he didn't hear it again.

"Thanks for tonight," Emma said and lifted her beer. "And all you've done for me. Because of you, I feel a lot more like myself. Maybe even ninety percent."

"That's pretty good. Shouldn't be hard to get you to one hundred."

"I'm good with the ninety."

He cocked his head. "You don't want more?"

She shrugged. "I'm lucky to be where I am."

"Not lucky. It's your own hard work." He paused because he could tell he was missing something. "Maybe we should talk about the hundred percent thing."

"Let's not."

He'd seen a lot of patients over the years. He knew the real recovery was far more mental than physical. "You still don't feel like you deserve that last ten percent," he guessed.

Their gazes met, hers wary and stubborn. "Thought this was a safe-space bubble."

He nodded slowly. "It is."

"Okay, then." She laid her head back, closed her eyes, and let the silence wrap around them once again.

Chapter 6

Step 6: Show up.

Emma had been at her new place for well over a week, and she was *still* feeling the daily effects of walking up and down the stairs to her apartment.

Her apartment.

In spite of herself, the words gave her a thrill.

The steps though, not so much. She'd been using the gym in the PT clinic, which Simon had encouraged her to do, specifically the treadmill. If she was ever going to get back to running, this was the only way. Yesterday she'd managed to walk full weight bearing at the heart-stopping rate of 1.25 mph. Sure, a long way from Usain Bolt speed, but progress.

She was in an Uber on her way to Paw Pals for a puppy training session with a new client when her phone rang with an incoming FaceTime call from her parents. With Hog up against her right side and her left arm still slow to accept commands from her brain, she almost missed the call.

"Hey, baby," her mom said with a smile. She had her hair piled on top of her head, half of it escaping. Her only makeup was a swipe of mascara and rosy cheeks from smiling. She line danced twice a week with her friends and taught water aerobics at her local senior center, and she was in better shape at fifty-five than her thirty-year-old daughter. "You okay?"

"I'm good. How are things there?"

Her dad just smiled. He rarely spoke a word. Probably couldn't get a word in being married to her chatty mom, who was beaming. "You have Hog with you! Hi, Hog!"

Hog leaned into Emma and smiled into the phone while breathing his hot breath on Emma's neck. "He says hi too."

"Such a sweetie. Did he stop eating your socks?"

"Mostly."

Her mom laughed. "I miss him. Oh! Guess what? We took first place at the annual country line dancing tourney."

"That's great, congratulations."

"Thanks. One of the judges is an attorney, and he said you should be suing the pants off the man that hit you. He said you should also sue the other car, the one that hit *him*. And also the city because the stop sign was partially covered by a low-hanging branch from one of the oaks lining the street. And—"

"Mom." Emma pressed her fingers against her eyelids. They'd talked about this a hundred times. Maybe a thousand. It was exhausting and it made her sad. "I was running. I ran right off that curb into oncoming traffic—without looking. I wasn't paying attention. The fault is mine."

"Emma—"

"Mom, the insurance companies all ran their own investigations, remember? Fault was undetermined. Which made it a no-fault. I got medical coverage and a small settlement."

"But at the end of the day, your so-called medical coverage turned out to be only eighty percent coverage."

"I know." Oh how she knew.

"I just thought if you sued now, all these months later so they could see how your life has changed, how you've suffered, you could get a settlement that would set us up for life."

Us. And she couldn't even get mad because her mom had given Emma a year away from her own life. She closed her eyes and tried to imagine suing the people she *knew* weren't at fault. She thought of Jack Swanson, the driver of the car who'd hit her. He'd lost a whole lot more than a family business and a job.

He'd lost his wife.

His entire life.

She'd tried to find news of him. She needed to know that, like her broken bones, he was healing. But the man had zero social media presence. So far all she'd been able to hunt up for him was a physical address. She'd Uber'd by his place enough times that she was going to have to cut back on her food budget, but she'd not seen hide nor hair of him. "I'm sorry, Mom. I know this isn't what you want to hear, but I'm still not going to sue."

Her mom was quiet for a moment. "My greatest achievement was having you. Raising you, watching you become the sweetest, kindest, warmest-hearted person I've ever met, so I'm not surprised. I understand, and I'm proud of you and who you are." Her eyes watered and she sniffed.

"Please don't cry," Emma whispered.

"I'm not. I just have something in my eye." Her mom swiped a hand over her tear and her dad wrapped an arm around her.

When they were gone, Emma let the smile slip from her face. Hog immediately licked her chin. "Thanks, buddy."

Talking to her parents was good, but it also reminded her of last year, most of which was a pain-filled blur. Thinking about it was hard, but she didn't want to get mired in the past. All she could do was focus on the here and now and work to build a future for herself.

Thanks to a lot of people, that future held a lot less pain than it could have. People like Simon Armstrong.

The car stopped a full block too early. "Thank you," the Uber driver said.

There weren't many Uber drivers in Wildstone and Emma knew most of them by now, but not this guy. She stared at him via the rearview mirror. "We're not there yet."

"This is where you wanted to be dropped off."

"No. Paw Pals is on the *next* block."

"This is the address you gave. Out, please, or I'll give you a one star."

"I didn't give you the wrong address. I—"

The man picked up his phone.

"Fine," she said tightly. "And wow." She pulled out her phone to show him he was wrong, but . . . he wasn't. She was wrong. She'd indeed typed the wrong street number. Thanks for nothing, left fingers . . . With a sigh, she got out.

Hog didn't. He knew they were going to have to walk.

"Come on," she said. "It'll be fun."

He didn't look convinced. As it turned out, he was right. It wasn't fun. She'd skipped her stretches last night and she hurt. The feel of Simon's extremely capable hands on her aching muscles would've been welcome right about now. He'd be both pleased and irritated with her, she knew. Pleased that she'd had any endurance at all and irritated that she wasn't listening to her body and giving it what it needed. The last few nights while trying to sleep, she'd considered and then rejected the thought of pain meds. It wasn't the pain keeping her from sleeping. She had other anxieties doing that for her just fine.

Like the fact that she suddenly wanted her Hard-Ass PT, a fact she was trying to convince herself was just her hormones coming back online.

Another problem? Income, or the lack thereof. But being anxious wasn't going to keep the roof over her head or food in her belly.

Emma walked up the street to Paw Pals. The building sat a block past the end of Commercial Row. Just the one block made a huge difference. Here the lots were bigger and mostly industrial. Once upon a time, the building had actually been a barn. Single story, it sat on an acre of land that backed up to one of the biggest cattle ranches in the area. If you were an early riser, you could still catch the occasional sight of the wild mustangs that ran free through it. Early meaning dawn.

Big surprise that Emma, not a morning person, had never seen one of the mustangs.

The building still had the feel and flavor of an old, beautiful barn and was perfect for a doggy day care. The front doors opened to a reception area, where people signed in, complete with a retail section that sold just about anything people might need for their beloved fur babies. A second set of doors opened to a huge room divided by fencing into different areas. They had big dog and small dog yards, along with a cat sanctuary. There was also a yard for dogs who weren't feeling . . . friendly. There was always someone watching over all of it, keeping the peace, cleaning up any messes, and adjusting attitudes.

Each yard had two areas, an "outside" pad with artificial turf and a bin of toys, and the "inside" portion, set up like a living room where pets could lie on sofas and watch TV.

In the reception room, Emma stopped to quickly check her email for the hundredth time, hoping to get word from any of her interviews from the week. Anyone.

"Still nothing?" Gabby asked sympathetically, coming out from the back.

Gabby Johansson owned and operated Paw Pals, the only doggy day care in town. She'd been born and raised in Switzerland, came to the U.S. in her twenties for a guy she'd kept around for a few decades while they procreated. Now single, she was in her fifties and very fond of animals, reality TV, and all things chocolate. That's how Emma could sometimes get the extra hours she needed—she brought chocolate. And not just any kind, but the expensive, imported-from-Switzerland kind. Sometimes Emma's chocolate fund was bigger than her Uber budget. She shook her head. "Jobs aren't falling from trees, unfortunately. Sucky week."

Gabby clicked her tongue in sympathy. "It gets worse. Your client canceled her puppy training. Something about she bought a book and thinks she's got it covered."

Emma nodded. Sounded about right. She turned back to the door.

"I could use you for a shift in the back today if you'd like."

"Really? That'd be great."

Gabby smiled. "Anything for you."

And Emma was grateful to have this job at all, as well as the twenty hours a week Gabby could afford to pay her.

It wasn't that her boss didn't make a decent living, because she did. It was that she had six kids, and something like twelve grandchildren, and she supported almost all of them. She also had two other part-time employees she was responsible for, Marco and Khloe, but at least among them, the place ran like clockwork.

At the moment, Marco was dividing his time among pens. Later, Khloe would show up and take over. Ever since her accident, Emma either trained clients' pets or worked the front desk, usually during the heavy drop-off and pickup hours, with Gabby overseeing the day-to-day operations.

At the moment, Gabby was drinking coffee and looking at the new shelves behind the front counter. "Damn, Rico did a great job on these for me."

Rico was Gabby's on-and-off—although currently off—longtime boyfriend.

"Are you back together?" Emma asked.

"Not yet. But I think he's wearing me down. Love's funny that way."

"Love is dumb," Emma said.

There came a raspy snort and she turned to look at the elderly woman in the recliner against the south window, knitting while soaking up the morning sun.

Katerina Johansson was Gabby's mother. She understood English but spoke only Swiss German. She was somewhere between eighty and immortal and went by the innocuous nickname of Miss Kitty, which she got because she could unsheathe her proverbial claws in the blink of an eye.

Miss Kitty scared the ever-loving shit out of everyone, including Gabby.

She pretty much lived at Paw Pals, usually knitting in that chair and enjoying the warm sun. Gabby often joked her mom came with the building, like it or leave it.

Miss Kitty looked at Emma and said something in her Swiss German.

Gabby translated. "She agrees with you about love being dumb. But for the record, I don't." She waved her coffee mug for emphasis. "There're certain things definitely worth living for. Giant mugs of coffee, having someone to bitch to, and falling in love."

Emma shrugged with her good side. "I'd settle for some freshly baked cookies and an orgasm. Oh, and a left arm that remembered it belonged to me."

"Okay, you might be on to something with the cookies and orgasm," Gabby said. "And hey, you could bundle fixing the arm and an orgasm by sleeping with your hottie PT."

Emma felt her face heat and give herself away. "How would sleeping with him fix my arm?"

"Let's just say after a night with him, you might not even notice your arm anymore."

Emma snorted to cover the fact that the idea more than intrigued her, and she moved behind the desk to look over their schedule. Busy. The yards would be filled to capacity. No room for Hog, who qualified for the big dog yard, but he was also shy, so he was usually more comfortable just staying out front with Miss Kitty, who'd been gracious enough to allow him to be her minion.

The minion was currently snoozing at her feet.

A warm feeling filled Emma's chest, in her happy place here every bit as much as Hog. "I love this place so much."

Gabby's easy smile faded some. "I've been wanting to tell you something . . ."

"Oh my God. You're firing me."

"No. *No*," Gabby said more gently. "But I'm tired of giving everything I make to my damn kids—"

Miss Kitty looked up sharply and pointed to the swear jar they kept on the counter.

Gabby winced, pulled a dollar bill out of her pocket, and stuffed it into the jar. The woman cost herself at least fifty bucks a week, but the money all went to the local humane society, so it was for a good cause. "My kids manage to go on vacations and have new fancy phones, and what do I have? Too much work. I'm retiring and selling the business."

Emma sank to the bench lining one wall. "When?"

"Soon as possible."

Emma's knees felt weak. "Who's buying it?"

"I don't know yet. I can only sell the business, not the lease to the building, which isn't transferable. If the new buyer wants to stay in this location, they need to qualify with the property management company that owns it. I'm hoping whoever it is, they keep the three of you on."

Marco had been walking through, carrying a French bulldog, who sat in his arms like a little princess. A princess who breathed like Darth Vader. He stopped and drew a deep breath. "I'm hoping that too, since I'm fond of eating."

"I want to buy it," Emma heard herself say. But the idea was already putting down roots. She could be with animals all day long, and animals never judged or let you down. She could be her own boss, and she was pretty damn great if she said so herself. Plus, she could stop hunting for a job that wasn't going to happen.

Gabby was grinning broadly. "I love this idea. I'd be honored, Emma. You'd be perfect."

Emma let out a low breath and struggled with tears. It'd been a while since she'd felt of value. "Yeah?"

"Oh yeah. But . . . can you afford it?"

If she could get a business loan. Running this place—with help—was something Emma could do in spite of her physical disabilities. And the more she thought about it, the more excited she got. "I'll talk to my bank, see what I can qualify for."

Gabby nodded and clapped her hands. "Then get to work on it. I need a buyer much sooner than later."

"How soon?"

"I need to give forty-five days' notice on my lease, which means if I'm going to get out of renewing, you've got about two weeks."

Emma's mind raced—two weeks!—but she nodded.

"And I love you, but it won't be cheap," Gabby warned. "I won't charge you a penny more than Paw Pals is worth, but this is my retirement fund. If you're really serious, I'll send you an email with everything you need to know."

Emma's heart was thundering in her ears. Nerves. But . . . also something else, something she hadn't felt in a long time. *Hope.* "I've never been more serious."

"Two weeks, girl. Make it happen."

Gulp. But hey, if she could nearly die in a single instant, then she sure as hell could figure out a new life for herself in two weeks, right?

Emma spent a few late nights creating a business plan and figuring out how to transfer over Gabby's current licensing and permits if she bought Paw Pals, not to mention actually qualifying for a business loan.

Two big ifs.

It was a pipe dream, but other than sex with Dream Simon, Emma had never wanted anything so much as Paw Pals. She wanted it so much she was almost afraid to believe it could happen.

Almost. She walked into the PT clinic for her next appointment and waited until Simon had her on the leg machine to say anything.

"I've got a new plan," she said, trying to ignore the pain of pushing her body.

He lifted his head and leveled her with those eyes of his, warm and curious. But still she hesitated because saying it out loud for the first time was going to make it real. "I'm going to buy Paw Pals."

"Yeah?" Simon smiled, his eyes lighting up. "That sounds perfect for you."

"It will be. If I can secure a business loan and lease for the building."

"You'll find a way. That's who you are."

Emma appreciated the words. But she was afraid he had more faith in her than she had in herself.

"My cousin manages a bunch of retail space, one of them being the building Paw Pals is in."

She sat up so fast she got dizzy. "What? Are you serious?"

"Yes."

She blinked, thoughts whirling. "That . . . sounds like a very odd coincidence."

"It's not. The property management company she works for owns a lot of buildings in Wildstone. It's my dad's company. Armstrong Properties." Simon said this like he was saying *it's light outside*, or *two plus two equals four.*

"*You're* Armstrong Properties?"

"My dad is." He paused. "But I'm running the company for him right now, until he's fully recovered."

She stared at him. "That's why you had to go to only two half days at PT."

"Yes."

Emma could see everything Simon wasn't saying in his eyes. How he'd rather be back at PT full-time, how he wished his dad could be back at work, that he felt stretched thin. But he didn't say any of that. Wouldn't.

"You know how you like dogs?" He shrugged. "I like helping people."

"So you're nice *and* a sadist?"

Simon smiled. "One of these days you're going to figure out I'm not either of those things."

Something to think about.

Chapter 7

Step 7: Be nice.

Allison sat on the first row of the bleachers lining the softball field in Wildstone's state park. The park was near the beach and a huge draw to locals because one could day camp, barbecue, lounge on the grass, walk to the beach, or play softball. She squirmed a bit, waiting for the game to start. She hated the first row. It left her open and exposed to everyone who walked by and wanted to talk.

And *everyone* in Wildstone always wanted to talk.

If she had her way, she'd be on the top row in a far corner. Or maybe in her car. Or better yet, at home in her town house that was the size of a postage stamp, but was at least all hers. Well, okay, it was the bank's, but in twenty-seven years it'd be all hers.

Except . . . the truth was that she'd never miss

Simon's weekly rec league softball game. For one thing, it was a huge stress reliever watching a bunch of hot guys being fiercely competitive about a little ball. But if Alison was being honest, she was really here for Ryan. He played on Simon's team, and no way would she miss the chance to see him. She hadn't seen him in the nearly two weeks since they'd broken up and she needed a glimpse. She needed more than a glimpse, but she'd take what she could get.

She'd come straight from work, which meant she was in full armor: makeup, her favorite suit that made her butt look good, and, thankfully, it was a good hair day. No one would be able to see that she'd had a rough couple of weeks. The roughest in a long time, and that was saying something.

When Ryan's truck pulled into the lot, she felt it all the way to her toes, which meant he was still making her feel things without even trying. She sure as hell hoped he was feeling things too—like devastation. Because why did it matter that she wasn't good at opening up with his friends and family, she wasn't dating any of them, she was dating Ryan.

Well, *past tense* dating.

"It mattered to Ryan." This from Simon's dad, her uncle Dale, who was sitting next to her. "That you didn't like anyone in his life," he clarified.

"Hey, it wasn't that I didn't like them. It's that there are so many of them."

Dale nodded. "You gotta point there. Maybe you could figure out a way to ease in. You know, soothe your introverted soul by starting small. I bet if you gave it any effort at all, Ryan would help you."

Alison wanted to believe that could be true, but after nearly a year of struggling together, he'd given up on her.

"Listen," Dale said gently. "I'm fine here by myself. I don't need a babysitter. Go sit up at the top of the bleachers and hide behind your big, fancy sunglasses while you think it over."

Dale was her mom's older brother. *Estranged* older brother. This had been mostly due to Alison's mom running away when she'd been fifteen, then coming back five years later with a kid.

Alison didn't remember much about those early years, except that she and her mom had struggled. A lot. She also remembered the both of them trying to hide that fact. Her mom had refused to accept help from anyone, especially her brother; she wouldn't even tell him she needed help as she hopped from job to job, making just enough for her and Alison to get by. The day Alison graduated from high school, her mom had taken off with some guy to backpack around Europe.

She popped in and out of Alison's life every other year or so, mostly when she needed money.

Alison had never told anyone about their struggles, but she suspected Dale had known. Little things gave him away. Like how he'd managed to sneakily give her a leg up whenever she'd needed it the most. Money for food when she'd been in high school. A job while she'd been getting her AA, one that had led to a career for her at Armstrong Properties. She loved him ridiculously. Maybe because when he'd been at his sharpest, he'd also been at his grumpiest, and she understood that on a core level.

Her uncle had played a lot of roles in her life, the most important being a pseudo dad, which she could never thank him enough for. But he'd also been a friend, an employer, and, during her wild teen years, also her enforcer. She was grateful for every single moment of it.

And now it was her turn to help him. "I'm good sitting here with you."

"Liar."

She smiled. "What if some hot chick texts you and you need help responding?"

"Then she should have called me instead of texted."

Alison shuddered in horror at the idea of having to talk on the phone instead of answering a text. "Barbaric."

He shook his head. "Terrible horrible death coming . . ." He pointed at her. "You too."

Dale was getting better after the strokes, but he was sometimes hard to understand, and his right side didn't always work the way he wanted it to. Every time he had an issue—which could be trying to button his own shirt or work his phone—he'd grumble with frustration and say "terrible horrible death coming." Then he'd point at Simon and Alison and tell them they should also prepare, because these things were hereditary and they too would someday face a terrible horrible death.

"Simon asked you not to say that anymore," she reminded him.

"Hey, I don't make up the rules of life."

Alison shook her head. He was the most stubborn man she knew. Simon was the second.

"Ryan's here."

Yeah, she was aware, because even if she hadn't seen his truck, she'd have known by her racing pulse. "And?"

"And . . . stop being crabby just because you're torn between your pride and what you really want."

"Gee, thanks, Dr. Phil."

Dale cackled. He was wearing trousers and a pressed button-down. He wouldn't wear pants in his house, but if he went anywhere, he had to look "spiffy." He'd been into work exactly once since the strokes. Simon had thought it might cheer him up, but Dale had gotten away on his own for a few minutes, and to the shock of everyone, had shut down and locked the company's entire system. He said he was just making sure everyone was on their toes.

It'd taken a week to fix.

In spite of pulling off that feat, he often couldn't remember his own address.

"You're afraid," he said. "Afraid to let love in."

And then every once in a while, like right now, he'd do or say something that told her his mind was sharp as a steel trap. "Just when I think you're not paying attention," she managed to say lightly.

"People don't think I see anything anymore, but I do. I'm not completely worthless, you know."

"You're not even a little bit worthless. You're a superhero," Alison said and took his hand. "*My* superhero."

"Then trust me now," Dale said. "Smile. You look ready to take someone's head off—the someone who's looking your way."

Pride ran hot in the Armstrong family, and she was not exempt. She was, in fact, choking on her own pride at this very moment.

Players were arriving, putting on cleats and warming up, joking with each other. The evening was warm with a light breeze coming off the water. It wouldn't get dark until nine o'clock, which was a good thing because the park didn't have lights.

Ryan had parked and gotten out of his truck and was indeed looking at her from across an expanse of a hundred feet. He lifted a hand in greeting.

She very maturely ducked behind her uncle, pretending to paw through her purse for something critical to this moment. Maybe a lobotomy.

"You look unhinged," Dale said.

"Yes, because terrible horrible death coming, remember?"

Her uncle snorted.

"Whatever," she muttered. "Is he still looking?"

"You mean after he waved to you and you pretended not to see him?"

"Oh my God. Some help you are."

"Here's an idea. Just be nice. Maybe even wave back." He watched her frantically search her purse for nothing. "Wow. When you're committed . . ." he said, sounding amused. "You sure you're okay?"

Alison turned her arm over and revealed the tiny script tattooed on the inside of her wrist: *I'm fine . . .*

Her reminder to herself that she was always fine. Always.

"He's still looking at you," Dale said ever so help-fully.

Shit. New tactic. Alison grabbed her phone and brought it up to her ear, pretending to be on it, smiling and talking to no one about a deal that didn't exist. She was still going at it, staring at her heels, when a dog let out a stream of yips that she'd have recognized any-where for the shrillness alone.

It was Killer. The six-pound Yorkshire terrier she and Ryan shared custody of took a flying leap at Alison, who caught her one-handed since her other hand was still holding her phone to her ear. "Killer, no," she whispered, trying to put her down. "You gotta go. Come on, baby, I love you madly, but pretty please scram before your daddy—"

Quivering with excitement, Killer was trying to kiss Alison's face. "Oh my God. Baby, this is the exact opposite of going away—"

Too late. Ryan was striding right toward them, Killer's leash in hand. He wore his team uniform: the blue jersey and the accompanying snug white pants that fit him like a glove, emphasizing a frame that never failed to make her mouth water. "Yes," Alison said quickly into her phone to no one. "Absolutely, I can make that deal happen—"

Her phone rang. While she was pretending to be on it. Closing her eyes, she answered quickly without looking at the screen. "*What?*"

There was a pause, then a female voice. "Is this . . . Armstrong Properties?"

Alison winced and took the harsh from her voice. "Yes, so sorry. Armstrong Properties, how can I help you?" She didn't look up. Nope, she might never look up again.

"My name's—"

Killer started yipping again, even more shrilly and loudly, if that was possible, putting out the alarm that a golden retriever was daring to cross the field. "*Shh! Sorry,*" Alison said into the phone, feeling beyond frazzled, so much so that she couldn't have repeated the woman's name to save her life. "How can I help you?"

"I understand that Armstrong Properties owns the Oak Street building that houses Paw Pals. I'm in the middle of getting a business loan to buy the doggy day care and I'm hoping to talk to you about getting a lease in my name for the building."

Simon had mentioned someone would be calling, as had Gabby Johansson, whose lease was up at the end of the month. "You'll need to qualify. Soon as I'm in the office tomorrow morning, I can get you the link to the application. Should I text it to this number?"

"Yes, please."

"Great, will do." Alison disconnected and stared at the pair of size twelve cleats now toe to toe with her heels.

"Hey you," Ryan said in that unbearably familiar voice, the *only* voice that had ever reached past her armor to squeeze her heart and leave her speechless. Then he turned to her uncle. "Hey, Mr. A, good to see you. How's it going?"

Her uncle nodded, then nudged Alison in the ribs.

She pasted a smile on her face. "Oh hey. Didn't see you."

"I waved to you from my truck. You were looking right at me when you answered your fake phone call."

"That was a real call, I'll have you know. And plus I forgot my glasses so I can't see much past my nose."

Ryan just shook his head, like she was a really bad liar. And it was true. She was a terrible liar. They both knew she'd had Lasik surgery and now boasted twenty-twenty eyesight.

Killer, still in Alison's arms, was bicycling her short little legs, trying to swim through the air to kiss her face.

Ryan watched as she nuzzled their little tyrant. "You can take her home with you for a couple of nights if you'd like."

It was a generous offer, one that completely contradicted the custody arrangement they'd both agreed to.

Alison hadn't gotten full, or even half, custody in the breakup, but that was her own fault. She spent much of her time in the Armstrong Properties offices, but a good part of her day was also out in the field, checking and showing properties, at all hours.

Normally, having a little dog that could fit into her purse would be perfect—except that Killer had a few behavioral issues they hadn't been able to cure her of. Less than a foot tall, she saw herself as the ruler of all living things, to be obeyed at all costs. She would go after a Doberman or nice little old ladies with equal fervor. In short, she was an asshole. The cutest little asshole Alison had ever seen. Yes, she wanted to take Killer home, but her calendar was full tomorrow. She was presenting at a city board meeting, trying to get approval for a permit for a piece of land Armstrong Properties owned on the north side of town. They'd kept it as a green belt for twenty years, but now they wanted to build on it. "I don't know if I can," she said apologetically. "Work—"

"Of course," he said evenly, like no skin off his nose. "Should've known."

"No, you don't understand—"

"Down, girl," Dale said.

Killer had hopped onto Dale's lap and was humping Dale's arm.

Which was reason number two that Alison couldn't take Killer to work. She humped anything in sight. It was adrenaline and excitement, or so the vet kept promising. They were to ignore the bad behavior rather than bring attention to it and accidentally encourage it.

But exactly how long was one to ignore the fact that six months later the dog was still humping everything in sight?

"She needs to be trained." This came from the old man sitting next to Dale. Mr. Olsen was older than dirt and owned the apartment building next to Dale's. They'd been Mr. and Mr. Bickering Bickersons for fifty-plus years now.

"Also," Mr. Olsen said, "your boys R and J blew your leaves onto my property again."

"That was the wind," Dale said.

Mr. Olsen curled a hand around his ear. "Eh?"

Dale turned and spoke loudly right into his ear. "The wind was blowing hard yesterday!"

"Speak the hell up!"

"I said you're a blowhard!" Dale yelled.

Dear God. Alison put a hand on Dale's arm and turned to Mr. Olsen. "I'll have the boys take care of the leaves, sorry about that." She looked at Dale. "Didn't you just tell *me* to be nicer?"

"Yes, to Ryan here."

"Don't worry about it, Dale," Ryan said. "Alison and I are fine. We understand each other now."

But that was the thing. He *didn't* understand her or he'd know how devastated she was about their breakup. Sure, she could just tell him—except that would be embarrassing.

"Why didn't you tell him about your big presentation tomorrow?" Dale asked after Ryan had walked to the field. "He'd have understood that, but now he thinks you just didn't want to make the time for him, like everyone keeps telling him."

"You know, you never used to talk this much before your strokes."

He gave a rough laugh. "Never had the time to dwell on your shortcomings."

Alison sighed. "It doesn't matter. He doesn't care *why* I am the way I am, he just cares that I *am* the way that I am."

"Or maybe he cares *too* much, and so do you, and I think that scares you. Also it wouldn't hurt you to assume good intent once in a while."

"I don't know how to assume good intent."

"Yeah, you also never knew how to be part of a family unit, but you and I worked on that, didn't we?" He held her gaze. "All anyone ever needs is some practice with their problems."

"And yet," Mr. Olsen piped up with, "after thirty years of practicing, you still haven't been able to figure out how to get your damn leaves off my property."

"Aren't you rooting for the visiting team?" Dale asked. "Their stand is on the *other* side of home base."

"Which was a longer walk from my car. Plus my daughter's over there, and she's mad at me."

"There's no amount of practice that can make me nice," Alison said. "You're either born with it or you're not."

"Now there's a load of bull pucky if I ever heard it," Dale said. "A girl who looks like you do, with the amount of brains and wit you have, just hasn't *had* to be nice."

"That's true," Mr. Olsen said. "Cuz if you were old and ugly like your uncle here, you'd have *had* to learn the skill."

Dale snorted. "You're older than me, old man."

"By one year. I was the football star. Got all the chicks, including your girlfriend."

Alison gaped at the two men. "You went to high school together?"

"Yes, but I was more popular," Mr. Olsen said.

"You were a bag of dicks," Dale said.

Mr. Olsen smirked. "That might actually be true. We were . . . what do you call it? Frenemies?"

Dale snorted. "Yeah. Sure."

"Frenemies," Alison said with a laugh. "Really?"

"You didn't have one?" Mr. Olsen asked. "I thought everyone had a frenemy in high school."

Oh, she'd most definitely had one. Emmie Harris. She'd been hugely popular, surrounded by a great family with money, and *still* had taken the time to steal Alison's college scholarship out from beneath her—the reason Alison had ended up at city college. And if that hadn't been enough to hate her, she'd had Alison arrested on false charges in front of the whole school.

Okay, maybe not exactly false charges. Sigh. Gee, such great memories. Luckily, the first pitch of the game was thrown and . . . hit.

Alison quickly scanned the field for Ryan. He was manning second base, concentrating on the fly ball, then *catching* the fly ball, and looking pretty damn sexy while he was at it. In a fast blur he threw to Simon on first, beating the hitter there.

The game went fast. She and Killer cuddled. Well, unless Ryan was playing, because when he was in the field or at bat, he had her full attention.

It was actually pretty pathetic.

She'd self-detonated their relationship. All he'd wanted was for her to try to fit into his life more, and with the people in it. He cared deeply about his circle. She'd just had no idea how big his circle actually was. But as Alison's own mom had shown the barest of interest in her daughter's life, this put her so far out of her league, she couldn't even see the league. Looking back, it shamed her actually, that she'd not handled Ryan's family with care, but with suspicion. The truth was that they'd intimidated her, and she'd never known what to do with that.

When the game was victoriously over, Ryan stood just off the field with a group of guys including Simon. "Wait here," she said to her uncle. "I'll be right back."

"Okay."

"I mean it," she said. "Don't move."

"*Okay.*"

Alison narrowed her eyes and Dale lifted his hands. Well, his left. His right just sort of twitched. "I *swear*," he said.

"Don't look at me like that. Last time I asked you to stay put, you begged a ride home from a stranger and I thought I'd lost you."

"I was hungry."

She pulled out a bag of trail mix from her purse and gave it to him.

"For a *burger*," he clarified.

"You and me both." She patted him on the shoulder. "After this though, I promise." She walked Killer onto the field for the handover, and her cousin met her halfway.

"Good game," she said.

"Yeah? Did you like that fly hit I got in the third?"

"Amazing."

"Uh-huh. I didn't get a fly hit. I got a home run."

Shit.

Simon laughed and turned to head to his dad.

"Wait," she said. "I'm still waiting for the lease of whoever you put in 2A."

"It's at the top of my to-do list."

"Your dad mentioned that he caught a glimpse of her the other day going up the stairs. Said she was pretty and that she held her left arm like he holds his right one. What does that mean? She have a stroke?"

Simon tugged playfully on a strand of her hair. "Good luck, Ali." And he headed to the bleachers.

"*Alison*," she muttered after him. Taking a deep breath, she moved toward Ryan and the other guys. They stopped talking and began to scatter.

Be nice, Dale had suggested. Sure. Sounded easy enough. She nodded to the tall, skinny guy. "Hey, Bill. How's it going? Did you ever get that boat you were always talking about?"

He blinked. "Actually, I was losing the boat."

Well, damn.

Bill shook his head. "As always, Alison, great to see you. Gotta go."

She turned to Ryan and discovered everyone else had left. Ryan was trying unsuccessfully not to laugh. She tossed up her hands. "Well, how was I supposed to know he was losing the boat? He just kept talking about the boat, on and on about the damn boat!"

Ryan's good humor faded away. "Because it was his dad's, but with the divorce, he couldn't afford the storage or dock fees. He had to sell."

Alison looked into his eyes and saw . . . pain. Pain *she'd* put there. In the breakup, he'd told her that she'd broken his heart. She'd thought that had just been words, but there was no denying he was hurting.

She'd done that.

Regret was a bitter pill. Not only had she lost him, she'd hurt him, all because she was a coward who hid behind her crappy upbringing, using it to convince herself she wasn't capable of showing love because *she* hadn't been shown it. That was bullshit and she knew it. She was better than her past, dammit. Great, and now she was sweating.

Ryan was watching Alison, his searing blue eyes hidden behind dark lenses.

"Sorry about the Bill thing." She swiped her brow. "You're making me nervous."

"Alison Pratt doesn't do nervous."

"You think I don't get nervous?" she asked in disbelief.

"I think you don't like to show it."

"Well, duh." She drew a deep breath. "And FYI, this is why people like me stick to fur babies."

He gave her a small smile. "That'd be a shame. I always thought you'd make a great mom if that's what you wanted."

Ignoring the lump in her throat and the tightness in her chest, Alison bent over Killer's soft head and gave her a kiss. "Love you, baby. I'll see you this weekend. Be good for Daddy."

"Daddy" snorted.

"She's not been good?" she asked.

"Sure. She only yakked up a stick in the middle of my bed at three A.M. last night. And then ate Michelle's shoe this morning."

Alison's head whipped up so fast she got whiplash. "Michelle, your cute, single neighbor Michelle?"

"Yes."

Alison's stomach hit her toes. What was his way-too-cute, *single* neighbor Michelle doing at his place this morning—*not* wearing her cheap knockoff Manolos? "She . . . spent the night?"

Ryan was quiet for the length of a single heartbeat, but it was long enough for Alison's heart to stop. She spun to walk away, but Ryan said her name.

She stopped. Didn't turn back.

"You and I broke up," he said quietly. "So not that it's any of your business, but no, she didn't spend the night. She was borrowing some milk."

"Code for hitting on you. And you broke up with me, remember?"

"I do remember. You were unhappy." His free hand settled on her arm. She hadn't even heard him approach. Slowly he turned her to face him. "And you've given me no indication that anything has changed in that department or that you'd like to talk about it—" He broke off when Killer licked his face. With a low laugh, he kissed the top of the dog's head.

And if Alison hadn't already melted from his touch, she'd have melted at that.

"*Do* you want to talk?" he asked her.

Did she? The horrifying, embarrassing truth was, she didn't know *how* to be happy. Nor did she know how to win him back. At least not without a complete personality change from introvert to extrovert, which she had no idea how to pull off. She stared at him, the words stuck in her throat.

After a beat, Ryan dropped his hand from her arm and stepped back, and she almost cried at the loss. "I thought . . ." she started, but had no idea how to finish.

"What? You thought what, Alison?"

She'd thought maybe she could continue to shut him out of her heart and still keep him. She'd thought . . . she'd thought he'd love her through this. Or beg her to stay. "I thought you loved me." Not what she'd meant to say, and horrified, Alison covered her own mouth with her hand.

"My love for you had nothing to do with what happened," he said.

She sucked in a breath at the past tense in that statement. A stab to her chest. The next and final stab came when he walked away, Killer eyeing her over his shoulder, her ridiculous little ears flopping in the wind, making Alison's eyes sting.

Simon watched Alison come off the field after talk-ing to Ryan. He hadn't been able to hear what she and Ryan had discussed, but he could tell by her defen-sive posture that it hadn't been good. He and Ali were family, but he and Ryan were close too, always had been, which was how he knew Ryan was hurting more from the breakup than Alison pretended not to be.

He hurt for the both of them, but God himself couldn't convince Alison to try something before she was ready—not even for the people who loved her. "You okay?" he asked as soon as she got within earshot.

She flipped her wrist to show him the *I'm fine* tat.

"I thought we talked about how using your words is necessary."

"Sometimes it's about silence," she said.

"Yeah?" His gaze flicked to Ryan walking off the field with a couple of the guys. "How's that working out for you?"

Behind his dad's back, Alison flipped her wrist again, this time so she could show him her middle finger.

"Ha ha," Simon said as his phone rang. Ryan. Slid-ing Alison a look, he answered.

"You coming to dinner with the team?" Ryan wanted to know.

He glanced over at his dad. "Sorry, can't."

"I've got Dale," Alison said.

Simon put Ryan on mute. "What?"

"I'll take him for you."

"Why?"

Her eyes narrowed.

"Okay, let me rephrase," he said. "I can't ask you to do that."

"You didn't ask, I offered. I promised him we'd marathon the latest season of *Total Bellas*."

Still staring at her, Simon unmuted Ryan, said he'd catch up with them and to save him a seat. Then he disconnected and looked at Alison some more. She hated reality TV. "What am I missing?"

She let out an exaggerated sigh. "Fine. I had an epiphany, okay? I realized that when I lost Ryan, I didn't have a lot of friends."

"And I'm what, chopped liver?"

"You're related to me. You have to like me."

He laughed. "No, I don't."

"But you do, right?"

She looked just a touch worried, so Simon tugged on a strand of her hair again. "I like you a whole lot, pissiness and all."

Alison rolled her eyes. "I'm looking to make someone *else* like me."

"Like a certain engineer named Ryan?"

"Well, yes, but I have to work my way up to him." She drew a deep breath. "I'm not supergood at this, all right? But it's not like I'm incapable or anything. I mean, I know how to love, blah blah. I'm just not good at peopling. So I'm going to practice."

He blinked and opened his mouth, but before he could do anything, she jabbed a finger at him. "Don't you dare laugh. This means a lot to me. And it's not just about a stupid guy either. I'm going to learn how to make and keep friendships going."

"Okay," he said, nodding. "I like it. How?"

"By practicing on you and your dad and anyone else I can think of. I googled some ideas during the game." She pulled out her phone. "Item number one," she read. "Get over yourself, the fear is in your head." She grimaced. "That might be true. Item number two: Be nice—which by the way, your dad also suggested. Number three: Listen." She nodded. "I could definitely do better there. And there're a bunch of little tips, like be aware of your resting bitch face."

He laughed.

"Whatever. There's lots more things to try, like put yourself out there, don't give in to the fear, show up . . . I can totally do this." She paused. "Probably. Oh and speaking of that, your contact called me about the lease for the Oak Street building and I was very nice. I'll get her an application and set up a time to meet with her."

"Great." Simon knew he should've told her right then and there that it was the same woman renting 2A. But he knew Alison. She'd drive him crazy about him pulling favors and want to know who this woman was to him. Frankly, he didn't want to explain it because . . . he didn't *know* what Emma was to him. A patient, yes. Also a friend. But there was more.

He wanted her.

He'd refused to acknowledge that for a long, long time now. But even when she'd been vulnerable and in so much pain, she'd been a force of bright light in a world that had become dark. She was resilient, determined, smart as hell, and incredibly, adorably sexy. And—and this was his favorite—stubborn as hell.

He'd told himself he could never have her, of course. She was a patient, and he wouldn't cross the line. But the line was getting harder to see. "She's the nicest person I know," he said. "So be . . . really nice."

"Hello, did you not hear my item number two?"

He shook his head and laughed. "Go for it. And you know what? I bet you two become good friends."

"Well, let's not go overboard."

Chapter 8

Step 8: Connect.

That night, Emma stood outside her apartment door, staring up the stairs to the attic. Might as well have been Mount Everest. She'd spent way too much time on her laptop today. Simon had told her from day one that sitting was death. He'd been correct, of course. She felt like a creaky skeleton. She needed to move.

But the stairs, the *steep* stairs, mocked her. The old Emma would have run up, no problem. Emma 2.0 wanted a nap. She sighed, but didn't walk away. She was going to do this. It was about pride now. She needed the sense of empowerment, and sitting on the roof watching the stars would go a long way toward soothing her aching bones *and* her equally aching soul. Determined, she pointed at the stairs. "I'm coming for you."

At her side, Hog huffed out a breath. St. Bernards needed daily exercise to keep their energy from turning destructive, but no one had ever told Hog that. "You do realize that someday, I *am* going to be back to running," she said. Maybe . . .

He plopped onto his belly and closed his eyes. Denial was his friend. Hers too. But she'd had enough of it. "Come on, big guy. Get up."

Hog gave a loud snore.

"You're faking."

He farted.

Emma sighed and fanned the air. "If you do this, I'll make you scrambled eggs after."

At the mention of his favorite, he opened one chocolate brown eye to gauge her honesty. She nodded.

With a grunt, he leapt up with surprising dexterity, making her laugh. "I think that's the fastest I've ever seen you move." She eyed the stairs again. "Okay, here we go." She held on to the handrail. "Yep. Totally doing this." Drawing a deep breath, she began. "One . . ." She was already exhausted. Like to-the-bone exhausted. She'd given up on job hunting and had turned her focus to acquiring Paw Pals. She'd created a business plan. She knew what she needed in the way of start-up funds. She'd applied for a business loan. And . . . she'd been turned down for a business loan. Refusing to let that get to her, she was already working on another application for a different bank, as well as filling out the lease paperwork Armstrong Properties had sent to her. She'd gotten stuck on the line requiring her to fill in her current source of income.

Simon had done a lot for her, but not even he could produce that, so she really needed to get to the roof and feel some sense of accomplishment, had to know that in spite of so much being out of her control, she'd be okay simply because she was breathing.

And not thanks to a ventilator.

At her side, Hog nudged her hand with his big, warm head, then licked her palm. She bent and hugged him. "You're right. We've got this." He licked her cheek in agreement. They had this.

Straightening, they kept going. At the halfway point, Emma was more than a little wobbly, but she forged on because she wanted to watch the stars, dammit. She wanted . . . well, what she also wanted was a little embarrassing.

She wanted Simon to be there.

At the landing, Hog dropped to the floor dramatically, panting like he'd just run a marathon. If Emma had the air left to laugh, she would have. Instead, she bent over at the knees and gasped for breath too. "Man, we're *so* out of shape."

Hog sent her a baleful look.

"Yes, *both* of us." The coma had taken a lot from her, including her endurance. Simon kept promising she'd get it back, but when? "One more flight to go." And with that, she drew a deep breath and started, Hog reluctantly at her side, her ever faithful wingman.

Even if he was only in it for the scrambled eggs.

Still, it felt like the very definition of love. Hog had no desire to get back into shape. Zero. None. But because she did, he was along for the ride, no questions asked.

If only the humans in her life had been half as kind.

There'd been more than a few nights over the past year when she'd let herself, in the deep dark of the night, mourn for what she'd lost. Her jobs, her livelihood. Her best friend. The man she'd thought she loved. No matter how much she pretended not to care, she *did* care.

She'd done her best to lift her chin and carry on, not to mention move on, but sometimes late at night the loneliness got to her. Not enough to want either of the exes squared back in her life, hell no. Life was too short. But enough to sometimes—only sometimes— question her no-more-relationships rule.

Ignoring the trembling in her limbs, Emma kept going. Halfway up the last set of stairs, she tripped.

With a gasp, she just managed to catch herself from taking a header.

Hog whined and nudged her shaking thigh with his head.

"I'm okay, buddy." Still breathing too fast, she clung to the rail and lowered herself to sit. How she'd done this before, she had zero idea.

Hog climbed into her lap. With a rough laugh that might have been almost tears, she dropped her sweaty face into the thick fur at his neck. Then she heard someone on the stairs below her and froze. A drop of sweat slid between her breasts, from exertion and now also nerves because she felt too exposed for public consumption.

And yep, those were definitely footsteps. She hadn't met any of her neighbors yet, but suddenly she wanted it to be anyone but Simon . . .

"Here. Sip this."

So of course it was him. Emma opened her eyes to find him holding out a smoothie. A green smoothie. She was not a fan of green, and he knew this.

"Tastes like bananas," he coaxed. "You like bananas."

She raised a brow. "You think drinking this is going to get me up the rest of these stairs?"

"No, I think your bad attitude is going to get you up the stairs. But the protein shake is definitely going to help."

"Again, it's green."

"Green is delicious."

"Sure, if it's Apple Jacks." She shook her head. "I feel like a gentleman would offer to carry me the rest of the way."

He gave her a considering look. "I'm either Hard-Ass PT or a gentleman, which is it going to be?"

The old Emma wanted Simon the gentleman because she really wasn't all that sure she could make it the rest of the way herself. Plus, she wouldn't mind having his hands on her outside of PT . . . No, wait. That was Emma 2.0 talking. "Can't I have both?"

He laughed. Then he got a better look at her face and his smile faded. Holding on to the smoothie himself, he passed her on by, stopping at the door at the top, where he once again held out the smoothie.

"Well, now you're too far away," she said.

"Did I mention I put peanut butter and a dab of chocolate in here?" He took a dramatic sip so that it left a liquid mustache. A green mustache. "Mmm." He slowly licked his lips. "Delicious."

"That's just mean."

He took another sip. "Sure hope you make it up here before it gets all melty."

Her mouth was actually watering, the bastard. She counted how many stairs were left. Eight. She pushed herself up and tackled half of them before having to stop and gasp for breath.

"You've got this, Emma."

She sighed and kept moving, stopping when she couldn't move another inch—one step from the top.

"Only one left."

"That last step and I haven't worked things out."

He just waited. Patient. Calm.

"You should know, I'm going to push you down the stairs when I get to you."

Another slurp of her shake was his only answer.

Hog hopped up onto the landing and she glared at her dog. "You're supposed to be on my side."

Simon pulled a dog cookie from his pocket.

Hog inhaled it without even chewing.

"That's low. Coaxing my dog to the dark side. How did you know to have the smoothie and dog cookie on you?"

"Maybe I'm looking out for you." He offered her a hand.

Stubborn to the bone, Emma shook her head. "I've got this."

"Just trying to help so you don't have to wrestle with that ten percent of you that isn't ready to be healed."

Oh, how she hated that he knew her so well as to be able to stomp all over her biggest fear. Hated even more how emotional it made her feel. Eyes burning, throat tight, chest aching, and worse, still sweating from the physicality of getting all the way up without dying, she ignored his proffered hand, took the last stair herself, and then . . . walked right into him and held on tight.

Simon stilled for a beat, then crouched to set down the shake and wrapped his arms around her.

"Sorry," she whispered, but not sorry enough to let go. "I'm all sweaty."

"I like it. It means you worked hard."

Emma snorted past the tears threatening. "You're a strange man."

She felt Simon smile against her hair. "That was a hell of an accomplishment, Emma."

Nodding, she didn't lift her face from where she'd pressed it into the crook of his shoulder, up against warm skin. He smelled good. Like guy good. His arms were strong and firm around her, and yet somehow also warm and welcoming. And something else, making her realize why this felt like such a moment.

It was the first time anyone had held her since . . . well, since Emma 1.0. She lifted her head and looked at him.

Cupping her face, he ran his thumbs along the sleep-deprived smudges beneath her eyes, his own softened now, showing concern. "Rough day?" he asked quietly.

Later Emma would tell herself it was his voice that broke her barriers. But that was the thing about losing the people closest to you, leaving you so vulnerable. There was no one in her life to express worry about her, to check in and make sure she was okay, and while she thrived on the independence, she missed . . . *connections.*

Having Simon ask about her day threatened to release the tears she'd been holding back. And like the tide, they couldn't be stopped. A tear slipped out, followed by another, each meeting his thumb. Brushing them away, he pulled her back into him, once again enfolding her in those warm, strong arms. Molding herself to him, she burrowed her face into his chest and let the tears fall.

He held her for a long time, rocking her lightly, his embrace a sweet comfort that made her heart ache even more. "I'm fine," she finally sniffed.

"I know."

"I just thought it'd be easier by now."

"It will be. Proud of you, Em."

She met his gaze. "You were watching me struggle the whole time, weren't you?"

"You needed to know you could do it yourself."

"I could've died."

"But you didn't."

She narrowed her eyes.

He smiled. She was amusing him again. "If you'd fallen, I'd have been there."

"I *did* fall."

"You tripped," he corrected. "And you caught yourself. You persevered. You did it, Emma, by yourself. Now you know you can do anything."

She let out a low laugh. She wanted to be pissed, but . . . he'd given her back something she hadn't even realized she was still missing—her independence. "You're a sneaky SOB, you know that?"

Simon didn't look bothered by this in the least. In fact, he looked . . . intensely focused. On her. That's when Emma realized she still had her hands on him, and not in a platonic on-his-table sort of way, which sometimes happened in PT in really tough sessions. She'd clutch at him like he was her only lifeline, while also secretly thinking about wrapping her hands around his neck and squeezing. Hard.

But this . . . this was *nothing* like that. His mouth was only a few inches from hers, and it was a great mouth too. He hadn't shaved that morning, and not yesterday either. Maybe even *several* mornings, and the scruff made her fingers itch to touch.

Emma lifted her gaze to his and found Simon's hazel eyes swirling with things that made her swallow hard.

She wanted to twine her arms around his neck and slide her hands into his silky hair. She wanted to pull his face to hers. She wanted to kiss him, and she thought maybe he wanted that too. "You stayed away from your spot on the roof all week for me, didn't you?"

He didn't answer, which really was his answer. He'd given up coming to his spot, the place he went to be alone and just be, so that if she made it all the way up here, she could have it.

She wasn't sure what to make of that. "This is your place. I don't want you to stay away because of me."

He started to shake his head, but she cut him off. "Promise me." She lifted her pinkie finger between them. "Pinkie promise."

"You need it more—"

"Pinkie promise me you won't stay out of your own space because of me, or I'll go back to crying at every single appointment I have with you."

"I hate it when you cry."

Emma waggled her pinkie.

With a shake of his head, Simon hooked his pinkie in hers.

"Say it," she said.

That got a smile out of him. "Why am I constantly surprised by you?"

"I'm easy to underestimate. *Say it*, Simon."

He met her gaze with his own half-amused but half-serious gaze. "I promise not to stay away from the roof because you might be up here huffing and puffing."

She laughed. "Thank you."

"You're welcome. And anyone who underestimates you is an idiot."

Their gazes locked and held, and she found herself more breathless now than she had been on the stairs. She liked that he hadn't pulled back. He could have no idea why this hug felt so important to her, and yet he let her have it, seeming content to hold her for as long as she wanted.

"Do you want to sit?" he asked.

"I'm not sure I can make it to the couch," she admitted.

"Put your feet on mine."

"I'll hurt you—"

He lifted her off the ground a few inches and lowered her again—onto his feet. Tightening one arm around her, he grabbed the drink in his free hand and walked her backward to the couch.

If she closed her eyes, it almost felt like they were slow dancing. It was the closest she'd gotten to dancing of any kind in a year, and it felt so good she almost cried. Nodding to how he hadn't spilled a single drop of the smoothie, she murmured, "That's talent."

"I'm a talented guy."

With a laugh, she sank gratefully onto the cushions.

He stood there a moment, looking down at her. "How you doing?"

When Emma gave him a double thumbs-up, Simon nodded and sat as well, handing her the smoothie. He was quiet while she drank, just letting her be with her thoughts, which she appreciated more than she could say. When she finished, she held up the glass. "What did you hide in here? I'm betting a bunch of icky stuff."

He took the empty glass and set it on the small coffee table.

"Hello?"

He met her gaze, his eyes amused. "Spinach, kale, and flaxseed."

She blinked. "No way."

"Yes way."

"You tricked me."

Amusement crossed his face. "Actually, no. I'd never trick you into doing something you didn't want to do."

"Are you kidding me? You do it every time I'm at PT." She lowered her voice to mock his timbre. "'One more, Emma. Another. Okay, again . . .'" She shook her head. "Until I've done exactly however many you wanted."

"That's not a trick. I tell you right up front what I expect out of you. Always."

This was actually true. He set expectations, gave her choices, asked for her input, and then . . . proceeded to do only what he'd promised her he would do, all while waiting patiently for her to do the same, assuming she was as grown up as he was.

Note: she was *not*. "So you're saying I just drank *spinach*." She couldn't even say this without grimacing.

"And kale and flaxseed."

She shuddered.

"You going to throw up?" he asked.

Fair question. In the beginning of their PT sessions all those months ago, there'd been plenty of times when he'd asked her if she was at her breaking point, if she needed a break or to stop altogether.

Pride had always made her reply that she was fine.

And then, almost without fail, she'd end up on her hands and knees throwing up into his trash can. He'd rub her back until she stopped spasming, then had always given her a break to recover.

Then, if she wanted, she could finish their session. Her choice.

The point being that he always, always, assumed she could handle herself and took her at her word. She'd learned a lot from that, actually. One, that there was no need for her to hide things from him regarding her physical being. Once she'd gotten to that point, where she trusted and believed in him fully, her progress had grown by leaps and bounds.

These days she'd progressed enough to cut back PT to once a week. But after all this time, there was still an ease between them, a comfort. They each knew their roles. He was her unbending but trusted enforcer.

All she had to do was let him help her get better.

But suddenly their roles felt blurred, at least in her mind. Because she wanted a hell of a lot more than just his PT touch. "No, I'm not going to throw up." Emma gave a wry smile. "The smoothie was the way to go. I would've grabbed something with caffeine and probably something questionable but fast to eat, like salami and cheese."

Simon gave a mild grimace. "And how do you feel now?"

She gave that some consideration. Her stomach wasn't feeling squishy or icky or bloated. In fact, she felt . . . really good. "If I tell you that I feel almost good enough to get up and try the stairs again, you won't actually make me do it, right?"

"I'd never make you do anything you don't want to."

The night was a dark one. No moon. Thick clouds hiding the glow of the stars. Disappointing, but even more so was the fact that she couldn't see his expression clearly. "Can I get that in writing so I can pull it out at our next session?"

"You don't need it in writing. And I'm talking in *or* out of the PT clinic."

Okay, so he wasn't feeling playful. She turned to face him on the love seat and found his eyes dark and serious, and damn. *Compelling.* "So . . . what happens here on the roof, is it like what happens in Vegas stays in Vegas?"

He let a beat go by. "I'm not sure I should answer that."

Probably smart. Whenever she was with him lately, she felt things she'd almost forgotten about. Hunger. Desire. Need . . . Made all the more shocking because it was centered in only a few select body parts that she hadn't thought about in a long time.

And then there was her brain. Everything she knew about Simon told her he was a good guy, one of the best. But the last time she'd let a man into her heart, he'd walked when the going got rough.

Okay, so the going had gotten *really* rough, but Ned hadn't just turned away. He'd taken her best friend, whom Emma was equally mad at. In fact, she'd be happy to never see either of them ever again. It'd been a painful lesson—her own heart couldn't be trusted.

As for her body . . . well, it had its own ideas. "I'm feeling conflicted," she finally said.

"Because . . ."

"Because I gave up relationships and commitments." Plus, she was pretty sure she'd no longer recognize either one if it hit her right in the face. Huh. Maybe she was feeling a little sorry for herself today. She'd work on that. *Tomorrow*.

Simon was looking at her thoughtfully. "You're trying to tell me something."

"Actually, I'm thinking show, not tell."

He paused. "Normally, I'd agree one hundred percent. But they say that making any sort of big decision after a traumatic event is a bad idea."

"No doubt 'they' are right," she said, using air quotes.

He gave a small smile. "Your small motor skills are coming back more and more each day. As is your left arm."

And she hadn't even realized. Emma stared at her hands. "I feel like I'm moving at a snail's pace."

"Nothing wrong with that. The tortoise always won the race, after all." Simon leaned back to stare up at the sky.

She mirrored his position, looking up, feeling her blood pressure immediately slow and calm. No idea if that was the view or the man next to her. Glad it was dark, she said, "About that no commitment thing . . . it doesn't mean no sex." She hesitated. Bit her lip. "Just thought you should know."

He turned his head and looked at her in a way that had heat moving through her body like hot lava. "You're in the driver's seat, Emma. The controls are all yours."

She stared at him and then huffed out a breath. "Great."

He smirked. "You can't control yourself?"

Emma turned back to study the sky again. "I'd rather drink more spinach than answer that question."

Simon laughed. *Laughed.* Because they both knew she had zero self-control. In fact, she was this close to crawling up his body to straddle him and ride him like a bronco.

He abruptly stood up.

"You're leaving?" she asked in disbelief.

He took a slow, purposeful breath, his eyes on her mouth. "I think that's the best thing I could do right now."

Not even close. Nope, the best thing he could do right now was *her*.

Clearly reading her mind, he let out a rough groan. His gaze, hot and dark, met hers and she sucked in a breath, bombarded by waves of sensations.

"Emma, if you knew what I wanted to do to you when you look at me like that . . ." His voice was low, husky. Sexy as hell.

Good thing she was sitting because all her bones melted. "What's stopping you?"

"I'm struggling to remember."

She swallowed hard. She wanted this. Wanted him. And he wanted her back. It was her secret every-night fantasy coming to life, but that was just it. It was fantasy.

Wasn't it?

Because here, in real time, there were facts to face. Logistics. The actual physicality of it all. The truth was now that she was thinking with her head instead of her needy girlie parts, she was remembering her body no longer moved the way she wanted it to. Being with Simon would be . . . magic. Erotic, sensual magic. It'd be full speed ahead.

But she didn't have that setting anymore. She needed to start slow. Use training wheels. Like maybe start with a date with her shower massager, where she could practice a solo run and see how things went. But then she met his gaze, his hungry, heavy-lidded gaze, and felt herself go damp. Her body wanted him.

But her brain whispered, *You're wearing ugly undies and you didn't shave your legs all the way up.*

Good thing Emma 2.0 didn't give a shit. "Simon—"

His cell phone buzzed. He pulled out his phone, looked at the screen, and swore beneath his breath. "It's a text from my dad." His voice was heavy with regret. "He broke the remote. Last time he did that, he threw it at the TV."

"You have to go. I understand."

He looked surprised. "You do?"

"Of course. Your dad comes first. Go."

"Let me help you down to your apartment."

"Not necessary," she said. "I'm okay."

Simon looked at her. "You're more than okay."

Emma smiled. It was true. And she had him to thank. Tonight he'd given her back something she'd needed—that missing connection. And if his phone hadn't gone off, they might've taken it to the next level. But for better or worse, he was gone and she wasn't going to have to decide between magic and reality after all. At least not tonight.

Chapter 9

Step 9: Try again.

Two mornings later, Alison stood inside Paw Pals, waiting to show the space to Simon's connection, a woman named Emma Harris who she sincerely hoped wasn't her old nemesis Emmie Harris. What were the odds? she wondered. Probably zilch. Hopefully zilch. It was only 6:30 A.M. and the place was still closed. Gabby had given her permission to let herself inside, as long as she locked up after.

Alison walked through the place, refamiliarizing herself with the building, her heels clicking across the floor. Everything was clean and painted in bright, fun colors. Oddly enough for a girl who'd never been big on animals, she felt very comfortable here.

She'd never had a pet. She and her mom had lived in a four-story walk-up, a one-room apartment consisting of five hundred square feet and a whole bunch of doom and gloom.

When Alison had struck out on her own after high school, getting a pet hadn't been on her radar. The only thing she'd concentrated on had been survival.

Until Ryan.

And by association, Killer.

They'd both stolen her heart.

"Arf!"

Speaking of the devil. Alison had met Ryan at their coffee shop for the handover. She supposed it wasn't actually "their" coffee shop anymore, but Killer had jumped up and down, thrilled to see her, and that was all that mattered.

The man hadn't jumped up and down. He'd been in her favorite jeans of his, soft and faded, lovingly caressing the body she sometimes dreamed about.

Okay, always dreamed about.

The name of Ryan's company was on the right pec of his untucked work shirt. He'd looked a little overheated, a little rough and tumble around the edges, like maybe he hadn't slept well. He'd still been the best thing she'd seen since . . . well, the last time she'd seen him.

"Thanks," she said, cuddling Killer into her. "Oh, almost forgot. Got you this." She handed him the four extra coffees she'd bought and had in a holder. "You know, for letting me have the baby a day early."

He took a sip from one of the coffees and softened in surprise that it was a Shot in the Dark, his favorite— drip brewed, black, with a shot of espresso. "Four?"

"I know you're heading to a job, so I bought the others for your crew. Slim, Joey, and Tank, right?"

"Right." Ryan cocked his head, looking curious. "What are you up to?"

"Remember when we broke up?"

"You mean two weeks ago? Yeah. I remember."

Alison gave a half smile. "Well, me trying to fit into your life was important to you."

He arched a brow. "So you *did* hear me."

"I did."

He'd pushed his sunglasses to the top of his head then, his eyes warmer now. Much warmer. "Thanks." He nudged a chin toward Killer. "And as for the baby, I told you. Anytime."

She nodded, and so began an awkward silence—on her part, not his. He didn't do awkward anything. She searched her brain for a way to break the silence, but didn't know how.

You've been studying for this!

But it was like high school all over again; she was about to take a final and her mind was blank . . .

Smile! Ask about him . . . !

She managed the first, then struggled for a question. "So. How's your mom and"—she tried not to pause or make any sort of face to reveal her thoughts on his nosy-ass family—"your sister."

But he'd clearly seen right through her because he'd snorted, kissed Killer on the top of her head, then met Alison's gaze for a long, charged beat. "They are annoyingly like Killer; they're fierce in their loyalty and slow to trust. Know anyone else like that?"

She gave him an innocent blink and he laughed. "I like the effort though." He tipped up her chin to look right into her eyes. "A lot. Thanks again for the coffee."

Then he'd walked away.

And she'd come here, still smiling like an idiot. If she'd known studying for something would work, she'd have done a lot better in school.

There was a rustling and Alison looked over to see Miss Kitty come out from the back. She sat in the recliner in the front window and began knitting so fast that her needles were nothing but a blur. She was the stuff of legends and just about everyone was terrified of her.

Alison included, which she wouldn't admit upon threat of death. "Morning."

Miss Kitty nodded regally.

From the floor, Killer gave a yip.

Miss Kitty narrowed her already narrowed eyes, and of course Killer started barking.

"Stop," Alison said.

Killer did not stop. Not until the old woman stood to her full five-foot height and stared Killer down.

Killer zipped it, but her pride wouldn't let her shut up completely. Instead, she shifted to growling, low and quiet beneath her breath.

Miss Kitty murmured something in German and Killer abruptly stopped.

Alison snorted, nodded her appreciation to Miss Kitty, and then went about finishing her walk-through. It was an interesting property, reminiscent of the barn it'd once been, but it'd be hard to rent when Gabby was gone. Alison hoped this new client worked out, though she had her doubts since she hadn't yet received the qualifying application. So she'd been unable to get a background check.

Her phone buzzed with an incoming text.

Simon: Don't be scary.

Simon: Don't let Killer jump on her.

Simon: And don't forget to smile . . .

Alison rolled her eyes and shoved her phone away. What did he mean, don't let Killer jump on her? Killer couldn't knock over a flea. She scooped up the little dog and nuzzled her in. "So here's the thing, K. You're it for me. I love you to the moon and back. But let's face it, we can be scary. We're going to fix that, okay?"

Miss Kitty harrumphed, but when Alison looked at her, the old woman was paying her no attention at all.

Killer licked her cheek gently, her eyes warm with affection.

"Okay then, it's a deal," Alison said, smiling. "We're both working on us." If only it was as easily done as said. She set Killer down. "We're going to practice on our hopefully new client. No barking, no growling. Got it?"

Killer cocked her head to the side.

"Yeah, yeah, *I'll* behave too. We just have to realize that our fear of rejection is all in our heads." She pulled out her phone again and brought up her notes app to look at the list she'd copied and pasted in for herself. *I WILL make a good impression. I WILL be receptive. I WILL smile and be nice. I WILL make a friend today.* She looked at Killer, who seemed doubtful.

"Whatever. It's happening." She kept pacing, continuing her pep talk, her words echoing off the walls, the click of her heels as she paced matched by Killer's little doggy nails tapping on the floor as she paced with her. "And hey, next time we go to the dog park, maybe you can find yourself a real friend too, instead of being the fun police all the time."

The front door opened. Alison turned and then froze in disbelief. Because damn, it *was* . . . "Emmie Harris," she heard herself say dully.

Emmie had gone statuelike as well. "It's *Emma*. And I did not see this coming." She shook her head. "Did *not* see this coming." She shook her head again, looking like she'd just eaten something sour. "Ali Pratt. Who'd have thought?"

"It's *Alison*." She too sounded like she'd eaten something sour, but being face-to-face with the unexpected blast from her past had knocked her off her game and sucked the air from her lungs.

"*You're* Simon's cousin?" Emma asked, clearly hoping there was some mistake.

Alison wished there was. "Yes." She shifted her attention to the hugest dog she'd ever seen, sitting at Emma's side, a St. Bernard the size of a VW.

"Hog," Emma said by way of introduction.

Alison nodded numbly, feeling like that hurt high school girl all over again, filled with an immature sense of hate and jealousy that she'd thought she'd long since gotten over.

Apparently not.

The thing is, Emma had *zero* reason to feel the same. It'd been Emma who'd ruined Alison's life, not the other way around. She opened her mouth to say hell no, get the hell out, there was no way she'd take her on as a client, but Killer, who'd been growling low in her throat at Hog, escalated to barking. "Killer, stop. Killer, *sit.*"

Killer did not sit. She charged forward, her little paws gaining purchase on the concrete before Alison could catch her.

The St. Bernard yelped and hid behind Emma.

This didn't stop Killer. The little thing flew after the bigger dog, chasing it around Emma in tight circles. Well, at least Killer went in tight circles. The clumsy St. Bernard couldn't get traction on the concrete, not to mention was lead-footed as . . . well, a St. Bernard. Giving up, he stopped short, lifted a leg, and . . .

"No!" Emma yelled. "Hog, no!"

Too late. Hog peed all over Killer.

"Oh my God!" Alison gasped, surging forward, but Killer was safe from the big dog, who was now running toward the door.

"I'm so sorry!" Emma called out, but before Alison could tell her where to shove that apology, Emma caught up with Hog. Dropping to her knees, she winced as if that movement hurt like hell, then wrapped her arms around the big guy and hugged him tight. "I'm so sorry, baby."

Wow. Okay, so she wasn't apologizing to Alison or Killer, she was apologizing to her big oaf masquerading as a dog?

Emma looked up. "I'm his emotional support."

Alison just stared at her in disbelief.

Emma kissed Hog on his massive head and said, "Stay, baby."

Hog sat. Stayed.

Emma moved to Killer and started to scoop her up.

"I wouldn't," Alison warned. "She doesn't like being picked up. She can get nippy with strangers, and—"

And nothing, because Emma had Killer in her arms. Not only did Killer not bite her, she instead immediately stopped growling and barking. What the actual hell?

Emma moved through the place like she already owned it, vanishing into the back.

Seriously, *what the hell?* Alison followed and found Emma and *her* dog at the wash station. Her nemesis was carefully checking the water temperature, then in less than five minutes, she had Killer bathed and wrapped in a towel. Impressive because she did most of it with her right hand, as if her left arm wasn't a part of her body. Something niggled at her about that, but Emma was cuddling Killer into her, distracting Alison. Her dog—so named because she was a warrior who hated everyone equally—gave Emma the moon eyes and . . . laid her head on the woman's shoulder.

"Aw," Emma said, stroking her. "What a sweet girl."

Killer was a lot of things. Too smart for her own good. Independent. High maintenance. But sweet? *No.* And frankly, Alison was boggled as Emma handed over Killer and then grabbed a mop and went back out front to clean up the mess on the floor.

Okay, fine. So Emma knew her stuff. Maybe she'd make the perfect person for this building. Maybe. She followed Emma out, watching as she waved at Miss Kitty and got a warm wave in return.

Huh.

"She comes with the place," Alison explained. "Not negotiable."

"She's welcome," Emma said in a tone that made Alison's spine go ramrod straight.

Miss Kitty bowed her head at Emma, for a beat actually looking sweet and compliant. Feeling oddly jealous, Alison crossed her arms. "Okay, I feel behind. Catch me up. You and Simon are . . . what exactly?"

"He's my PT."

The memory concerning Emma's arm suddenly clicked in for Alison as she flashed back to the news stories about Emma's accident.

Killer, who'd caught sight of Hog again, now standing as close to the front door as he could get, was back to growling low in her throat.

"Stop before you get peed on again," Alison told her.

Killer did not stop.

Emma headed toward Hog—the strangest name for a dog Alison had ever heard—and glanced at Killer on her way. "Hush now. I know he's scary big, but I promise you, he'd never hurt you."

Killer leapt from Alison's arms right into Emma's, while Alison just stared because her dog—whom Alison counted on to hate everyone—had just made a friend before her.

Emma kissed Killer's cute little face. "Sweet girl. I'm going to set you down now, and you're going to be nice to my baby. There's enough love for everyone here. Yeah?"

Killer blinked her two lovestruck-puppy eyes. Emma laughed, kissed her again, and set her on the floor. Then she pulled Hog away from the door he'd hugged himself up to. No easy feat given that he must've weighed well over a hundred pounds. Emma crouched in front of him. "I know she was mean, but she's sorry. It's going to be okay. I've got you."

The big oaf licked her from chin to forehead and Alison shuddered at how much slobber must've been involved. Emma simply smiled and kissed her dog between the eyes. "Remember, we don't give in to bullies. We've got this."

"Hey," Alison said. "You think *we're* the bullies? Are you kidding me?"

Emma looked up. "You told everyone in our entire school that I *put out* to get A's in AP Biology and AP History."

Alison bit back her wince. "You have no proof that was me."

"You keyed 'bitch' into the car I drove to school."

When Alison had woken up that morning, she'd never in a million years known she'd be facing her past later. Which she hated to do on a good day. But now it was a bad day and it was all coming back to her, flooding her head with the miserable memories.

In their junior year of high school, Alison had volunteered at the local women's center, logging hours for scholarships. Once she'd had enough on the books, she'd quit so she could get a job bagging groceries for actual money, which she'd needed, badly.

Emma had taken over Alison's volunteer position at the women's center. And when someone from the scholarship board had called to verify Alison's hours, Emma had said Alison didn't work there. Not "she *did* work here for a time" . . . just "she *doesn't* work here."

Alison had lost the scholarship—and the chance to go to her dream school, UCLA. She'd ended up having to stay in Wildstone, which she hated.

So yeah, she'd started the rumors about Emma. Keyed her car. She wasn't proud of it, but she'd certainly paid the price. And in the end, none of it had hurt Emma, though it'd nearly destroyed Alison. "We're not here to talk about our history."

"Maybe we should," Emma said. "Get it all out in the open. And actually, you'd be helping me since I've got some serious holes in my memory. To be honest, high school's just a blur."

What kind of bullshit was that? She'd ruined Alison's life and didn't even remember doing it? "Great idea. Let's ignore the past."

Emma stared at her. "That's literally the opposite of what I just suggested."

"Look, do you want to lease this building or not?"

Emma laughed roughly and sat. Right there on the floor, like maybe her knees were weak or something.

She took in a shaky breath and began to rub her thigh and calf muscles.

"What are you doing?" Alison asked as Hog plopped at Emma's side and pressed up tight against her.

"Sorry." Emma ground her teeth. "*Cramp.*" Sweat broke out on her temple and she went pale. So pale she was nearly see-through. Alison pulled out her phone to call 911.

"Don't."

"Do you need help?"

"Not from you."

Okaaaay. Alison slid her phone away and wondered how to proceed. A tactful person she was not. "I, uh, heard about your accident last year." Hard not to, it'd been all over the news. Emma had been out for a run and stepped off a curb. The stop sign had been hidden behind an old, gnarly, overgrown oak tree. An oncoming car missed the sign and hit Emma before spinning out of control, in turn getting hit by a second car in the intersection.

Someone had died. Emma had nearly died as well, but after a coma, she had made a miraculous recovery. "I saw that the town sent you a life-size card with a bunch of get well signatures. I go to the town hall meetings to represent my uncle and his business, and it came up."

"Did it?" Emma asked, rubbing her leg. "Because I didn't see your name on the card."

"There were hundreds of signatures on that card, how could you possibly know I wasn't one of them?"

"Because I read all the signatures."

"All of them?"

Emma sighed. "Look, I know you can't possibly understand unless you've gone through it, but try to imagine being in a coma for two months, during which time you were kinda sorta aware of what was going on around you, but mostly felt like you were living in a weird, distorted nightmare. For fifty-nine long days and nights, completely and utterly alone, unable to move. Then you wake up and learn that not only can you not go home, but you have to go to a rehab facility. For the rest of the year."

In spite of herself, Alison felt sympathy well up. "Um—"

"And then maybe after this accident, you need to relearn things, like how to walk and eat without horrifying people. And on top of all that, when you're finally released to go, the two most important people in your life are gone because your fiancé fell in love with someone else during your stay at the rehab center—your best friend. They've moved in together in the apartment you shared with said supposed best friend. They have noisy sex that sounds a helluva lot better than any sex you've ever had. So yeah, I did read each and every signature on that card. I kept it too. There are nights that those signatures are my only company."

Hog climbed onto her legs and she wrapped her arms around him. "I'm okay," she told him softly.

All while Alison stared at her, eyes burning with an emotion she didn't want to name. "You're right," she said quietly. "I didn't sign it. I never thought you'd actually read it, because truth is, if I'd been you, I wouldn't have. I'd have felt sorry for myself and angry at the world." She hesitated. "And while I'm being honest, I wouldn't have known how to sign it to you anyway."

"Sure you would have," Emma said. "'Hope you rot in hell, forever, *not* yours, Ali Pratt.'"

"*Alison*." She had to laugh though. "But okay, yeah. Fair, and possibly accurate." She drew a deep breath. "Are you . . . doing better?"

"The cramp's gone."

"I mean . . ." She gestured at Emma's body, which by all accounts had been badly broken.

"Sure," Emma said. "I'm running in a half marathon next week, just like I'd been planning before I got hit."

Alison's eyes widened in surprise before she realized

Emma was being sarcastic. "You . . . don't want to talk about it."

"I do not. So. The lease?"

"You have to qualify. Like I said, I didn't get the application."

"Working on it." Emma got stiffly to her feet. She looked around with a barely there smile. "I work here. Did you know that?"

"No," Alison said. "Because again, no application back from you." She paused. "Is that why you want to buy Paw Pals?"

"I want to buy it because it'd be perfect for me. Plus no one else wants to hire me." As she moved, Hog stayed at her side, but lagged a little, like he needed Emma as a shield from Killer, who was standing smack in the center of the room glaring at Hog.

Emma was still looking around with an expression Alison couldn't quite read, but hell if she was going to ask another personal question after being shut down on the last one.

"What are the terms?" Emily asked.

"First, last, and a security deposit."

Emma hesitated. "That's a big chunk at once."

Alison shrugged. Not her problem.

"Can you give me some time to come up with the money?"

"Until you put down a deposit, you risk losing it." This probably wouldn't happen. They had a lot of vacancies right now.

Emma met her gaze and called her bluff. "You *just* found out Gabby's not renewing her lease. This won't be an easy building to fill. So I don't imagine it'll suddenly be snapped up tomorrow." She looked around again. "I want to negotiate the monthly rent."

"It's nonnegotiable," Alison said automatically. Because the hell with this. She picked up Killer, who licked Alison on the chin, lowering her blood pressure. *Stay calm. Don't think about how you'd like to send her packing.*

Emma gave Alison a smile. "Okay, then. I guess I'll have to keep looking. Thanks, Ali. It's been . . . interesting."

"*Alison.*" But she grimaced, fought with herself, and lost. "*Wait.*"

Emma and Hog looked back in unison.

"How much were *you* thinking?" Alison asked.

"In this economy?" Emma smiled. "Ten percent off the top."

"And why exactly should I give *you* a deal?"

"Because the art studio next door is closing, which means two open places on the same block." Emma shook her head. "Not very good for your bottom line."

Oh no she didn't. "It's on a good street, and this space is updated and has the huge glass front, *and* a dedicated parking lot in the back."

Emma went behind the counter and grabbed a pad and pen. She scribbled a number down before holding it up to Alison.

Alison laughed. She set Killer down and snatched the pad and pen. She crossed out Emma's number and wrote one of her own, halfway between the original offer and Emma's counteroffer.

Emma looked at it, shook her head, and wrote another number.

Alison stared at it. "Are you kidding me? That's only one dollar difference."

"Do we have a deal or not?"

"It's a dollar, *Emmie*."

"It's a *dollar*, Ali."

Okay, let it go. "Fine, whatever. It's just a dollar." She held out her hand.

"It's the principle of the thing," Emma said and then, having had the last word, shook Alison's hand.

Alison opened her mouth to say something that no doubt would blow the whole deal, but Hog took that very moment to lean against Alison's legs, looking up at her with . . . damn. Sweet adoration. It melted her black heart, and she stroked his soft, clearly well-taken-care-of fur, liking that she didn't have to bend down like she did with Killer. "Aw. You're just a big sweetie."

"He's trained to pick up when people are losing their shit."

Alison looked up at Emma. "I'm not losing my shit, *you're* losing *your* shit."

Emma rolled her eyes, but smiled fondly at Hog, whose tail was now sweeping the floor.

Clearly proud of himself for changing the energy in the room, he panted up a smile at both of them as a line of drool made its way from his mouth to the floor in slow motion, and Alison felt her heart melt a little. *Don't you fall in love with the dog belonging to the devil herself.* "You going to send me your app?"

"Yes."

Alison nodded. "Are you going to keep Gabby's other employees?"

"Why?"

"Just trying a hand at being friendly."

"Well, don't," Emma said. "You scare me when you do that."

Hurt bubbled up, which surprised Alison. She didn't usually feel things like hurt. She drew a deep breath. *Step 9: Try again,* Google had told her. She drew a deep breath. "This is a big venture to take on by yourself."

"Easier than finding a job that'll allow me to take Hog to work."

"Tell me about it," Alison said. "My ex got custody of Killer for that exact reason." She kissed Killer on the nose. "But we have today, don't we, baby?"

"My ex got custody too," Emma said softly.

"Of Hog?"

"No. My best friend. I'm pretty sure he fell for her because she didn't come with any baggage, and I've got so much I should have to pay extra fees."

"That part didn't make the news," Alison said.

"Nope."

She narrowed her eyes. "If you're playing with me, I swear—"

"It's all pathetically true." Emma shrugged with mostly just her right shoulder. "My ex was never a good multitasker when it came to relationships. The moment I get scooped up off the pavement by the paramedics, my life became one task too many for him to handle."

"Wow, he sucks." Alison sighed. "And dammit." She pointed at Emma. "Okay, you win. But this is the one and only time."

Emma looked pleased. "You aren't going to scratch 'bitch' into the side of my car, are you?"

"Depends. Are you going to play nice?"

"TBD."

"Then same."

Emma laughed. "Good thing I don't actually have a car."

Damn. If she didn't hate her, Alison might have even liked her. It wasn't until later that night that she suddenly realized why Emma's left arm not appearing to work as good as her right made sense—she was Simon's new renter.

Chapter 10

Step 10: Be yourself.

The next morning, Simon woke up to his phone buzzing. He knew it was Alison by the level of annoyance in the cell's vibration.

"Did I wake you?" she asked.

"Do you care?"

"Not even a little bit, since you didn't call me back yesterday. I met Emma."

Since he'd just been dreaming about Emma, dreaming about what might have happened between them if his dad hadn't needed him, Simon drew a deep breath. "I didn't call you back because I was swamped all day and then fell asleep."

"Let me repeat—I met Emma."

"And?"

"*And* she's the girl who had me arrested in high school."

Simon sat straight up in bed. "Run that by me again?"

Alison told him the story from all those years ago, and, boggled, he shook his head. He'd already been away at college when all that happened, and though they'd remained close, his cousin had never told him any of this before. "Why didn't you tell me back then that you were having problems?"

Silence.

He sighed and answered his own question. "Because you're an Armstrong and therefore stubborn to the bone." He ran a hand over his face, hating that she'd gone through all of it alone, though he wasn't exactly thrilled about the shit she'd pulled on Emma either. "Why did you vandalize her car?"

"Did I start this story with 'let me tell you some great stuff about me'? No, I did not." She sighed. "Look, it happened and she had me *arrested*. So I'm going to need you to be on my side."

He needed caffeine for this. "You said the charges were dropped."

"Yes, because they couldn't prove it was me. And that's not my point."

Right. Alison liked her grudges. She liked to hug them, hold them close. This of course was why she had only him and his dad. People didn't understand how big a heart she really had, and how easily she could be hurt. "Okay, well, since you're already mad, you should probably know that Emma's renting 2A."

"Oh, I figured that one out for myself, no thanks to you."

"Look," Simon said. "It doesn't matter what happened all those years ago. You need a tenant for that building and Emma wants to lease it. And you're trying to be more open to people, right?"

"Maybe."

"Definitely. So start with Emma. Just a suggestion."

Alison told him where he could put his suggestions and disconnected.

Simon shook his head, rolled out of bed, fed his dad, let Jodie in, reminded his dad to keep his pants on until he got home, and then left. It was a PT day, which made it a good day. He got to the clinic early enough to get his own workout in first. He saw two patients in a row, then had a thirty-minute break before his third patient—Emma. So he was surprised to find her in the front reception area, sitting in a corner with a laptop and a mug of steaming tea.

Something in his chest warmed at just the sight of her. And that wasn't his only reaction. He felt himself smile, like really smile.

You got it bad.

"Hey," he said. "You're early. On purpose. In the morning. Everything okay?"

She jerked and pulled out her earbuds. At her quick movement, Hog scrambled behind Emma, hiding.

"I'm sorry. I didn't mean to sneak up on you guys."

"No, it's okay." Emma reached behind her to put a hand on Hog. "I was about to throw this thing out the window anyway," she said of her laptop.

Simon ruffled the dog's big head. "Sorry, buddy."

Hog licked Simon's hand. He was forgiven.

"I'm stealing your internet," Emma said. "I still haven't gotten signed up at the apartment."

"Feel free to use mine. The network's Malicious Virus, and the password is cookies, no caps." When Emma laughed, he smiled. "It's the only password my dad can remember. What are you working on?"

"Getting a business loan. Oh, and I met your cousin Ali."

"She let you call her Ali?"

"No. But I did it anyway."

He laughed. "Because . . . ?"

"Because when I knew her, I knew her as Ali. And also because it irritated her."

He laughed again and sat next to her. "Bet that was fun."

"It had its moments. So . . . you're Ali's boss?"

"Temporarily."

"Small world. Did she tell you that we were mortal enemies in high school?"

"I didn't know you two had a past when I suggested you call her," he said. "But yeah, she told me the story."

"Okay, that's good news. Maybe you can fill me in on why she hates me so much."

This gave him pause. "You don't know?"

"I know she accused me of putting out to get good grades. I know she scratched 'bitch' into the car I drove to school."

He knew this wasn't his fight. It was, however, his circus, his monkey. "She has some issues."

She snorted at the understatement.

"Look, I'll just say that she had had it rough. Nothing in life has ever come easy for her. Making friends is a challenge, and I imagine it must've irked her that the friendliest girl in school, and one of the most popular, didn't like her."

Emma was brows up. "She told you all that?"

"I filled in the blanks."

"It's not that I didn't like her. We just didn't hang out in the same circles. The only reason we knew each other at all was because I replaced her at the internship at the women's center. We overlapped for maybe a day?

She never said a word to me. Then she was gone and suddenly people were gossiping about me. It turned out that she'd spread a bunch of hurtful rumors, which never made any sense."

Damn, Alison. "I'm not going to even attempt to give excuses for her, but I can tell you that she's a different person now. She's still got a pretty tough exterior, but if you're lucky enough to get to know who she is on the inside, she's good to have by your side. She's fiercely loyal and would lay down her life for you."

Emma shook her head. "I'm going to have to take your word on that." She drew a deep breath. "Look, I'm willing to leave the past in the past. I'm much more worried about the *now.* I've got an interview at North Bank later. I want to get this one right. I had no idea how hard it would be to get a business loan. Turns out being in a coma isn't an excuse for not working for an entire year, and I've been turned down twice already. I think this might be my last shot."

He hated that for her. "I'm sorry, Emma."

"Me too. I was excited. For a minute I actually thought I'd finally found my thing. My new place in the world."

"Have you tried options other than traditional banking? There are lots of other options."

"I hope you're right," she said.

"Just don't give up."

"I won't."

"Should I make you pinkie promise?"

Smiling, Emma stuck out her pinkie. When they touched, an electrical current went through them both.

"Still there then," she murmured.

Yeah. It was still there, big-time. And the other night they'd gotten way too close to the fire. So Simon gestured to the gym. "You ready?"

"Sure. What's a little more torture in a day anyway."

After the PT session was over, Simon watched Emma head to the locker room and then he walked out to the juice bar, where he found Kelly brooding over her books. "Everything good?"

"Better than," she said. "Business is up."

"So why don't you look thrilled?"

She moved over to make room for him. "It's grown so fast. It's too much for me to manage on my own." She paused. "The hospital offered to buy me out."

He was surprised. "And you're thinking about it."

"Yes."

"I thought you wanted to be your own boss forever."

"I do," she said. "But I also want to live my life."

Simon got that. All too well. He spent most of his waking hours working these days, no real life to speak of.

"Forget about me," she said. "How's Emma doing?"

The interest was sincere. She'd been there throughout Emma's entire treatment, from the time she'd first come from rehab and could barely move, to now when she was close to starting to run again—if she wanted. "If" being only because Simon had his doubts she was actually ready. She was holding back from full recovery, he knew this. What he didn't know for certain was why—though he had his suspicions.

Survivor's guilt. He knew she blamed herself for what had happened, which left her struggling with being alive when someone else hadn't gotten so lucky. Guilt was a bitch, as he knew all too well. "We're working on legs," he said. "She's still cramping sporadically. She's changing. She's going to need a juice."

"Of course," Kelly said, getting up to go behind the bar. "But . . . very *interesting*."

"What?"

She waggled her brows at him. "That you know exactly where she is and what she's doing."

Simon pointed to the open double doors into the gym area. "She was right there for all to see as of five minutes ago."

"Uh-huh. And the way you were sitting together out here before your session?"

"She's working on some personal stuff."

"You make her laugh," Kelly said. "But even more interesting . . . she makes *you* laugh."

He shook his head. "Don't."

"Don't what?" she asked innocently.

"Don't do your shrink thing on me."

"Well, I was one for five years before switching lanes. It's in my blood." She gave him a knowing look. "There's something between you two. Always has been."

Because he didn't know what to do with the truth of that statement, Simon turned away. The last thing he wanted to talk about was his feelings for Emma, especially when he had no business having any feelings for her at all. Even without the conflict of interest, his life was not his own. "You of all people know I don't have time for a relationship."

"Simon," she said gently. "You didn't have time for me because I wasn't in your heart. You love me, but you were never *in* love with me. You've yet to find the woman you care enough about to make a place in your life for."

He hated that it was true. But it just proved to him that as much as he could feel himself falling for one adorably sexy Emma Harris, it couldn't ever happen. "You think you'll sell?"

"You're changing the subject."

"Trying."

"Look." She stopped working on Emma's drink and looked Simon in the eyes, her own earnest. "It's been a long time since you let yourself live a little. All I'm saying is there's a spark between the two of you. Why not go with it?"

"It's not that simple. She's a patient."

"And I was your boss. That didn't stop us. You can't deny that when you're both in the same room, the heat factor goes up exponentially. I walked by the two of you a bit ago and got so much static electricity I nearly electrocuted myself going into my office." Kelly smiled at him. "I like it. You need it. You need to act on it."

"It seems unethical."

"It's not like you're a doctor. Or a shrink. So what if you're helping her get back to herself? And I've seen her look at you. Trust me, it's two-sided."

"She's . . . not ready."

"Maybe. Maybe not." Kelly shrugged. "That's up to her. But I'm talking about you. You're too stubborn to let yourself be happy, like . . ." She cocked her head as she looked at him. "Like maybe you think you don't deserve it."

He opened his mouth, but she cut him off. "You do realize you've pretty much given up your life to help your dad. But, Simon, your dad never gave up his life for yours. He wouldn't want this."

"What would you have me do, Kelly? Put him in a facility? Let his business fall apart so he has no income?"

"No, I'd get help. I'd get a full-time aide for him. Several. One of them should take an evening shift or two so you could have a life too."

"I'm fine."

"Are you?" Kelly asked.

Emma came out of the back locker room, moving more easily across the floor than she had even two weeks ago. She had her things in a backpack on her shoulders, looking . . . damn. Better than she had in a long time.

Kelly gave him a meaningful look that said *get your shit together.*

Emma came their way and sat on the stool next to Simon. At the sudden silence between him and Kelly, she gave them a second, longer look. "Am I interrupting?"

"Yes," Kelly said. "I'm lecturing Simon about getting a life, and how important that is."

"Food," Simon said to Emma. "You need food to refuel."

Kelly rolled her eyes and turned to the fridge to pull out two chicken avocado salads, the toppings, including two small containers of crumbled blue cheese, and a small loaf of homemade blueberry-lemon bread.

"I'll take his crumbled blue cheese," Emma said, snatching it up.

"Because . . ." Kelly looked at Simon with faux guile. "He's lactose intolerant?"

Emma snorted. "No, he doesn't eat it because"—she lowered her voice to imitate his—"*that stuff'll kill you, Em.*"

Damn. Why did he love it when she made fun of him?

Kelly laughed. She'd been trying to push Simon's buttons. Instead she'd proved a point. That he and Emma had gotten close enough that she knew him better than . . . well, most people.

He'd let her in.

Yeah, yeah, fine. He had. But he hadn't meant to, and until the other night on the roof, he'd had no reason to think she might feel the same about him. As for what he *did* feel for her, that was still a big hot ball of messy emotion the weight of an elephant sitting on his chest. Best to ignore.

Emma reached over and stole his pickle.

Kelly started to laugh again, but at Simon's deadpan look, she pretend-coughed to cover it.

"He hates pickles," Emma explained.

"Oh, I know," Kelly said. "I'm just finding it funny that you know it too." And with that, she smirked and walked off.

Emma watched her go. "What was that about?"

"Nothing."

"Seemed like something."

He shoveled some salad in.

"Think that's going to save you?" she asked, once again mimicking him, using the very words and tone he often used on her in their sessions.

It made him laugh, and damn, Kelly was right. Emma *was* good for him. And something else too. He was no longer surprised by how comfortable he felt when he was with her. Yeah, so much of his life wasn't his own right now, but this, *her*, was. Their working relationship had been built slowly, over months and months, on honesty and trust alone. It'd begun with Emma having no choice but to fully trust Simon, and he'd done his best to live up to that for her. Their ensuing friendship was also built on honesty and trust, but ironically, this had been *him* having to trust *her*, at least at first, and he'd been rusty at that. Still, it'd worked and it was good, so he saw no reason to give up either the honesty or the trust now. "Kelly thinks we should make a move on this thing happening between us."

She stared at him. "And you?" she finally asked. "What do you think?"

Honesty. He told himself that was the only thing he had in his favor. "That we can't do this and still work together."

She nodded and set down her fork. "Well, that settles it then."

Okay, good. One of them was thinking straight. She'd drawn the line in the sand, and neither of them would cross it. That was the smart thing to do. The right thing. The *only* thing, so he nodded, hoping like hell his disappointment wasn't showing.

"Simon?"

"Yeah?"

"You're fired."

He blinked, compliant when she stood and pulled him to his feet, then stepped close and looked at him with those beautiful eyes that he'd never been able to resist. She went up on tiptoe and, hands to his chest, brushed her lips to his.

A simple touch, and his heart thundered in his chest. He wondered if she could feel it beneath her hand, but then he could wonder about nothing because she kissed him again, deeper, and his brain ceased functioning. God. Her mouth, her taste . . .

When Emma pulled back, Simon's first instinct was to tighten his hold on her as they stared at each other. He finally cleared his throat. "That was a long time coming."

"What, me firing you?" she asked innocently.

That got a laugh from him. "Smartass."

She smiled and stopped his heart.

Maybe, *maybe* if they'd never kissed, he could've walked away. He wanted to believe that, but it was too late now.

Her smile got bigger. *She knew.* "You wanted that too," she said.

"Hard for a man to hide it."

She let her gaze run over his body and took a shaky breath when she discovered that yep, indeed, he was hiding nothing.

"Emma—"

"Shh." She bit her lower lip and stared at him some more. "I need to see something." She slid her hands up his chest and into his hair, kissing him again, a little less tentative, a whole lot more intense. With a rough groan, he hauled her in closer and kissed her back until they were both breathless.

After, she pressed her forehead to his chest and took a deep gulp of air. "Holy cow."

"Yeah."

Her fingers tightened in his shirt. "No, you don't get it." She lifted her head. "This is . . . um. Well, I don't really even know how to say it."

"Emma, it's me. You just say it. Whatever it is."

"Okay." She nodded. "So . . . you're the first person I've felt even a tingle with that didn't have to do with damaged nerves." She paused. "You know, down-stairs."

His reaction to that had nothing to do with being a PT and everything to do with being a man. Not ready to acknowledge that given where they were, he smiled and teased, "Downstairs . . . ?"

She narrowed her eyes at him. "If you laugh at me and my downstairs—"

He caught her hand just as she whirled to walk off. Tucking a strand of hair behind her ear, he dropped his voice to a barely there whisper as he looked right into her eyes. "I would never, ever, ever laugh at your downstairs. Drop to my knees and worship at it, yes. Laugh, no."

She stared up at him, eyes a little glazed over. Then she blinked and shook it off. "You're lethal in close."

Simon smiled.

Emma looked away, inhaled, and then looked back. "I haven't felt much like a woman in a long time. What

I went through, it's . . ." She searched for a word. "Dehumanizing."

He gave a slow shake of his head. "From the first moment I saw you, Emma, you were all woman."

She drew a shaky breath. "Thanks—even if you're just being nice, I appreciate it."

"Have I ever lied to you?"

"No. You've omitted or redirected, but never lied."

"I've omitted the statistics and chances for you to run again because they weren't encouraging, which wouldn't have helped you. I've misdirected when you've been on a self-destructive path."

"So . . . for the greater good and all that?"

"Yes," he said, knowing she was teasing him, but he wasn't. Not about this, not about her.

"Well," she said lightly. "Okay then. Great chitchat, thanks."

Again he pulled her back when she turned to go. "Remember the other night when I said you were in the driver's seat?"

"Yes."

"You still are. Always will be. Nothing happens unless you want it to."

"And only if we're not working together," she said clearly.

He nodded.

She continued to stare up at him, thinking so hard he could almost smell something burning.

"Good to know," she finally said.

Which didn't tell him much. He had no idea which way she was going to go with this thing between them. And then she whispered his name.

"Yeah?" he whispered back.

"You're still fired."

Simon considered skipping that night's ball game because his home care help had called in sick. And with Alison still at work, he had no one to sit with his dad on the bleachers. But he also didn't have a sub, and he didn't want to let the guys down. So he and his dad piled into the car and headed to the park.

When they got out, Simon looked his dad in the eyes. "Remember. Ali's running late. All you have to do is sit on the first row of the bleachers and wait for her."

Dale eyed the bleachers and scratched his jaw. A sure tell that he was up to no good.

"I mean it, Dad. No wandering off. No telling tall tales. No—"

"No living. No enjoying myself. Got it, son. Just sit here and wait for my terrible horrible death."

"Dad." Simon rubbed his left eye, which was twitching. "I just don't want you to get hurt."

"Life hurts, son. Get used to it."

A truck parked next to them and Ryan got out and smiled. "Hey, Mr. A. How are you feeling?"

"Like I could handle first base. Gonna sub me in?"

Ryan grinned. "We might. If your son sucks."

"Don't encourage him," Simon said.

"Right," his dad said, "because the only fun to be had is yours."

Simon sighed.

Ryan eyeballed them both. "Okay, I feel like I missed something."

"Simon kissed the new girl and he liked it," Dale said.

Simon stared at his dad in shock. "What did you just say?"

Ryan's eyes had nearly fallen right out of his head. "What new girl?"

"The cutie pie neighbor he moved into our building," Dale said. "Oh, and she's a patient of his too. Coma Girl."

"She has a name," Simon said, giving his dad a dark look. "And how do you know all this? Shit, don't tell me. You saw Kelly yesterday at PT."

Dale scratched his jaw again.

"Let me guess. You just remembered she also told you not to tell me she told you."

Ryan was cracking up big-time and leaned into Dale. "What else do you know? Tell us everything."

"I know he's mooning over her like a lovesick puppy."

"Keep talking, Dad, and I swear I'll put you out to pasture."

Dale grinned. He knew an empty threat when he heard one. "I also know that even after all she's been through, she's sweet and kind and funny. Kelly said she's a keeper. So you tell me, boys, how many keepers have you two met?"

Ryan and Simon looked at each other.

"See?" Dale said triumphantly. "They're rare. They're unicorns. So if my son was smart, he'd keep her. But I worry." He looked at Simon. "I love you, son, but you've never been the sharpest tool in the shed when it comes to women."

Ryan snorted.

"You shouldn't talk," Dale said. "Because you're the best friend my son's ever had, but you're no sharper than he is. You let the most amazing woman I know slip right through your fingers."

Ryan opened his mouth, but Dale jabbed a finger at him. "And yeah, maybe Alison's not all sweet and kind and soft on the outside, maybe she's got sharp edges that can cut like a knife, but you know what? She'd lay down her life for the people she cares about. She's got what it takes on the inside, and you cut her loose. So yeah, you're as stupid as Simon in my book."

"I agree with you there," Ryan said seriously, smile gone. "But you know her. Until she's done pushing me away, there's nothing I can do."

Dale just shook his head in disgust at the both of them. "It's a sad day when an old geezer like me is smarter than you two idiots put together. Don't know your asses from your own noses." And with that, he stalked off toward the bleachers.

"Did he just call us idiots?" Ryan asked.

"Idiots who don't know our asses from our noses. And you know what else?"

"What?"

"He's right."

Chapter 11

Step 11: Be kind.

Afew nights later, Emma and Hog were on the roof, stargazing. Okay, so Emma was stargazing. Hog was doing what Emma couldn't seem to—catching up on his beauty sleep. What she *could* do was think about seeing Ali Pratt and how it had made her feel like a stupid teenager all over again, including all the messy emotions surging through her. She shook that off and thought about Paw Pals, and how much she wanted it. Thought about making a future for herself.

Thought about Simon.

He'd kissed her. No, she'd kissed him, and then he'd taken control of the kiss and rocked her world in the very best of ways. She'd known it'd be good, but she hadn't known it'd be earth-shattering, rattling her to her very foundation. She had no idea what to do with that.

Eventually hunger got her to her feet. "Time to figure out dinner."

Hog scrambled to all fours and trotted excitedly across the roof.

"You do realize you only move with any sort of speed when I mention food, right?"

Hog pleaded the Fifth. He was nose to the door, eyes fixated on it as if it might open for him if he stared at it long enough.

She opened it for him and then stared in surprise. The staircase was lit by strings of twinkle lights wrapped around the handrails, lighting up her way. The next set of stairs was lit too, making her reverse commute warm and cozy, and magical.

R and J were just finishing up on her floor near her front door when she got there. "Wow," she said. "It's beautiful. But why?"

R shrugged. "Simon asked us to do it."

J handed her a brown bag. Whatever was in it smelled amazing. "What's this?" she asked.

He just smiled bashfully and looked at R, who answered for him. "Simon's working, so he asked us to help you celebrate making the climb."

She was stunned. When was the last time someone had thought of her like this, gone out of their way to make her feel special? She couldn't even remember—literally. "But how did he know I'd gone to the roof?"

J pointed to a security camera mounted high on the wall in a corner of the stairwell.

"There's one on each floor," R said.

She'd never even noticed.

"He said the lights would hopefully bring some cheer," he said. "And the food's his personal favorite Thai takeout. He thought you'd be hungry after all that work. Oh, and if you need dessert, I'm supposed to get you the ice cream out of his freezer."

Suddenly the hallway wasn't the only thing warm. She was too, from the inside out. "Does he offer dinner and dessert to all the tenants who climb the stairs?"

"Uh . . ." Clearly sensing he was about to step into a minefield without the proper gear, R looked like a deer in the headlights.

J shook his head at his twin, but R said, "He thought you could use some happy and . . ."

Emma arched a brow. "I'm going to need the rest of that sentence, R."

"And . . . he likes you?"

J sucked in some air, leaned into his brother, and whispered something.

"Right." R grimaced. "*Don't* tell her that last part."

J smacked his brother upside the back of his head and then they both escaped, racing to the stairs, shoving each other into the walls for apparent fun before they vanished from sight.

Emma stood there a moment, taking in the sparkling lights with a silly smile on her face, melancholy gone. She'd gotten both up *and* down the stairs without stopping once. She had another loan application in. She'd kissed a really hot guy . . . She had dinner in hand. Things were looking up for her.

Way up.

So she made an about-face. Instead of letting her and Hog into her place, they took the stairs down to the first floor, because maybe Simon was working from home and she could thank him personally. She knocked, then realized she was probably imposing. For one thing, if Simon was here, he'd have shown up himself, and—

The door opened and Alison stared at her. "What the hell?"

Emma stared back. "You live here too?"

"No. I'm Uncle Dale's caretaker tonight."

"Hey, I take care of myself, thank you very much," a male yelled from inside the apartment. Uncle Dale, presumably. "I just won twenty bucks off your lousy poker face, didn't I?"

Alison made an annoyed sound. "I forgot that you live in this building now too—though how I forgot that, I've got no idea. Simon is way too soft." She eyed the brown bag in Emma's hand and stopped frowning. "Is that Thai takeout?"

"Yes." Emma hugged the food closer to her. "I wanted to thank Simon for the food, and also for putting up the strings of lights—"

"Hold up. *Simon* bought you Thai, but I'm stuck cooking dinner?"

"Because you lost to him at poker last night," Dale yelled from within. "You promised to cook dinner tonight if you lost, which you did. Badly. In case you're wondering, it's because you always let your emotions get the best of you."

Alison looked Emma straight in the eyes. "I'll take one percent off your future monthly lease if you tell me you're here to share the Thai."

"Uh . . ."

"Great." Alison dragged her in and Emma found herself standing in the middle of a living room much the same as hers, except more lived in.

"Good news, Uncle Dale," Alison called out. "You don't have to suffer my cooking after all. We got delivery."

Dale came out of the kitchen. He was wearing a white T-shirt under a brightly colored Hawaiian shirt, paisley boxers, and black socks.

No pants.

Alison waved in his general direction. "Uncle Dale, Emma. Emma, Uncle Dale—who's fundamentally opposed to eating dinner with pants on." Then she took the bag of food from Emma.

"Pants hinder my eating prowess," Uncle Dale said. He patted Hog on the top of his big head and sat at the dining room table, expectantly eyeing the food. "You're the new girl."

Emma moved closer. "Yes. I'm renting upstairs."

He nodded. "You're also dating my son."

"No." Kissing him, yes. Dating, no. "He's my physical therapist."

He just smiled.

Emma knew he'd had two strokes. And she could see it in the right side of his face, which didn't quite line up with the left side. His speech was a little halted, but she could still understand him.

"Let's see what we've got," Dale said, pointing to the bag.

Alison pulled everything out and sighed dramatically. "He really should've gotten us some too."

"Nah," Dale said. "You'd have modified everything, making it a pain in the ass to order." He looked at Emma. "Simon hates to order for her."

"Hey," Alison said. "I have some allergies."

"Yeah. Allergies to going with the flow."

Alison slid him a look. "Okay, first, why in the hell do your doctors keep telling us that your mind is frail? You're the least frail person I know."

He beamed. "Thank you."

"Not a compliment."

"Thought you were working on being nice to get Ryan back before he starts going out with his nice neighbor."

"Okay, first of all, he's not dating his neighbor." Alison said this in a tone that suggested she wasn't actually sure if it was true, but that she hoped it was. "And second of all, I *am* working on being nice."

Dale chuckled.

Emma tried really hard not to laugh as well, especially when Alison leveled her with a dark look. Emma bit her tongue and opened the container. "Glasses?"

"Do you mean plates?" Alison asked.

Shit. She flushed. "Yes. Plates."

Dale was looking at her thoughtfully, a new light in his eyes. Understanding. "You know what I hate more than saying the wrong word?" he asked.

"People assuming that because I can't always find the words that I'm dumb. So they talk to me real slow and loud, like I'm deaf and need to ride on the short bus."

"Oh my God." Alison shook her head at him. "We've talked about the kinds of things you can't say anymore. Short bus being one of them."

"Bah. People are too sensitive." He looked at Emma. "I also walk like a zombie sometimes. I suppose I'm not allowed to say that either."

"My left arm refuses to obey my brain," Emma said. "Especially when I don't do my exercises that your son gave me to do."

Dale laughed. "I hate that. You know why? Because it makes him right. Which I hate even more than exercises."

Emma leaned in. "I secretly call him Hard-Ass PT."

Dale gave a hoot and slapped his knee. "I like you." He dug into his food, spilling half off the fork before it got to his mouth. "My son must like you too. He doesn't usually bring anyone home. He says I scare them off."

"He didn't bring her home," Alison pointed out. "She just showed up. And as for scaring people off, he *has* asked you a million times to wear pants."

Dale waved this off as inconsequential.

Emma found herself smiling, feeling more alive than she had in a long time. Well, except when she'd been kissing Dale's son. That had made her pretty damn alive. The only thing that would've made this evening better was if Alison was gone and Simon was home.

At the moment, her nemesis was helping Dale get more food, making sure he had everything he needed. Which, if Emma was being honest, was actually kind of sweet.

Dale must have thought so too because he patted his niece's hand and smiled at her. "You're a good girl. When I get back to work, I'm going to give you a big fat raise."

Alison smiled. "You already pay me too much. Keep your money and just get better so you can come back already."

"Why?" Dale asked. "You got your eye on another job or something?"

"More like following advice from a certain uncle about improving my personal life, and maybe I need some time freed up for it." Then she leaned in and kissed his cheek.

Emma was fascinated. She'd had no idea that Alison was even human, much less . . . gentle and loving.

"You should let Ryan see this side of you," Dale said.

"Yeah, well, it's not that easy," Alison muttered.

Dale raised a brow. "Why not?"

Her eyes narrowed. "How about this. I'll show Ryan that side of me when you show Simon that same side of *you*."

Dale rolled his eyes. "Rubbish."

"That's what I thought." Alison caught Emma's curiosity. "You remember how I was in high school?"

"*Was?*"

"Whatever," Alison said when Dale snickered. "Let's just say I came by it honestly. Uncle Dale here taught me everything I need to know about pushing away those who love you the most."

"Hey," he said.

Alison looked at her uncle. "You know you were hard on Simon growing up, *really* hard."

"Hey, the boy was bound for trouble. He needed direction, discipline, and sometimes a keeper."

Alison shook her head. "He was smart, driven, focused, and needed to know you loved him."

"Would've made him soft."

Alison just rolled her eyes. "You know I'm right. You were awful to him." She pointed at her uncle. "I know you loved Aunt Jenny. I know you love me. I even know you love your stubborn-as-hell son. But it'd be nice if *he* knew it too."

"*Phfft.*"

"I give up," Alison said and dug into her food until her phone buzzed with a text. She eyed the screen and sighed. "There's a security issue at one of our buildings."

"Go," Dale said.

"I can't. I promised Simon I'd stay until he got home."

"I could stay," Emma said.

Alison paused, looking torn.

"You don't trust me," Emma guessed. "But I did just share my food with you."

"That has nothing to do with trust." Alison scrubbed a hand down her face. "But I don't see a choice here, so fine. You'll stay until he's in bed? You have to make sure he looks you right in the eye and promises not to get up or cause any trouble. And check that his fingers aren't crossed."

Dale snorted. "A guy sneaks out one time . . ."

Alison glared at him. "You walked to the corner drugstore, bought a pack of cigarettes, and then smoked them on the walk back. You got apprehended by a cop for smoking in a no-smoking zone, and you very nearly got arrested for refusing to put out the cigarette."

"I'd just bought it!"

Alison tossed up her hands.

Emma was soaking all this up, aching because she missed her parents. These guys bickered and fought and loved as crazily as her family did. "I've got this, Alison."

"You'll make him promise?"

"Want it in writing?" Dale asked dryly.

Alison didn't take her eyes off Emma. "I've got him," Emma said. "Go."

Alison nodded and turned to leave, but then hesitated. "Thanks. You know, for doing this for me."

The words sounded like they'd been torn from her throat. "You're welcome," Emma said. "But I'm not doing it for you. I'm doing it for Dale."

"Understood."

When she was gone, Emma and Dale finished eating and then did the dishes together, joking that Emma's good right hand and Dale's good left made them one whole person. Dale entertained her the whole time by telling bad dad jokes that continued to the bedtime routine. She waited in the hallway while Dale showered.

"What's the difference between snowmen and snow-women?" he yelled from the bathroom.

"I give up."

"Snowballs!"

Emma laughed in spite of herself and was grateful when he came out fully covered in pj's, top and bottoms. "What now?" she asked him.

"I'm going to go watch my shows in bed, where I hereby solemnly swear I'll stay put. I'd ask if you could join me, but that's on the list of things I'm not supposed to say to anyone, especially females."

"You've got a whole list?"

He nodded. "It's in the notes app on my phone. Alison and Simon keep adding to it. Mostly Simon. He's got a lot of stupid rules. Stuff like no more online poker games and no driving. He's ridiculously strict."

"Sounds like maybe he learned from the best."

He scrubbed a hand over his jaw, his expression rueful. "Yeah."

"Good night, Dale."

"Night." He started into his bedroom, then turned back. "I like you for him, you know. You're sweet and kind, but I suspect you've got a backbone of steel."

"Along with some platinum and titanium," she quipped.

"Tough too." He smiled. "Yeah. You'll do."

"It's not like that."

"Uh-huh." He walked into his bedroom and shut the door. "Night, Coma Girl," he said through the wood.

Emma smiled. "Night, Dale." She turned to leave and ran smack into Simon.

"Hey," he said, putting his hands on her arms to hold her steady. "What are you doing here?"

Good question. She couldn't remember what excuse she'd given herself to knock on his door *knowing* he wasn't home. Curiosity? Nosiness? "Wanted to thank you for the lights," she said. "They're lovely."

He smiled and she soaked him in. Dark jeans, a button-down. Jaw dark with sexy scruff. Eyes holding a look of hunger . . . all of it hot as hell.

"Where's Alison?" he asked.

"She got a business call and had to leave."

"Shit. I'm sorry." He shoved a hand through his already tousled hair. "She should've called me, not conned you into helping."

They hadn't talked since they'd kissed, and she was trying really hard to concentrate on his words, but her gaze drifted to his mouth of its own volition.

"Emma."

She loved the way her name sounded like a growl on his lips. "Hmm?"

With a low groan, he shifted in close, sandwiching her between the wall and his body. His hands slid along her jaw and into her hair, causing a delicious full-body shiver as he tilted her face up to his.

Yes! Kiss me again!

Simon stared into her eyes, then at her mouth, and with another rough groan, he stepped back, letting his hands fall from her.

"What?" she whispered, her lips tingling from the kiss he hadn't planted on her.

Expression intense, he held her gaze. "You're really okay with this?"

Emma's life goals and fears had changed after the coma. Once upon a time, she hadn't wanted to make waves. Now, she just wanted to live, waves and all. "If you mean more of the heart-stopping kissing and what hopefully comes after that, then yes please."

He gave a rough laugh. "Heart-stopping?"

"Like you don't know."

Emma felt her pulse kick into gear when Simon pressed every inch of him into her—and he had a lot of really great inches—and finally kissed her. She was well on her way to forgetting her own name when he stopped.

She made a sound of protest and tried to pull him back into her, but he resisted. Meeting her gaze, his voice was husky but quiet. "I'm sorry."

"For . . . ?"

"I'm thinking blueberry pancakes," Dale said, and Emma nearly jumped out of her skin.

"Hey," she said, pointing at Dale. "You promised."

Dale looked sheepish. "I got hungry."

"Dad, can you give us a minute?"

"Sure, but hurry up. You're holding the kitchen hostage."

Simon let out a breath, brushed a kiss to Emma's temple, and put space between them. "I can't let him cook for himself, he tends to set off the fire alarm. The fire department isn't thrilled with us."

Emma shook her head and squeezed his hand, even if she'd wanted to climb him like a tree. Which was fantasy anyway. Her reality was that she hadn't been with anyone in so long, she wasn't actually sure she remembered how. "It's okay."

Simon nodded, but looked surprisingly, and endearingly, unsure as to whether she was being honest about understanding. So she went up on tiptoes, gave him a soft good-night kiss, smiled when he groaned and reached for her, and backed away from him. "See you," she whispered.

His solemn expression softened. "See you."

For the first time ever, Emma climbed the stairs with a smile. Halfway up, she started to doubt what had just happened. Started to think maybe it hadn't been about Simon's dad, but about . . . him purposely putting the brakes on.

Then her phone dinged an incoming email and distracted her. All day she'd been trying to load her email but she'd not had enough reception. She glanced at the screen. The first email was from her bank and she could see the first two lines in preview. It started with: "We regret to inform you . . ."

She tripped on the next step and nearly went down. Nearly. She caught herself.

Hog whined and nudged.

"I'm fine." But the truth was, she was the furthest thing from fine.

Chapter 12

Step 12: Be open.

The next morning, Emma unlocked and opened Paw Pals, pretending she wasn't an inch from a panic attack about her uncertain future. *It's not uncertain at all; you're going to have to move to Florida and live with your parents.*

She moved woodenly through the building, turning on lights, booting up the computer, filling water bowls, reloading the snack bins, making sure everything was still spotless from the previous night's cleaning. In the back, surrounded by the adorable, colorful play yards, she stopped to just take in the fact that this really wasn't going to happen for her, this future she'd hoped for, the one that would've put her on her feet, given her a purpose and a hope.

Gone.

Hog leaned on her, eyes warm with love and worry. "I know, big guy," she murmured. "We'll figure it out."

She heard the bell on the front door ping as it opened, and then came the click-click-clicking of heels on the concrete floor that made her groan. Sure enough, she went to the front to face Alison. Did the woman wear heels every single day as her armor? Not that Emma was one to judge. She had her own armor of self-deprecating humor—which was a lot cheaper than great shoes. "Morning," she said in automatic professional greeting.

"Name one good thing about it," Alison said.

Ha. Okay, so Emma wasn't the only one with a bad attitude today. If Alison hadn't been the bane of her existence all those years ago now, she might've liked her for that alone. "You here to book Killer for the day?"

"No, she's with her dad today."

"That must be hard."

Alison shrugged. "Life's hard, right?"

"Believe it or not, I actually agree with you there."

Alison snorted. "Heard Simon came home not too long after I left."

"Yes."

"Simon has nanny cams in his dad's apartment. It's to keep Dale safe. But Dale's a smart guy, even if he can't always access all those smarts. He likes to watch the feeds."

Emma stilled, pretty sure she knew where this was going. "And?"

"And he caught you two kissing." Alison grinned. "Then he interrupted because he can't help himself. He's a nosy busybody when he's bored."

"You're a scary family."

Alison laughed, sounding pleased. "Yeah." She picked up a bedazzled pink collar from a display. "Don't be surprised if you end up infamous for this."

"The collar?"

Alison snorted. "The kissing." She cocked her head at Emma's look of horror. "Have you forgotten what it's like to live in Wildstone?"

"Yes."

"Seriously?"

"I've forgotten lots of the little things, yeah."

"Right. The coma." Alison's smirk faded. "Sorry. Well, to remind you, you can't sneeze and fart at the same time in this town without making it on the stupid Facebook page that everyone pretends to be too cool for but follows religiously anyway." Alison paused and looked her over. "You know if you hurt him, everyone will know and you'll answer to me."

Emma laughed.

Alison didn't.

"He's my PT," Emma said. "And my friend." *Maybe . . .*

"You fired him. And friends don't kiss with tongues."

Emma shook her head. She really had forgotten what Wildstone could be like. One of those little details her brain had filed away somewhere during her coma, along with a lot of other things that might be helpful about now, leaving her feeling deeply out of her league.

"I just don't want his head messed with again," Alison said.

"Again?"

Ignoring that, Alison turned in a slow circle, looking around. "I talked to Gabby about you. She said you're a natural, that she can't see anyone else taking over this place. You make her customers feel like family, and she feels her repeat business is almost exclusively thanks to you." She faced Emma. "So. About your lease." She pulled an iPad from her shoulder bag. "You're approved. Ready to sign and write me a big fat check?"

"I got rejected for a business loan."

Alison paused, clearly surprised. "Did you fill the applications out correctly?"

"Yes!" Emma took a deep breath. "I'm going to have to pass on buying Paw Pals." It took everything she had to keep the emotion out of her voice.

Alison was just staring at her. "Or . . ."

Emma shook her head. "Or what?"

"Just how short are you?"

Emma had half of her estimated costs to take over the business, and that was only if she used the bulk of her insurance settlement.

Eyebrows raised, Alison was waiting for an answer.

"Half," Emma said. "I have half of what I need."

"Huh." Alison walked the length of the place and then back again, standing in the center of the room to turn in a slow circle. "Huh," she said again.

Emma and Hog looked at each other.

"I could get the other half," Alison said.

"The other half of what?"

"The business costs."

Emma gaped at her. "What does that even mean?"

"I've got business skills, good ones. And you, for whatever reason, have the intangible ability to make people like you. You always have. You inspire loyalty. You bring people and their pets into this business like flies to honey."

Emma was boggled. "Did you hit your head or something?"

"We have opposite strengths that would actually complement each other. Plus, I make decent money. I've socked a bunch of it away because . . . well, no husband or kids, so what am I going to spend it on, you know?"

Emma shook her head in bafflement. "Are you saying you want to go into business with me?"

"Historically Paw Pals has done well and you have a solid business plan."

"A second compliment in a row," Emma said, truly stunned. "Are you morning drinking?"

"I just know a smart investment when I see one. Even if I don't like you."

"You have a job," Emma pointed out.

"I do, and I love it. But I got into Armstrong Properties because I'm the CEO's niece. And great as that is, I want to invest in something on my own as well."

Emma laughed without mirth. "You do realize that this would never work between us."

"You'd let pride come before the business of your heart?"

Emma looked at Hog, who'd gotten bored and slid to the floor and was already snoring. He was depending on her. If she couldn't get a job, and she couldn't get a business loan, what was next for them? Driving across the country to live on her retired parents' sofa . . . She looked at Alison. "You're serious about this."

"Very." Alison still stood in the middle of the room, hair perfect, makeup perfect, outfit perfect, looking every bit as sure of herself as she'd been in high school.

"Even if we set aside all the logical reasons why this wouldn't work," Emma said, "there's also the emotional reason. My armor is humor. Your armor is to look perfect. That's a lot for me to try to beat with only my wits."

"You think I'm perfect?"

"I think you want everyone to believe it."

Alison laughed. "You want to know just how not perfect I am? Everything I have right now is thanks to my uncle. Everything. Without him and Simon, I'd be nothing. Don't get me wrong, I'm incredibly grateful to them, but like I said, this place . . ." She looked around. "This place would be mine alone."

"Well, and *mine*," Emma said dryly.

Alison waved that off as inconsequential and Emma had to laugh as her phone buzzed in her pocket. She held up a finger to Alison and pulled her cell out, answering it without looking at the screen. "Hello?"

Nothing.

She pulled the phone away from her ear and looked at the caller ID. *Ned?* Dammit. "What?"

Silence.

"Ned?"

"No. It's . . . me," Cindy said quietly. "I lost my phone. I used Ned's to try and find it. I hit 'Babe' in his favorites."

"And got me?" Emma asked in horror. "Seriously?"

Cindy's only answer was a soft sniff.

Emma sighed. "Look, I meant it when I said I'm not interested in him anymore. He's all yours."

There was a beat of weighted silence. "I know how much I hurt you, Emma, and I want you to know I didn't mean for this to happen. I've regretted it every single day since. I'm so sorry."

"Sorry enough to do me a favor?"

"Yes," Cindy said. "Anything."

"Delete my number from his phone." Emma disconnected and did what she'd asked Cindy to do, what she couldn't believe she hadn't yet done—she deleted Ned out of her phone.

But not Cindy.

"You've got a set, I'll give you that," Alison said with approval. "Where were we?"

Emma let out a breath. "Paw Pals. Out of morbid curiosity, what kind of a partner do you see yourself being?"

"A better one than the exes squared, I can promise you that. Plus, I'm awesome at numbers and marketing, *and* I like to work my ass off. And bonus—I have my current job, which I'm not giving up, so I'll be mostly an invisible partner."

"And in this crazy scenario, I'd do what exactly?" Emma asked.

"You're the face, the day-to-day operations. *And* the people pleaser."

Emma laughed. "I'm not a people pleaser anymore. And come on, you don't even like me."

"What does liking you have to do with making money?" Alison responded. "Think of it this way. What will you do if you *don't* take my deal?"

Her parents' short, uncomfortable couch flashed in Emma's mind . . . "And what is this deal *exactly*?"

Alison smiled. "Fifty-fifty ownership, of course."

Emma laughed. "No. Twenty-eighty, and once I pay down your loan on the same terms I'd have taken from the bank, you're out."

"Fifty-fifty ownership on the business or no deal." Alison didn't fidget, didn't move, just held Emma's gaze, her posture relaxed. Waiting. Patient.

Like a snake . . .

But the woman really did have sharp business sense *and* knew how to make money. *Dammit.* "This is never going to work unless we promise to be honest with each other."

"I don't have a problem being honest," Alison said.

Emma gave her an *are-you-kidding?* look.

"I'm not the same girl I was in high school."

"Is that an apology?" Emma asked.

"Absolutely not."

All right then.

"Also, I have stipulations," Alison said.

"I haven't agreed to anything. But sure, let's hear them."

"*I'm* the business manager. When it comes to the money, you have to trust me to know what's best."

"*Not* that we're doing this," Emma said, "but *my* stipulation is that you stay out of my way. In other words, we are *not* friends and we each remain in our own lane."

"Well, look at that. Miss Goody-Two-Shoes grew claws."

"Out of necessity. Also, I'm confused. Are we still mortal enemies?"

Alison shrugged. "I do like to keep my enemies closer than my friends."

"You have friends?"

"One more stipulation," Alison said. "No jokes."

"Who was joking?"

"Ha ha. Yes or no, Emma. You in, or do I take my money and walk away?"

Emma opened her mouth, then shut it again. God. Was she actually considering this? It was insanity.

But no more than *not* doing it . . .

Chapter 13

Step 13: Say nice things to people.

Alison found herself holding her breath. She'd been wanting something of her own on the side, something to prove to herself she could bring true value—and make money—without the benefit of nepotism. If it worked out, it was a chance at something no one could take away from her, or cut her out of for not being good enough.

Paw Pals would be so perfect.

She prided herself on being cool as a cucumber, but something about this place really drew her in, made her feel . . . warm and cozy, which, let's be honest, she rarely felt.

Yep, Emma had said they wouldn't be friends, and Alison had agreed just to save face. She knew she had a lot of learning to do in the way of creating and maintaining relationships. But she wanted this, badly. The only thing she wanted more was Ryan.

"You really believe we could be partners and *not* kill each other," Emma said, still heavy on the skepticism.

"I look horrible in orange jumpsuits, so yes. I believe we can do this." Alison paused. "You don't?"

Emma looked away. "Partnership hasn't worked out so well for me in the past."

"There's always a first time for everything, right? And you don't know, maybe we'll even like it."

"Doubtful," Emma said. "But luckily for you I'm desperate."

"Is that a yes?"

Emma didn't answer. Her color was suddenly off and she appeared to be breathing oddly as she shifted, standing on just her right leg, like a flamingo. "Hey, you okay?"

"Yes." Emma gritted her teeth. "Shit. No. *Dammit.*" She clasped her left leg with a strangled sound of pain. When she hit the floor, Hog woke from a dead sleep, jumping to all fours looking very confused and befuddled. He searched wide-eyed for his human, found her on the floor, and scrambled over to her, whining as he nudged his face to hers.

Alison ran too, skipping the face nudging. "Another cramp?"

Emma rolled around, face twisted in agony. Hog tipped his head back and started howling.

Alison tried to drop to the floor at Emma's side, but her pencil skirt was too tight. She had to stop and hike it up to her thighs before she could drop to her knees. "Talk to me."

Emma did not, so Alison yanked out her phone. "Okay, this time I'm really calling 911."

"No! Don't! And Hog, *stop*, I'm okay."

Alison sat back on her heels, watching Emma roll back and forth for a few long minutes, face pale, holding her breath, eyes shimmery with unshed tears. "This is more than a cramp, Emmie."

"I'm fine, *Ali*." Emma ground her teeth. "Fucking insurance—"

"*What can I do?*"

"You can get up. You're flashing me your yoo-hoo."

Alison looked down. "Yoo-hoo? Who calls it a yoo-hoo?"

"My mom," Emma grated out, digging her fingers deep into the muscles of her leg. "She thinks it's cuter than va-jay-jay or hoo-ha."

"Wow. And talk to me."

"It's . . . just a cramp."

"Bullshit."

"I need another surgical procedure," Emma said tightly, "but I've had a bunch already, and now my insurance is dragging their feet with approval."

Okay, enough of this. Alison pushed Emma's hands away and dug her own fingers into the spasming muscle of Emma's thigh. She'd never admit this, but several years ago she'd taken a deep-tissue massage class for a so-called healthy sexual relationship with an old boyfriend. He'd turned out to be a dick, so he'd not gotten any use out of the class. But Ryan sure had . . . Well, until she'd chased him off.

Emma groaned in pain but Alison didn't stop. "Don't hold your breath. Inhale for four." Alison inhaled slowly and deeply as an example, all while keeping at the spasming muscles. "Now exhale for four," she demanded.

Emma did. "*Jesus*," she gasped.

"Again," Alison ordered and kept working the muscles until finally, she felt them start to give.

"I feel like we're having a baby together," Emma managed.

"Bite your tongue." Alison watched Emma's face as she slowly used less pressure, then backed off entirely. "Better?"

"Yeah. Thanks."

Alison helped her sit up. "How often does this happen?"

Emma shrugged and absently patted Hog, who was trying to crawl into her lap. "It doesn't matter. It's better than being in a coma, right?"

Alison knew she was kidding, but she couldn't smile. "That must have been . . ." She shook her head, unable to imagine. "Awful. Do you remember any of it?"

"Look," Emma said, slowly getting to her feet. "Thank you. Really. You've got magical hands. But I don't want to talk about it."

Alison was hands on hips, scrutinizing Emma, who was shaking, damp with sweat, and clearly still in pain. "You need another surgical procedure and your insurance won't pay? You can't take that lying down."

"My surgeon's resubmitting for approval. It's just a waiting game."

"So if you get approval, you can have the surgery."

"Eventually, yes," Emma said. "But it took me four months just to get on the surgeon's surgery calendar. When we had to postpone because the insurance didn't approve, I lost that slot, and this time they won't put me back on the calendar until I get the approval. When that happens, I go to the back of the line again for a surgery date. No idea how long the wait'll be."

Alison shook her head in disgust. "That sucks. If you need anything . . ."

Emma snorted. "Yeah? What would you do?"

"I'd start with calling your insurance to tell them where to shove their approval."

"Okay, I'm definitely going to be our customer liaison here at Paw Pals."

Alison stilled, afraid to joke about this. "So . . . you're interested?"

There was an arrested silence, and then . . . Hog farted audibly, amplified by the concrete floor and the fact he was sitting on it. At the sound, he leapt up and craned his neck to stare at his hind end in surprise. This was followed by two more toots, then an odor that had Alison's eyes watering. "Dear God."

Meanwhile Hog was trying to walk away from his own ass, the whites of his eyes showing, clearly afraid of his own butt. Emma caught him and hugged the big silly lug. "You're crazy, you know that, right?"

It took Alison a minute to realize Emma was actually talking to *her*, not Hog.

"We'll never work, Alison," she said. "We're too different."

"Maybe that's what would make us work."

Emma buried her face in Hog's neck. Which . . . gross, but not Alison's problem.

"I'm really done having friends," Emma said quietly.

Once again, Alison tried not to let that penetrate, but it did. "Just partners then," she said back just as quietly.

Emma nodded. "That's a little easier to fathom."

Alison knew the truth always hurt, but man. She was so awful that the girl who, at least in high school, could literally befriend *anyone* thought that being Alison's friend was impossible. She drew a deep breath. "Personal feelings aside, you have to know that you being the face of this thing and me being the back end just makes good business sense."

Emma nodded and turned away to look out the window. At first it appeared to just be a delay tactic, one Alison had used plenty of times herself. But then she realized that something had caught Emma's attention. A man. He was walking past the big picture window. Maybe fortyish, alone, and at the sight of Emma watching him, he stopped short and stared right back.

At the sudden eye contact, they both immediately looked away from each other. After an awkward beat, the man resumed walking, vanishing out of view.

Emma moved closer to the window, practically pressing her nose against the glass.

"Who's the guy?" Alison asked.

No response.

Alison frowned and moved closer. "You okay?"

Emma sucked in a breath. "Great."

"Wow, that was so believable."

Emma closed her eyes. "Please stop. I can't handle your . . . Ali-ness right now."

Alison opened her mouth, then took a breath because she might actually deserve that. "I was being sincere."

Emma thunked her head on the window. "His name is Jack Swanson. And I haven't seen him since . . . *since.*"

Alison took in Emma's stricken gaze. "Since . . . ?"

Emma gestured to the length of her own body.

"Since you got hot?"

Emma raised a brow.

"Well, you were kinda scrawny in high school."

Emma let out a rough laugh. "Since the accident. He . . . was driving the first car."

Oh shit. He was the guy who'd hit her. And what was Alison supposed to say to that? She searched her brain, sifting through her research on making and keeping relationships, but her mind had gone blank. Saying *I'm sorry he almost killed you* seemed woefully inadequate. "What can I do?"

"Nothing." Emma rubbed the spot between her eyes. "It just shook me for a second, seeing him, that's all."

"For good reason."

Emma shook her head. "It's not what you think. I just . . . for a second I felt the weight of his loss."

"*His* loss? Are you kidding me? He seemed just fine. Meanwhile you're still waiting on procedures."

Emma turned her head and bowled Alison over with the amount of sheer emotion on her face. Alison assumed it was anger, until Emma spoke again.

"I stepped off the curb right in front of him. He didn't see the stop sign. He tried to swerve to avoid me but couldn't. He clipped me and then spun directly into oncoming traffic, and a car hit them head-on. His wife died on impact."

Ah, so not anger. *Guilt.* "You blame yourself for her death."

"I already saw a therapist for six months, thanks. But of course I blame myself. I set everything in motion."

"By stepping off a curb at a crosswalk where you had the right of way?"

"You don't understand." Emma turned away. "His wife *died*."

"You *nearly* died too."

"But I didn't," she said very softly, a few tears escaping to trail down her cheeks that Alison knew Emma hadn't even realized she'd shed.

Another reason to hate her—no red blotchy skin or ugly sobbing for this one. Nope, she was one of those pretty criers. Ugh.

"I *didn't* die," Emma said again, angrily swiping at the tears. "It just felt like it." She moved to the front door and stepped out, staring down the street. Obviously not seeing Jack anymore, she came back in, looking pensive and reflective.

Alison was surprised to find that she could actually feel her pain, though she didn't want to. "You're not okay."

"Yeah, well, *you* try coming out of a coma and being normal."

"Oh, you're perfectly normal," Alison said. "And nice try on the deflection, but you should know my uncle and cousin call me a pit bull. You're upset because you lost so much: your fiancé, your best friend, and nearly your ability to function—"

"Hell of a pep talk," Emma murmured dryly.

Feeling *way* over her head, Alison searched her brain for how to proceed. But as much as she'd been studying, this situation hadn't come up. "Maybe instead of fixating on what you've lost, what *both* you and Jack lost, you could concentrate on the fact that you lived. I mean yeah, so obviously your life isn't what you'd planned, but hey, at least you're still kicking."

Huh. That sounded pretty damn smart if she said so herself.

Emma was just staring at her. "Did you get that off a fortune cookie or something?"

That was just close enough to the truth to have Alison squirming. "Let's just say that on a much, *much* smaller and far less traumatic scale, I understand guilt and loss. More than I want to."

Emma studied her for a beat. "Go on."

"It's embarrassing."

"All the better."

"Fine." Alison drew a deep breath. "I told you I lost the love of my life. Only it wasn't because he was a complete asshole. It was me. *I'm* the complete asshole. I self-destructed our relationship and hurt him, and I hate myself for that."

"How did you self-destruct it? Did you cheat on him?"

"No. Worse. Before Ryan, I'd never . . ." How to say this? "I'd never really let anyone in. But then we got stuck in a snowstorm together for a week. Just the two of us in a ski cabin. Twenty-four, seven . . . It was both terrifying and the very best thing to ever happen to me."

It'd been nearly a year and Alison hadn't forgotten a single moment of it, not sticking together through the long hours of the eight nights without power, not how they'd made the most of their daylight hours as well, hauling wood in to keep warm, making snow angels, having snowball fights . . . God, she'd loved having snowball fights with him because he was competitive and he appreciated how she was the same . . . They'd always ended up breathless, wet, half frozen together, and then he'd warm her up . . .

She cleared her throat. "He got past my guard, and believe me that wasn't easy," she added. "But somehow he managed to bring out the best in me and I fell hard. Even more unbelievably, he fell hard for me." She shook her head, still marveling at that. "He used to joke that he knew he was going to marry me from that first night we met." Alison smiled in memory even as her heart squeezed so hard she could barely breathe. "He's got a million friends, a huge extended family, and everyone loves him. There's always some family gathering, a birthday, an anniversary, *something*, and there's so damn many of them . . ."

Emma arched a brow. "Let me guess. You didn't let yourself fit in."

She flushed a little, because okay, yeah, that had been her in high school too. "I didn't even try. Over and over again I made him choose between the people in his life and me, and he always, always gave me the benefit of the doubt."

"So what happened?"

"He finally gave up on me," Alison admitted. Not happy to find her own cheeks wet, she swiped angrily at them.

"So you were dumped. If you want him back, why not fight for him?"

"Not so good at that."

"And yet you're full of advice for me," Emma said.

"Always easier to see someone else's flaws. I've got to get back to work." She stuck out her hand. "We doing this or what?"

Emma stared at the extended hand and then looked at Hog.

Hog rolled over onto his back for a belly rub.

Emma sighed. "He's not very good at advice either." But she shook Alison's hand. "For better or worse."

Chapter 14

Step 14: Don't give up.

Simon's day had been long and unsatisfying. It'd begun at dawn when he'd been yanked out of a dream by the sound of banging. He'd found his dad lying on the bathroom floor, head beneath the bathroom sink fixing a leaky pipe.

With a hammer.

After playing plumber, things had gone downhill from there. Running Armstrong Properties wasn't particularly difficult, it just meant managing a lot of people with a lot of balls in the air, balls that continuously affected their bottom line.

He wasn't a big fan of the people-managing part of the job, or the hours it added to the actual work. And then there was what was really on his mind. Or *who.*

Emma. Sweet, sexy, amazingly resilient, strong Emma—whom he hadn't seen since the other night. Feeling grumpy, starving, and not a little frustrated, he pulled into the parking lot behind his apartment building.

At the same time as Alison.

Great. Perfect. He loved his cousin. He did. But he was already completely off-balance and out of sorts as he got out of his car with a bag of food he'd picked up from the diner.

Alison's eyes lit up. "Yes. I knew I could score dinner here."

"You know where else you could find dinner? At your place."

"Sure, but I'd have to cook it first. I tried calling and texting you all day. I've got questions for you. And stuff to tell you."

"Good or bad stuff?"

"Um . . . depends on your mood."

"I'm in a not-in-the-mood-for-questions-and-stuff mood."

"Oh, I'm sorry. Did I give you the impression that this was optional?" She smiled. "It's not." She followed him through the lot toward the building. "So . . . you and Emma?"

"Not going there."

She kept pace with him. "You do realize you kissed my mortal enemy and business partner."

"It was a onetime thing, and—" He stopped short when her words kicked in. "*Business partner?*"

"See, if you'd called me back, you'd know this by now. I'm going into business with Emma."

"*My* Emma?"

She went brows up. "*Your* Emma?"

He worked at giving his blank face, when he was feeling anything but blank. "She's a patient and a friend."

"Ah, but she's no longer your patient. She fired you, remember? And as for being her friend, like I told Emma, I don't know any friends who kiss with tongue."

Simon ran a hand over his face. "I've got to delete that security app from Dad's phone. *And* get Kelly to stop gossiping. They're like two middle schoolers."

"Yeah, good luck with that. Also, I'd have paid money to watch Emma fire you."

"We're not discussing this." Not the firing, and not the resulting kisses, which were currently in heavy rotation in his nighttime fantasies. "The partnership with Emma. Go."

"You're hangry, so I'm going to forgive the asshole alpha tone. I get it. But yes. I'm trying to tell you something. You know I've been looking for something I could take on that was separate from Armstrong Properties."

"No, I didn't know that. I thought you were happy there."

"I am. I'm very happy there, and I love the work. But I've been needing something more. Something that's just mine."

"Makes sense."

Alison smiled because she could always count on Simon to cut right to the chase and support her no matter what. "Emma and I are buying Paw Pals together. Gabby agreed to our terms, and with our blessing, she's retired as of today, eager to be at home with her grandbabies. I'm in this fifty-fifty with Emma. She's the face of the place and the day-to-day operations. I'm the behind-the-scenes, running-the-business side of things."

This was hard to imagine. Alison didn't stay behind the scenes for anyone. But he could admit, if he'd been the one starting a new business, his cousin would be the first person he'd want at his side, irritating or not. She was smart, fiercely loyal, and knew her stuff. But what he couldn't see was her dealing with someone she didn't like. "You're going into business with someone you don't trust."

"Well, to be fair, I don't trust anyone."

"*Why*, Ali?" he pressed.

"*Alison*." She dropped the smile. "Listen. Don't take this the wrong way, okay? I don't really want to talk about it, but I'll say this—you and your dad . . . you've given me so much. And I was honest when I said I *love* my job. I do. But everything I have has been handed to me because you guys felt sorry for me."

"That's not even close to true," Simon said, stunned that she felt this way and even more frustrated with himself that he'd never noticed. He opened the front door of the building and let them into the foyer. "Hey."

She turned to look at him.

"You're incredible at your job. You regularly increase profits, which Dad has always reflected in your year-end bonus. You've earned everything you have. I just want you to know that."

She swallowed, nodded, and looked away, which he knew was because she was never comfortable realizing how much someone might care about her.

"You're really doing this?"

"Yes. Because maybe I don't always trust my own instincts, but I trust yours?" she said. "And you trust Emma." She pointed at him. "You also like her, a whole lot, even if you were stupid enough to kiss her and then blow her off."

"I didn't blow her off." He paused. "Wait. Is that what she thinks?"

"It's what *anyone* with half a brain would think. You let her leave because your dad wanted blueberry pancakes. And if I didn't need this to be all about me right now, I'd tell you how dumb you are. Look," she said, softening. "My own believe-in-people barometer might be broken, but yours is solid." She followed him as he went to the mail table, her smile fading when he slid off his sunglasses. "Wait." She took off her own sunglasses and stared at him, eyes narrowed. "Shit. You almost fooled me. You're not okay and you let me go on and on? What's wrong?"

Was Alison right? Had he blown Emma off so they didn't take things too far, to a place they couldn't recover from? Because if he held her at arm's length, then he couldn't mess them up and she wouldn't walk away from him?

Shit. He had. Which meant he was 100% fucked up. Simon grabbed their mail and walked to 1A, juggling the food and mail in one arm while he unlocked his front door.

"Slow the hell down," Alison said breathlessly. "These heels look fantastic, but aren't meant for high speed."

He didn't slow down.

She swore and kept up with him. "Okay, so you're not a normal person," she said, not telling him anything he didn't know. "You're remaining silent because you won't lie and say nothing's wrong when something is. Nor will you complain about it."

He gave her a long look. "So you're a shrink now?"

"Well, I've paid for enough of them over the years that I should be. Hold up a minute," she said, putting her hand over his on the door handle before he could open it. "Talk to me."

"Can't. Jodie quit. Dad's been alone for fifteen minutes."

"Oh, shit. Why didn't you call me?"

"You shouldn't have to always come running when I've got a problem."

"So I'm not part of this family?"

He took in the hurt in her gaze and felt like an ass. "You are. You know you are."

"Then prove it by letting me be there." She pushed ahead of him into the apartment. "Uncle Dale?"

The living room was neat and quiet. Simon moved past her to the kitchen, stopping short in relief when he found his dad standing at the sink, staring out the window. "Dad. Hey. How's it going?"

"Shitty."

Simon's stomach sank. "I'm sorry Jodie had to leave early. Did something happen?"

"They moved *Family Feud* from four o'clock to three."

"Okay."

"*Family Feud* didn't tell me."

Simon looked at Alison, who shrugged. They both knew Dale loved *Family Feud*. Since the strokes, that love had turned slightly obsessive. He talked about *Family Feud* contestants as if they were close personal friends. Simon turned back to his dad as he set the bag on the counter and pulled out containers of food. "But three o'clock is still a good time, right? You're always home at three."

"But I didn't know, so I missed it. I missed today's show."

"We'll make sure you don't miss tomorrow."

Dale waved his hands and raised his voice. "But I missed a show! *Family Feud* never missed a day for me, I can't miss one for her!"

"I'll find it for you online. Don't worry."

"Come on, Uncle Dale," Alison said gently, taking his hand. "Let's go into the living room and sit down. I'll get it on my phone and cast it to your TV. You can eat in front of the show. How's that?"

Dale shrugged off her hand and stalked off in his halting way into the living room.

Simon walked to the fridge and took out two beers, handing one to Alison.

"So Jodie just up and quit on you?" she asked. "Who does that?"

"Her daughter was diagnosed with cancer, so she's moving in with her to help with the baby."

"Oh, no," she breathed. "What are you going to do?"

Simon shrugged.

"I can take care of myself," Dale yelled from the living room. "No one needs to do anything with me."

Simon and Alison looked at each other. Then Simon took his dad's dinner to him in the living room, setting him up with a tray. "It's spaghetti squash lasagna from Kelly." He opened the container and cut it all up before handing his dad a fork. "Eat up."

His dad got up. "I'm getting water."

"I'll get it," Simon said.

"I can get my own damn water!"

When he'd vanished into the kitchen, Alison looked at Simon.

"I'm going to have to hire someone new to add to the team," he said. "Maybe two someones."

"He hates new people."

As Simon well knew. They'd lost good caretakers because Dale couldn't be nice.

A crash came from the kitchen.

"It's okay!" Dale yelled out. "It's just a glass."

Simon tipped his head back and stared up at the ceiling.

"Hey," Alison said, putting her hand on his arm. "I'm going to stay and watch *Family Feud* with him. Go up to the roof. Or anywhere. Take some time for yourself. I'll get him to bed and make sure he's settled before I go home."

"I can't ask you to do that."

"You didn't ask, and I want to."

"Thanks," he said with genuine gratitude, then slid her a look. "Is this because you don't want to talk about you and Emma being partners?"

"Probably every bit as much as you don't want to talk about kissing her."

Touché.

Emma staggered to the top of the third set of stairs and leaned on the roof door to gasp for air. The sun was just barely dipping down behind the bluffs in an explosion of glorious reds and purples. Just looking at it had her relaxing, which was when she realized she'd already caught her breath. The stairs were becoming easier and easier, as was walking, two things she'd never take for granted again.

Sure, she had lingering aches and pains that she knew might never go away, but maybe that was her penance for surviving. Maybe it was supposed to hurt a little. Along that vein, in a moment of insanity earlier, she'd signed up for a 5K in the fall. Three months away. She told herself it wasn't about proving to Simon that she was back to herself because she was fine and didn't feel the need to prove that to anyone, even him.

It was about proving it to herself.

With that, she stepped out onto the roof and found the man himself on the love seat, head tipped to the sky, eyes closed. His button-down was a midnight blue, untucked, sleeves rolled up. He'd been shoving his fingers in his hair again. Between that and the roughness at his jaw, he looked disheveled, sexy, and dangerous as hell to both her heart and soul. Feelings stirred, affection and desire both in the lead and tied for first place.

Scary.

A bottle of rum sat in front of him on the coffee table.

Emma walked over, but Simon didn't say a word. She was trying to decide if he was asleep when he spoke without opening his eyes.

"You're not out of breath." His voice was low and deep like he'd been nearly asleep. "You're doing better."

She'd started getting up early in the mornings and walking. She told herself she was prepping for the 5K.

She'd started with one square block, then slowly expanded. She was up to four blocks, which was exactly how far Jack Swanson lived from her.

But she'd not yet caught sight of him again. "If I'm doing better, it's thanks to you."

Simon shook his head, whether to say that he didn't credit himself with her success, or he just didn't need the thanks, she had no idea.

"I'm sorry about the other night," he said.

Emma nodded, not that he could see it. "The only reason to be sorry is if you regret it, and in that case, I don't think I want to know."

He snagged her hand and pulled her down to sit beside him. "I'm *not* sorry for kissing you." He gave her fingers a gentle squeeze until she looked at him. "Kissing you was . . ." He gave his head a little shake. "The best thing to happen to me in a damn long time."

She smiled and he slowly smiled back. "You're the highlight of my day, Emma."

"Same." She waited, hoping he'd make a move, or suggest they pick up where they'd left off the other night. Instead, he gestured to the bottle of rum in front of them. "Would you like a drink?"

"Rum makes my clothes fall off."

This got her a slow and wistful smile, like he'd really enjoy seeing that, the stubborn, needlessly noble idiot.

"Are you and Alison really partners now?" he asked.

"Looks that way."

"She's lucky to have you."

"She doesn't *have* me. It's not a personal relationship. Just business. That's it."

He gave a small smile. "You're still serious about no personal relationships."

She shrugged. "Actually, I'm feeling disturbingly open to one relationship in particular." One she knew he was feeling leery of and worried about. So she turned to him, carefully tucking her legs beneath her since she was in a sundress. She looked into those deep hazel eyes and saw exhaustion, the kind of soul-deep tired one gets when their world isn't right. She knew it. She recognized it. She'd felt it every single day after waking up from her coma, fighting her way back to the living. She'd felt it on the first day in the rehab facility where she'd met Hog. He'd been scared, not liking the lights or the slippery floors. Having a down day herself, she'd gotten out of bed and on her knees to hug the huge, shaking dog, and she'd never forget how he'd laid his massive head on her shoulder and drooled down her back while melting into her with relief. They'd been together every day since.

Remembering that first hug now, and how it had literally turned her life from her world revolving around just her misery to suddenly being responsible and in charge of another living being. One simple hug had changed her entire perspective, gotten her out of her own head.

So Emma did the only thing she knew how to do. She climbed into Simon's lap and set her head on his shoulder. She did not, however, drool.

His arms immediately came around her and pulled her in even closer as he let out a deep, shuddery breath against her temple. "Are you emotionally supporting me?" he asked, sounding amused.

She had her face pressed into the crook of his neck, one of her favorite spots on him because he always smelled so good. "Actually, I don't know what I'm doing."

His hands stroked up and down her back, soothing *her* even though she'd intended to be the soother. "Makes two of us," he murmured.

"Do you want to talk about it?"

"Talking is the last thing I want to do." His hands were on her bare legs now. "Which is a hell of a good reason for me to stop touching you."

She tightened her grip on him so he didn't get any ideas about being stupid and noble right now. "Or," she said, "maybe it's a hell of a good reason to keep them on me."

"Emma." Lifting his hand, he cupped her jaw and made her look at him. His gaze was dark and heated. "It's been a really long day. I'm drained and I'm not thinking straight. I don't want to do anything to hurt you."

"You'd never hurt me."

He groaned and pressed his forehead to hers. "I'm just worried that this is going to get all messed up."

"How? I'm not looking for a label." She met his gaze, let him see what was on her mind. "But . . ."

He ran a finger along her jaw. "But . . . there's something here between us that we can't seem to shake," he finished for her.

She nodded and gave a little rock of her hips, which had a ragged groan rumbling up from deep in his chest. "No labels," she repeated. "No pressure. No games. Just this, just you, Simon, in the moment, for right now."

He slid a hand into her hair at the nape of her neck and looked into her eyes for a long moment before slowly tugging her mouth to his for a sweet, slow kiss that had her curling into his body as closely as she could, wrapping her arms around his neck.

This won her another one of those groans she loved. "Simon?" she whispered.

"Yeah?"

"We're doing this."

He smiled. "You going to be gentle with me, Emma?"

"Absolutely not."

He laughed, the sound very male, very sexy. He still had a fist in her hair, using it to tilt her head so his mouth could make its talented way along her throat. "Love this sundress," he whispered, running his fingers over the tiny delicate straps holding it up.

"I'm hoping you also love what's beneath it."

"Guaranteed," he said in that husky voice that had her body wound up tight with anticipation. "Count on it." He nudged the straps off her shoulders to her elbows, encouraging the lightweight material to fall, baring her breasts. "Emma." His voice was both strained and thrillingly rough. A big, warm hand glided up her thigh as he covered her mouth with his, his tongue stroking in the same sensuous rhythm as his fingers.

In a shockingly short amount of time, he had her on the very edge, her hands gripping his biceps like he was her lifeline, her body tense and poised to let go, had her gasping out his name, so close, only a few heartbeats away, and then she felt it hit. Not an orgasm, but a vicious leg cramp, holding her in its grip as pain, so much insidious pain, threatened to wash over . . . "*Oh my God*," she gasped.

His mouth was at her throat, nipping, kissing, sucking. "I prefer Simon."

She let out a half laugh, half sob as she twisted out of his arms, lost to the threat of sharp, fiery pain about to shoot through her left leg. She heard Simon swear as if from a long distance and his hands slid down her leg, his fingers searching for the cramp.

"No!" she cried, furious at her body. "Don't touch me."

At her sharp tone, his head came up, studying her.

"I'm fine!" She pulled her leg into her body, unable to handle him touching her like he would a patient, not now, not here.

She held her breath, but then realized . . . the cramp was gone.

Or maybe it'd never come. "I . . ." Confused, she shook her head. "I don't know where it went."

"The cramp?"

She nodded miserably.

"All that matters is that it isn't here," he said, watching her face carefully.

"Yeah." Confused, her breathing hitched and there was a pain in her chest. "I'm sorry, I don't know what's happening to me."

"It's . . . your first time, right?" he asked softly. "Since the accident?"

She closed her eyes. "Yes."

"Hey," he said gently, cupping her face. "It's okay. We're not going to do anything you're not ready for—"

"I'm ready!" Realizing she'd yelled that while still hugging herself tight, Emma let out a long exhale and purposefully and mindfully relaxed her body. "I want this," she said much more quietly. "More than anything. Please don't make me go home and use the shower massager again. I want the real thing from a real live breathing person." She stared at him, daring him to laugh.

To his credit, he didn't. Instead, he gave her a little nudge so that she lay beneath him on the love seat, then met her gaze. "Still with me?"

So relieved that he understood, she fisted her hands in his hair, hard. "Yes."

"Good." His mouth came back to hers, his body moving against her, one hard thigh sliding between hers as he deepened the kiss. It was . . . perfect, and she let herself get lost, let herself forget time and place, conscious only of Simon: the taste of him, of his skin, the heat of his body, and the possessive yet protective touch of his hands. She felt his teeth on her neck, his lips tracing her throat, his hands . . . everywhere, exploring, teasing her to the edge, holding her there.

Mindless, her heart hammering in her chest, desire pooling low in her belly, hot tendrils of lust consuming her as she touched him back, getting her greedy hands on everything she could reach, loving how his reaction made her feel sexy and empowered.

"Emma."

She managed to drag open her eyes.

"Be sure," he said.

His eyes were hot, his body drawn tight with desire and hunger, but he'd stop right now if she wanted. "I've never been more sure."

He leaned over her and kissed her deep, and then they were shoving clothing out of their way, making room for the essentials. And oh God, the essentials . . . He produced a condom and she'd never been so grateful one of them was still thinking. And then he was inside her, mouth at her ear telling her in a thrillingly rough whisper what he was going to do to her. Her toes were already curling again as he began to move because there was no holding back now, not with him.

And then she was shuddering in his arms, a little shocked at how fast she'd come when she realized that one, Simon hadn't. And two, there were sirens. They came closer, and then closer still, splitting the night with the wails and flashing lights.

They stopped in front of their building.

She froze.

Simon did not. He was gentle as he disentangled himself from her, but moving with quick efficiency, he ran to the door, straightening his clothes as he vanished.

Chapter 15

Step 15: Smile.

Simon raced down the three flights of stairs, heart still pounding from watching Emma fly apart beneath him, but it was also lodged in his throat because he knew.

The sirens were for his dad.

He hit the ground floor and stopped short. Their front door was wide open. "Dad," he yelled, already knowing he wouldn't find him inside. Whipping around, he rushed to the front door of the building—also open—and found his dad outside, sitting on the curb being looked over by an EMT. He had a bloody knee and a scrape on his head and was holding his arm to his chest. The EMT flashed a light into his eyes. Mrs. Bessler, their elderly nosy busybody tenant from 2B, was hovering at the EMT's side.

"Dad. You okay?"

"No thanks to you," Mrs. Bessler said, her beehive hair quivering with indignation. "Leaving an old man on his own at night to trip on the front porch steps to his death. Shame on you."

"I'm not old," Dale said. "And I didn't die."

Simon bent to look right into his eyes. *"Are you okay?"*

"Of course I am."

Of course. "What happened?" Simon asked. "What were you doing out here?"

"He was taking out the trash," Mrs. Bessler said and turned to the EMT. "Can you imagine? Asking this sweet old man to do that after he had a bunch of strokes?"

"Only *two* strokes," Dale said. "And for God's sake, woman, I'm *not* old. And I *like* taking out the trash."

"You were taking out the—" Simon drew a deep breath. "Where's Alison?"

"She tucked me in and I told her to skedaddle. I don't need no babysitting while I'm sleeping."

"So why weren't you sleeping?"

"Because I had to take out the trash."

Simon pinched the bridge of his nose and stared down at his feet for a moment. He was barefoot. Shirtless. Because he'd been screwing around—*literally*—instead of looking after his dad. "I thought we agreed you'd call me if you were leaving the house."

"I did call you. You didn't answer. You were on the roof with that pretty girlie of yours, Coma Girl. Hope you got some." His dad looked him over. "Though by the uptight look on your face, I'm guessing not."

Both Mrs. Bessler and the EMT gave Simon very judgy, deadpan stares, which he deserved.

"It's a good thing I was watching from the window and saw him fall," Mrs. Bessler said. "I called 911 right away."

His dad turned to the EMT. "Sorry you had to come out this late."

"No problem." The EMT looked at Mrs. Bessler. "Are you his wife or caretaker?"

"That's me. I'm the caretaker," Simon said, feeling like the biggest asshole on the planet. Because that was what he was, a caretaker. Not some single guy who could come and go, casually hooking up with . . . whatever Emma was to him. No labels, apparently.

His dad was loaded into the ambulance. Simon hopped in after to sit by his side just as Emma rushed out the front of the building. The skirt of her dress was wrinkled from where he'd shoved it up to her waist. Her hair was wild, as were her eyes. And maybe it was his imagination, but she had a sort of dazed, well-satisfied look to her.

Under any other circumstances, he'd have basked in the memories of the feel of her in his arms, those sexy little sounds she'd made when he'd touched her, how it had felt to be buried deep inside her . . . but all he could think was his dad had just been loaded into an ambulance and it was his fault.

Emma waited up, but Simon didn't come back that night. She texted, she called, but nothing. A part of her wasn't surprised. She'd seen the look on his face as he'd climbed into the ambulance with his dad.

Guilt.

Something she knew a little about. Then he'd looked up and seen her on the porch and something new had hit his eyes.

Regret.

He regretted her. She'd been a mistake.

Her worry about his dad overrode her embarrassment about how the night had gone. Because if she thought about it too long—including how she'd gotten hers and he hadn't . . . gah.

But damn. There for a moment, it had been sheer magic.

At midnight she gave up trying to sleep and ordered an Uber.

She got dropped off at the hospital, where she tried to get info on Simon's dad. But HIPAA laws, not to mention COVID-19, had changed the way one could walk into a hospital and get information on a patient.

Frustrated, she had to Uber back to her apartment without any news at all. Once again she tried to sleep, but it wasn't going to work. So she made a call.

"It's the middle of the damn night," Alison answered groggily. "Our place better be on fire."

Our place. Normally, that would both thrill and terrify Emma. But she couldn't think past the look on Simon's face and not worry about his dad. "I'm not calling about the shop."

"Are you calling to once again grill me on customer service protocols for our soft opening the day after to-morrow? Because I think I can handle it."

"No, though I still think you could use a lot more practice. I want to know if your uncle's okay. From his fall earlier."

Long pause. "How did you know about that?"

"Please just tell me."

Another long pause, as if Alison was deciding how much to say. "He's okay. Or at least he will be. Broken wrist, and a thankfully mild concussion."

"And Simon?"

A much longer pause. "I think we need to set some rules for this business relationship. Such as hours. Eight to five sounds good. After that, and certainly after midnight, I'm unavailable. Goodbye—"

"No, don't hang up! I need to know that Simon's okay, that—"

"I'm going to do you a favor, by disconnecting and pretending this call never happened."

"Alison, please."

Alison sighed. "Okay, listen. First of all, Simon and I? We have our own rules. They involve trust and loyalty, and *never* talking out of turn. So if you thought I was the weak link and a cheap way to get deets on my family, you were wrong. And second . . ." She softened her voice. "Simon could have a limb literally falling off and he wouldn't admit he *wasn't* okay. And that's as close to an answer as you're ever going to get from me. Goodbye."

"But—"

But nothing. Alison was gone.

"*Dammit.*" Emma reminded herself that she had her weekly PT later that day. All she had to do was make it until then and she could talk to Simon herself.

Morning took forever to arrive. When it did, the first thing she did was check her phone. Nothing.

She went downstairs and knocked on Simon's door. More nothing. Pushing away the hurt and unease of not hearing from Simon—which did not bode well for future social orgasms with him—she took yet another Uber, this time with Hog, and they went to Paw Pals. They were closed today in preparation for tomorrow's soft opening. The "grand" opening would come next week. It was the first thing in Emma's life she'd had to look forward to in a long time.

It was odd to think she had Alison to thank for that.

Her new partner was behind the counter on the computer, going through the books, setting everything up to suit her.

Emma walked toward the front desk, Hog following more slowly and cautiously, clearly looking for Killer.

"She's not here today," Alison told him. "She's with her dad. You can relax."

Hog did just that, plopping onto the floor at Miss Kitty's feet in the sunny spot.

Emma turned to Alison. She'd heard the longing and hurt in her voice, which was interesting. Back in school, Alison had never revealed her personal feelings, ever. "Anything new on Dale?" Emma asked.

"No."

Emma nodded, then looked around, realizing that as of today, she wasn't just an employee anymore. She *owned* the place—well, half—and her heart squeezed. "Oh my God."

Alison lifted her head. "What now?"

"I think I'm actually . . . happy." Well, not 100% happy. Ninety percentish—same as her health. That last 10% was worrying about Dale.

And Simon.

"Well, good for you," Alison said.

"No, you don't understand. Happy is a rare commodity. We need to soak it all in. Take pictures so we never forget this moment. Quick," she said, pulling out her phone. "Stop what you're doing and fake a smile, we need a pic for our new memory board."

Alison slid her a look that said she was probably not yet caffeinated and that Emma was giving her a headache. "I don't think you understand the difference between want and need," she told Emma. "Like, I want a nap, but I need to work. Another example— I also *want* abs, but I *need* food."

Emma's stomach grumbled. "You're right. We should celebrate. With a big feast."

"It's seven A.M."

"And?"

Alison shook her head.

Emma moved behind the counter and bent to the shelves beneath. "Hey, I left a bag of sour cream and cheese chips here, but it's gone."

"I ate it."

Emma stared at her. "The whole bag?"

"If it's not in a resealable bag, then it's one serving."

"Oh my God."

"Hey, I don't make the rules."

"You owe me chips," Emma said. "A whole bag." She looked around. "And I was serious. I really think we can make something of this. Don't you?"

"Obviously, or I wouldn't have dropped my entire savings into it."

Emma rolled her eyes, but the gesture was wasted on Alison, who kept working.

"Stop staring at me" was all Alison said. "And celebrations are for *successes*. This is still a wait-and-see thing."

"Anyone ever tell you that you're a buzzkill?"

"Many. And I'm so glad I learned about parallelograms in school instead of starting a business. It's really coming in handy this week." She looked up from the computer. "Also, subject change—coupons for Paw Pals for new clients. What do you think?"

"Genius," Emma said, surprised.

"I'm going to remind you that you said that."

"Actually, we could print a bunch of coupons and put them up all over town. You could even take one to Ryan."

Alison blinked. "Why would I do that?"

"So he'd have an excuse to come see you here when he brings Killer in on his days with her."

"Seems desperate."

"Desperate times . . ."

"I'm not *that* desperate. I'm never that desperate."

"If that's true, I'm going to need the secret," Emma said.

An alarm went off on Alison's phone. She looked at it and swore very creatively.

"What is it?" Emma asked, heart kicking. "Simon? Dale?"

"No. I set a reminder for something."

Emma gave her the *go on* gesture.

Alison rolled her eyes. "To . . ." She coughed and said, "Remembertobeniceandfriendlyandopen" at the same time.

Emma stared at her. "Was that even English?"

Her partner sighed. "I set the reminder to remember to be nice and friendly and open."

Emma stared at her, and then laughed. She laughed so hard she had to sit down on the welcome bench and gasp for air.

"Whatever," Alison said, clearly entirely insulted. "I'm a delight."

Emma swiped her tears of mirth. "It's cute that you think that's true. But why the alarm? Why not just stick with being your usual ray of sunshine?"

"Fine." Alison tossed up her hands. "Because I know I'm not a delight, okay? And I'm . . . trying to fix that."

Alison actually seemed genuinely earnest, and Emma's smile faded. The bigger surprise was that her heart actually squeezed. "Okay, I think it's sweet that you're trying. But . . . your execution might be a tad off."

Alison made a face that said she was aware.

"We both agreed to this for our own various reasons," Emma said. "We might as well get used to it."

"Yeah, but . . . it's weird, right?"

Emma laughed. "Very. Hey, maybe if we told each other something about ourselves now, as adults."

"Such as?" Alison asked suspiciously.

"How about we share our weaknesses and strengths? I'll even go first. My weakness is . . ." She searched her brain. She had so many to choose from. "My old need of being a people pleaser still raises its head when I'm not looking. And also that I don't want to be a burden. On anyone. Not ever again—which still makes it hard for me to ask for help. And by hard, I mean I'm stubborn and sometimes obnoxious about accepting said help. As for my strengths . . . I think that's my sunshine nature and the ability to make people feel good." She smiled, proud of herself.

Alison was frowning.

"Your turn," Emma nudged.

"My strength is that I never admit my weakness."

Emma rolled her eyes. "Lame. Come on, let's hear it. Strengths and weaknesses. Or would you rather I say them?"

"Oh, do tell."

"Your strength is you're smart as hell and you aren't afraid to go after what you want. You're brutally honest."

"Not exactly flattering, but accurate," Alison said. "And my weaknesses?"

"Easy. You hide behind a thick armor of sarcasm and cynicism, and that scares people off, which you're fine with because then you don't have to deal with them."

"But not you apparently. I haven't scared you off."

Emma smiled. "I'm a product of desperation. I needed you, plain and simple, which sucks for me." She moved closer, leaning on the counter. "Also, I'm really trying to be cool here, but *please* tell me something about your uncle."

"How did you know about him getting hurt anyway?"

Good question. Emma wanted to say never mind, but her need to know that Dale was okay outweighed her pride. "Last night I was with Simon when we heard sirens."

Alison's brow nearly vanished into her hairline. "Define 'with.'"

Oh boy. "We were on the roof when we heard sirens. Simon ran downstairs, so I'm not sure, but from what I can gather, Dale fell."

"The roof?"

"Stargazing."

"Uh-huh," Alison said.

"I think Simon feels incredibly guilty about it."

Alison blew out a huge breath. "It's not Simon who should feel guilty. I'm the one who put Dale to bed and then left him." She looked away. "It's what I've done before, but even though he promised, I should've stayed longer to make sure he was really asleep. He's wily. I should've known—"

"You couldn't have known," Emma said, putting her hand over Alison's. "It's a tough situation. I'm sure neither Simon nor Dale blames you—"

Alison pulled her hand free, stood up, and closed her laptop. "I'm due at Armstrong Properties. I'm covering for Simon today. He had meetings on top of meet-ings, so I've gotta go, but I'll come back later."

"Don't worry about it. I've got this."

Alison's frown faded. "Thanks."

Emma worked until it was time for her late-afternoon PT appointment. She got a little anxious as she parked in the PT clinic lot, hoping last night hadn't ruined everything between her and Simon.

"Love it that you're always on time," Kelly said when Emma signed in. "I'm all ready for you in the back."

Emma's heart thumped heavily. "No Simon today?"

Kelly paused and cocked her head. "I'm sorry. I was under the impression that you wanted to work with a different PT from now on."

Emma felt herself flush. Okay, yes, she'd "fired" Simon, but she hadn't been serious. "It's just a silly misunderstanding. I'd really like to see him, if that's possible."

Kelly's pleasant smile never faded as she nodded and eyed the schedule screen. "As of right now, he's no longer working regular days, just on a client-by-client basis when he can fit them in."

Emma's stomach dropped. His dad must be really bad for Simon to give up scheduled days.

Or . . . maybe he'd just given up her. "Can I get fitted in?"

"I'll leave him a message to get back to you on that."

Okay, then. She followed Kelly to the back and they got to work. Kelly was doing leg stretches on Emma when she said, "I consider Simon one of my favorite people. He values privacy and loyalty above everything. So I'm really speaking out of turn here when I say . . . don't give up on him too soon."

Their gazes met, and Kelly gave a little smile. "You dig him, right?"

Emma wrestled with a response, but couldn't figure out how to answer.

"You do," Kelly said into Emma's silence.

Emma grimaced.

"I'm sorry." Kelly lifted her hands. "I know, I should just keep my mouth shut, but he's been through a tough time. I knew when I first realized how attracted he was to you that he'd find a way to keep his distance."

"I think he's just got a lot on his plate right now."

"Yeah. Listen . . ." Kelly moved closer and lowered her voice. "I'm going to give you some advice you didn't ask for. If he means anything to you, don't let him get away with not making time for the two of you, okay? He's bullheaded. He does what he thinks is right over what he might need or want, and he *never* takes the

easy road. Not for himself anyway. In his past relationships with women, he let them come last in the lineup,
myself included."

Emma drew a deep breath. "I . . . don't know what
to say."

Kelly smiled. "Just say you'll hold on to him better
than Maggie or I did. Even if Maggie wanted to, which
okay, maybe deep, deep, deep down she did, she had
no idea how to do that, how to hold on to him, especially when she could barely hold on to herself."

Chapter 16

Step 16: Friendship is the new romance.

Emma left PT knowing she needed to find a way to talk to Simon. It was early evening when she got home, but his car wasn't in the lot. Since she knew she couldn't sit at her apartment window and wait until she saw him drive up—it would take her too long to get down the stairs—she decided she and Hog would stay outside and enjoy the warm summer day.

The wind had whipped up some big surf. White-caps dotted the water under a sky so clear and pure and stunning, it almost hurt to look at it.

Emma led Hog down the street to Commercial Row, where they moseyed past cute shops and galleries until she got her steps in. Or, more accurately, until Hog lay down in the middle of the bike lane—the sidewalk was blocked with outdoor café tables set up for eating—and refused to go another step.

A biker shouted from a hundred feet away with a warning, "Lady, your dog's sleeping in the road!"

Hog was utterly unmoved.

"Hog," she said, tugging on his leash. "Get up."

"I'm not unclipping from my pedals," the guy warned.

Fifty feet.

"*Hog.*"

Nothing. He was playing dead.

The biker screeched his brakes and skid to a stop an inch from Hog's nose, indeed having to unclip so he didn't tip over. Which he did while swearing. Loudly.

Hog didn't care. It was like he'd totally melted into the sidewalk. Emma bent and slid her arms around his middle and tried to tug 110 pounds of dead weight upright. Breathing heavily, she gave up. "If you get up right now, I'll give you a doggy treat."

He leapt to all fours with a dexterity that had to be seen to be believed.

The biker shook his head with disgust and rode on.

Emma pulled the treat from her pocket—which Hog inhaled without even tasting—and she walked him back home, where they sat on the wide front porch of her apartment building. While Hog snoozed at her feet,

Emma worked on a surprise for Alison on her phone—creating a coupon for new customers at Paw Pals.

After an hour, Mrs. Bessler came out onto the porch and handed Emma a plate with a grilled cheese sandwich cut neatly into four perfect squares.

"Wow," she said. "Thank you so much."

Mrs. Bessler sat next to her and watched Emma take her first bite and moan over the warm gooey cheese. "So . . . you and my boy, huh?"

"Uh . . . who?"

"Simon."

Emma choked. "You're Simon's mom?"

"No, his mom died of cancer when he was in high school. But I look after her family for her. They're very important to me, which is why I have to ask—what are your intentions with him?"

Emma had already known about his mom, but she still felt swamped with emotion at the thought of Simon losing her so young. Unable to fathom the pain of that, she set her square of sandwich back onto the plate. "My . . . intentions?"

"Yes, because Simon's the real deal, a genuine keeper. They're rare these days, you know. I just want to make sure you're in it with him for the long haul, not any of this new age, loosey-goosey, fear-of-commitment thing all you young people seem to have going."

Emma picked up a second square of the amazing grilled cheese sandwich. "We're just friends." Or at least they had been. After last night and also PT, it was seeming more and more doubtful.

"That's a very disappointing answer," Mrs. Bessler said and took the plate *and* the grilled cheese square in Emma's hand, and . . . walked back inside.

Damn. She'd really wanted the rest of that grilled cheese. And what was she doing? If Simon wanted to talk to her, he'd answer a call or a text, or come see her. She couldn't make him talk to her. "Come on, Hog. Alison was actually right about something—there's never a need for this much desperation."

He jumped up, happy to finish his napping inside.

But on the second-floor landing, Emma kept going. She needed the roof. It took her a bit since she was already worn out from both PT and her walk down Commercial Row. But eventually, she got there and collapsed in gratitude onto the love seat, where she assumed her favorite thinking position: head back, eyes closed, body completely done in.

She had no idea how much time had passed when she woke up, but it was dark and Hog was asleep on her feet, which were dead.

Then Hog leapt up with a happy "woof" and she realized what had woken her. They weren't alone.

Hog bum-rushed the man leaning against the protective railing wearing faded jeans and a long-sleeved white T-shirt that emphasized the body she'd begun to crave more than air. He crouched down to hug her ridiculous dog, who'd flopped onto his back for more love.

Simon obliged, rubbing Hog's belly before finally lifting his gaze to Emma.

"How's your dad?" she asked quietly, sitting up, rubbing her eyes, her voice gravelly from sleep.

"He'll come home tomorrow. The hospital kept him because he hit his head pretty good."

She let out a rough breath she hadn't even realized she'd been holding. "I'm so sorry, Simon."

He shook his head. "Not your fault."

"Not yours either."

"You're wrong there." He rose to his feet.

Emma stood too. "Alison told me that she'd promised to watch him. She's blaming herself too. The way I see it, you're both just doing the best you can."

"Yeah, and maybe one of you could explain to me how you two are suddenly friends now."

"We're not."

He snorted and rubbed a hand over his unshaved face, his body language heavy, like he was exhausted beyond measure.

She opened her mouth to express some sympathy, but what came out didn't match her intentions. "You quit me."

An emotion crossed his face, gone too quickly to read it. "You quit me first, remember."

"You know that was a joke." She was hands on hips. "Did you dump just me, or was Kelly being honest about you having to give up your regularly scheduled days?"

A pained expression crossed his face. "That was the truth. And yeah, I know you were joking about firing me, but . . ."

Her stomach hit her toes. "But . . . ?"

Simon shifted closer and met Emma's eyes, his own revealing an easy and deep affection for her and . . . much more. Relief swamped her. So much that she stopped breathing.

Until he spoke.

"It can't be a joke, Emma. I really can't be your PT anymore. It's gotten far too personal for us to be involved professionally."

Her relief died a quick death. "Could you get in trouble?"

He shook his head. "Technically, there's no law against this, but ethically, you need a new PT."

"Because . . ."

"Because I crossed a line, Emma."

"Actually, if we're being *technical*," she said, "you didn't cross the line. At least not the *finish* line . . ."

His eyes warmed for a beat, and an almost smile quirked his lips.

"I'm sorry about that, by the way," she murmured.

He shook his head. "Don't be sorry for anything that happened." He did smile then, a small but genuine one. "I'm not."

Just like any other day, he wore a calm, quiet authority, which always made her feel secure and safe. It was part of what made him a great PT. Using that calm to help her feel brave had also made him a good friend. He was more than the guy she'd sort of, kind of hooked up with. The truth was, Simon was one of the most important people in Emma's new life, and she was afraid to lose him. "I know you're feeling guilty, even though there's no reason to," she said, stepping closer, putting a hand to his chest. "We've both had a lot taken away from us. So much, Simon. And I don't know about you, but I'm tired of it. What's wrong with taking a little bit of something just for ourselves?"

"Nothing," he said firmly. "And I hate how much of your life you lost. But you're the most amazing, resilient woman I've ever met. You deserve far more."

"More than you?" When she saw the affirmative answer in his eyes, she shook her head. "That's for me to decide, not you."

"Emma, my life's . . . complicated."

"Yeah? Join the club."

"No, I mean . . . we can never be more than this."

She shook her head, confused. "Why?"

He stared at her, then let out a rough breath. "Because I completely lose myself around you." He shoved his fingers in his hair. "Every single time."

The words were a thrill even as the tone of his voice scared her. "And that's a bad thing?"

"Yes, because you're not ready, Emma."

"Hey, I signed up for that 5K."

"Ready for an 'us.'"

That took her back a step and had her going from confused to ticked off. "Wow." She shook her head. "Did you decide this before or after what we did on the roof?"

He closed his eyes. "This is what I'm telling you. I can't tear myself away from you, even when I should. You . . ."

"I what?"

He opened his eyes and met her gaze. "You nearly had a panic attack instead of an orgasm."

"You mean a leg cramp."

"No." His voice was gentle. "That was panic, Emma."

Feeling embarrassed and stupid, she crossed her arms. "I got over it pretty quickly." Thanks to him . . . "If you don't want me, just say so."

"It's the opposite." He met her gaze, his own warm. "You make me smile. You make me laugh. You make my day, every single day." He shook his head, looking marveled. "You're so full of life that it reminds me my own life is so busy I don't ever take the time for things like . . ."

"Sex on the roof?"

Simon reached for her, but Emma stepped back. "No." She knew that she was a lot of things, but the type of woman to beg for a man's attention was most certainly not one of them.

"So I got nervous last night, so what. It'd been a while. It's perfectly normal."

"It is normal," he agreed. "For someone who's still healing from a trauma."

"I'm nearly all better!"

"Right. Ninety percent. *Ish.*"

She stared at him and then shook her head, too pissed off to speak.

"You need more time," he said. "You're holding back from getting fully healthy. Once you turn that corner, then—"

"Then what?" she challenged.

His voice lowered, gentled. "What happened to you didn't just create physical scars, Em, there are emotional ones too. You're not ready to open yourself up and let someone in."

"Yeah, well . . ." She looked away, hating that that was probably true. Hating even more that he was using his professional voice. "Who doesn't have emotional scars, huh?"

He murmured, "Touché."

"And by the way," she said. "I heard about two of your emotional scars."

He rubbed a hand over his jaw. "Kelly has a big mouth."

"She cares about you."

"I know. But *you* should know, I wasn't scarred by either of my past relationships. I'm still friends with them, it's all good."

"Okay, but if you weren't scarred, it means you weren't emotionally invested," Emma said, voicing what she'd just realized. "So maybe it's *you* who can't open up, Simon. You ever think of that?"

He remained impassive, just looking at her, and she wondered how it was possible to feel worse now than when she'd woken up from a coma and discovered her life was upside down. Damn, she needed a good fast exit. Hard to do when she was sore and achy from PT, and being emotional on top of it all. "I'm going now."

He reached for her. "I'll help—"

She glared at him. "Not a chance in hell." She opened the roof door. "I'm going to storm off now in righteous indignation, but we both know it's going to take me a minute, so please let me have it with as much dignity as possible. Come on, Hog."

Hog gave Simon one last longing look, then trotted to Emma. When he was through the doorway, she shut the door behind her with a satisfying thud.

And caught the hem of her sweater in it, trapping her.

"Shit." Wrestling to get the door open again while still caught in it was a joke. "You've *got* to be kidding me."

The door opened. Simon, of course. "Are you—"

"*Fine!*" She yanked her sweater free. "I'm fine!" She nudged him back onto the roof. Maybe *pushed* was a better word.

"Let me—"

"*No!*" She took a deep breath. "I'm trying to make a dramatic exit here, dammit."

He gave a slow nod and backed up.

Emma nodded back with as much dignity as she could muster—which wasn't much by now—but hey, pride was pride. The man had taken her to heaven and then decreed they weren't going to do it again. She wanted to be mad, but if she was being honest with herself, she was hurt.

Hell if she'd admit it.

You've been through worse. Way worse. So suck it up.

When Emma finally made it to her apartment, she kept going, accessing her Uber app to get a car. It was ten P.M. and she had nowhere to go, but that wasn't going to stop her.

Twenty minutes later, she and Hog stood outside Paw Pals. The day before Alison had put in a new security system, and they each had a new passcode to get in.

But Emma's didn't work. She tried it again. And then again. On the fifth attempt, she was politely but firmly locked out of the system.

Great. Fantastic. Thumbing through the contacts on her phone, she stared at Alison's name. Ground her teeth. Then hit the number.

Her mortal enemy and business partner answered with "Something better be burning. What is it?"

"My life," Emma said and her eyes filled. She sniffed and swiped at the stupid tears.

"Shit. Are you crying? Tell me you're not crying."

"I had a really shitty night."

"And you're calling *me*?"

"Men suck."

"Yeah, well, tell me something I don't know."

Emma sniffed again and then blew her nose. "You think men suck too?"

"Dumped by the love of my life, remember?"

"For being mean."

"Yes," Alison said softly.

Emma sucked in a breath. "I'm sorry. But . . . they say knowing the problem is half the battle. Maybe you can fix things. You know, by being *not* mean."

"Again, is there a real reason for this call?"

"Yes," Emma said. "Would you say I . . . use my emotional scars to keep people at a distance?"

"You're asking me? I don't even know you."

"Yes you do. I'm the same Emma I was in high school."

"Then I'd say you do the opposite of keeping people at a distance. You could use a little more of keeping people at a distance."

"Gee, thanks. Maybe you could tell that to your cousin."

"Oh, no. No, no, no . . . I'm not getting involved. If you've slept with him and are trying to tell me about it, our partnership is *over*."

Emma bit her lower lip.

"Oh my God," Alison breathed. "*That's* what this phone call is about? You slept with him?"

"Kind of. Well, minus the sleeping part. But then Dale got hurt, and I think he's blaming himself because he came up with some dumb reason why we're not going there again."

"Oh my God," Alison said. "He's still doing that?"

"Doing what?"

Alison sighed. "He's got some stupid notion that he has to give up his life to watch out for his dad."

"That's not stupid. That's admirable. But . . ."

"Where are you?"

"Paw Pals. My code won't work. I need you to come down here so I can work instead of think about your stupid cousin."

"If the code isn't working, it's because you didn't do it right."

"No kidding. Help me. I *need* to work, Ali."

"Call me Ali again and you're *never* getting in." Alison sighed. "Why do you need to work? You've got everything all perfectly set up for tomorrow. And by the way, the twinkly lights hung in the shapes of puppies and kittens in the reception were a stroke of genius."

"Wow, was that a compliment?"

"Yeah, but don't get used to it. I hate the new sappy bedazzled leashes and collar line you brought in."

"They're going to sell like hotcakes."

"Uh-huh. I'll believe it when I see it."

"*Please*, Alison."

"Fine. I'll be there in a few. I'll accept payment in blissful silence from you."

Emma snorted. "It's comforting to know some things never change."

"Right?"

Chapter 17

Step 17: Be vulnerable.

After disconnecting with Emma, Alison looked down at herself. She was in sweats, and not a cute pair of sweats either. Nope, these were her just-been-broken-up-with, aka laundry-day, aka have-to-kill-anyone-who-sees-me-in-them sweats.

She'd planned on wine and bed. She'd not planned on going out in public because her partner was having a bad night. But . . . there was something about even thinking the word *partner* that gave her pause.

In a shockingly good way.

She got to Paw Pals in six minutes and found Emma and Hog standing by the front door under the security light. Well, Emma was standing. Hog was lying down, snoozing. It made her miss Killer, who was with Ryan tonight. Probably having a great time. Maybe moon-light paddle-boarding past the surf break. Killer loved to stand on the front of the board in her little life vest, leading the way like she was captain of the ship. It never failed to make Ryan laugh. And damn, she missed his laugh.

Emma was watching her walk to the building from her car. "Whoa."

Alison narrowed her eyes. "What?"

"Uh . . . nothing."

"Say it."

"Okay . . ." Emma looked her over again. "I've never seen you looking like a normal human being who *possibly* had a bad day. I like it," she said and left Alison standing there with a boatload of defensiveness ready and nowhere to sling it.

"Where's Killer?" Emma asked. "Ryan's?"

Alison nodded and unlocked the front door with her code. Then she shut it again and gestured for Emma to try.

Emma, also wearing sweats, but somehow manag-ing to look supercute, entered her code and . . . the door didn't open.

Alison sighed, really not in the mood for this. "What's your code?"

Emma shifted on her feet.

"Hello?"

"I don't want to say."

Alison stared at her. "If it's the numeric equivalent for Simon, I swear—"

Emma crossed her arms over her chest.

"Oh my God. Are you twelve?" Alison whipped out her phone, accessed the security app, and then held it out to Emma. "Enter a new password. Something that is *not* Simon."

Two minutes later, they were inside. Alison turned to Emma. "To be clear, we're *not* talking about your and Simon's sex life."

Emma nodded, but her eyes went suspiciously shiny.

Dammit. Alison headed to the counter and pulled herself up to sit on it.

Emma ducked behind the counter and came up with two red Solo cups and a bottle of red wine. "Gabby left this for us." She opened the bottle and poured two very generous portions. Then she handed one over, taking the other for herself before gently knocking it into Alison's in a toast. "To independence."

"I'll drink to that," Alison said and they drank. "Since we're not going to talk about stupid males, what *do* you want to talk about?"

"Well, I did come up with a good idea earlier," Emma said.

"Your last idea wiped out my savings, so . . ."

"Right now we have big dogs and little dogs separated," Emma said, ignoring the sass. "We have it like that because the little dogs terrorize the bigger, sweeter dogs. But some of the big dogs *like* being with the little dogs, so I think we need to rethink it. What do you think about labeling the yards 'sweet' and 'salty'? We'd have to be careful with the scheduling for the salty dogs, of course, scheduled yard time and all that, but we do that anyway."

It was a damn good idea, but Alison just looked at Emma. "Why do I feel like you're thinking you're the 'sweet' and I'm the 'salty'?"

"Well, I do get dehydrated just looking at you."

Alison thought about that and had to shrug. "Fair."

Emma laughed. "So . . . yeah?"

"I can't believe I'm going to be the voice of reason on this issue, but it's possible you'll insult people with those labels."

"Only the salty people though."

"Hey, salty people have feelings too."

Emma snorted. "Let's ro-sham-bo."

"The last time you and I competed for anything was in our sophomore year. We didn't even know each other. It was the cartwheel challenge, remember?"

"Yeah," Emma said. "Winner got to be homecoming princess. I won. I did one hundred cartwheels. How many did you do?"

Alison sighed. "Twenty-five. I got dizzy. And you should know I still do them sometimes at the gym. I mean, I'm down to ten in a row, but still. You really think you could still beat me?"

"Doubtful since I recently broke a whole bunch of bones and ended up in a coma."

"Oh my God." Alison shook her head. "Fine. You win, but that's the last time you get to play the sympathy card, Coma Girl."

"Do you really go to a gym?"

Alison lifted a shoulder. "I went once."

Emma laughed and moved to unpack the latest deliveries of inventory.

Alison sat on the counter sipping her wine. Wine made her melancholy. Not that it had stopped her from drinking it. But the loneliness felt . . . insidious, a deep, unsettling ache in her chest. Actually, scratch that. It was more like a huge, gaping hole.

The reason was simple. She missed Ryan's easy affection. His laughing eyes. The way he said her name . . . She'd never been the type of woman who couldn't live without a man. She had a perfectly good vibrator, thank you very much. But sometimes there was nothing like being held, desired, hungered for.

"Dammit," she whispered and pulled up her Find My Friends app. Ryan's dot was at Whiskey River, a bar and grill hidden off the highway far enough that it was mostly locals only—just the way the locals liked it. Him being there was a sure sign he was on a date, maybe with his pretty neighbor. Which, for the record, she hated.

"Who are you stalking?"

Alison looked up and found Emma had come close, standing at her elbow, looking over her shoulder. "Jeez, it's called personal space. And no one."

"You mean Ryan."

"Okay, yeah. Ryan." Because Alison was a glutton for punishment, she stared at his dot. It was late. If his date was going well, they'd probably leave soon and go make merry somewhere. Just the thought had her belly cramping. And then the little dot changed positions.

"He's on the move," Emma said. Captain Obvious.

Feeling a little sick, Alison put her phone away.

"You're stopping now? It was just getting interesting."

"I don't want to see where he ends up."

"Yeah." Emma nodded. "I get that."

This reminded Alison of Emma's exes squared. "People suck."

Emma shrugged. "Not all of them."

Alison gaped at her. "You can still say that after what happened to you?"

"If it hadn't happened, if Ned and Cindy hadn't found each other, I might still be with him."

Alison wasn't used to looking at the positive side of things. It wasn't where her brain lived. But maybe there was something to it. Okay, so . . . playing the what-if game, if she and Ryan hadn't broken up, she'd . . . still be with him. "Nope, thinking positive doesn't work for me."

"Maybe because you haven't learned whatever you needed to."

Afraid that was actually true, Alison hopped off the counter and grabbed her purse. "Whelp, this has been fun, but I've gotta go." Even though she didn't really want to. Apparently setting her lack of physical intimacy aside, she was also missing an emotional connection.

She hadn't seen that one coming. "Lock up when you go."

"Thanks for coming and saving me. That was nice of you."

"Nice had nothing to do with it," Alison said. "Now you owe me a favor." She moved to the front door to go out into the night and . . .

Came face-to-face with the man she missed beyond bearing.

Behind her, Emma made a sound, but Alison didn't even breathe. All she could do was stare up at Ryan.

He had one hand above him, braced on the doorjamb, the other holding Killer against his chest, his tall, leanly muscled body at ease and confident. He was always at ease and confident, whether he was wearing his reading glasses to look over a set of engineering plans, or chasing a baseball, or in bed. Maybe *especially* in bed. The man made love like he did everything else, with dedicated purpose, easy affection, and utter abandon. Anything goes. Nothing outside his comfort zone.

It'd been addicting.

He was addicting.

He wore jeans and a leather jacket, his hair wind tousled, his dark eyes calm. Ryan didn't waste a lot of energy with things like worry and anxiety, and certainly not the bone-deep self-doubt that sometimes threatened to drown her.

His gaze met hers and slowly trailed south, which was when she remembered what she looked like, and with an undignified squeak, she jumped behind the door and shut it.

"Mature," Emma said.

"Shh! Maybe he'll leave."

"He's not going to leave," he said through the door.

Alison bonked her head on the wood several times. "You should have called," she said.

"If you're with a guy in there, just say so," Ryan said.

Tempting as it was to her pride to let him think that, she couldn't do it. "No. I'm . . . not dressed for company."

"I've already seen you. And since when am I company?"

"Since you dumped me."

"Alison. Open the door."

"I'm wearing laundry-day clothes."

"So? I've seen you in nothing."

Alison looked over at Emma, who was grinning. Alison gave her the "shoo" hands.

Emma didn't shoo, instead she stood there riveted as she soaked up every word. Alison rolled her eyes and turned back to the door. "I look good in nothing. I don't look good in laundry clothes."

Ryan gave a rough laugh. "You look *great* in nothing. But you look cute when you're not all done up in your armor. I like it."

Emma covered her mouth with her hand to hide her laugh. Alison jabbed a finger at her to knock it off. "*Cute?*" she repeated back to Ryan. "You need to take that back."

"Can't. Also, the way you look right now is actually one of my favorite looks on you."

This finally got her opening the door again. "Yeah?"

Ryan looked Alison over from wild hair to her bare toes and smiled. "Yeah. And definitely cute."

"You're a nut." A nut who owned her heart . . .

Ryan caught sight of Emma and nodded to her. "Hello. You're the new partner."

"Emma Harris," Alison told him, watching Emma smile easily and welcoming in an effortless way Alison couldn't have managed on her best day. Maybe she should be taking lessons from Emma instead of Google. "We're working late."

"Well, one of us is," Emma teased. "The other is flirting."

"I'm not—" Alison started, then sighed when Ryan laughed along with Emma. Then her so-called partner caught sight of Alison's face, clearly read the murderous intent, and smirked. "I'll be in the back if you need anything."

Alison waited until they were alone. "What are you doing here?" She cupped Killer's face and kissed her little button nose. "Hi, baby. It's so good to see you."

"Thanks, baby," Ryan said.

She rolled her eyes, but those two words, spoken in that low sexy voice of his, made her quiver. And ache. She missed their late nights in bed together, talking. Not talking. He'd made her feel good, inside and out. She hated that she hadn't done the same for him. "I thought you were on a date."

"Why?"

"Because you were at Whiskey River."

"And you know this because . . ."

Alison winced. "I might still have you on Find My Friends."

"I was there with Simon." His gaze held hers. "I'm here because I've got an early morning with a new client. I was wondering if you wanted to take Killer for me."

"It's almost midnight. How did you even know where I would be?"

Ryan gave a small smile. "I've still got you on Find My Friends as well."

She stared at him for a beat, saw the reluctant good humor in his eyes, and smiled back. She took Killer from him and kissed the dog's face all over.

Killer smiled her rare, sweet doggy smile and soaked up the love like it was her due.

"I missed you so much," Alison told her. "You ridiculous mini Napoleon you."

"She missed you too."

Alison looked up into his eyes. "Thanks," she said softly. "Means a lot."

He nodded and turned to go.

"Ryan?"

He paused.

"Do you really have an early morning, or did Simon open his big fat trap and tell you that I'm sad?"

"Are you sad?"

"No," she lied.

He tugged playfully on a strand of her wild and crazy hair. "What if I told you I was sad too?"

She stopped breathing.

He stared at her for a long beat, then dropped his hand. "Night, Alison." And then he was gone.

"But . . . are you?" she whispered at the closed door. Damn, now her heart hurt. He *was* sad. And that was on her. She set Killer down, who immediately raced over to a sleeping Hog and started yelling at him with her shrill bark.

Hog jumped up and tried to run around the counter, but slipped and fell. This didn't slow him down. He scrambled to his feet and nearly mowed over Emma, who was coming to his rescue. Crouching down, she hugged Hog tight. "Baby, all you have to do is stop running." She cupped his huge face and looked into his sweet, worried eyes. "Just stand up and stare her down, one time, and she'll stop."

Killer was still barking.

"Killer," Emma said calmly but firmly. "Stop."

Killer stopped.

Hog blinked in surprise.

"See?" Emma said. "You just have to let her know she's not the boss of you." She looked over his head at Alison. "We're all equals here."

"Hmm."

Emma smiled. "Ryan misses you."

"He didn't say that."

"He brought you Killer in the middle of the night. The man misses you."

"You were eavesdropping."

"Of course I was."

"Then you know he brought me Killer because he has an early meeting."

Emma rolled her eyes. "If you believe that, you're not nearly as smart as I thought you were."

"You think I'm smart?"

"Not anymore." Emma paused. "Okay, yes, I think you're smart. Smart and bitchy."

That ripped a laugh from Alison. "Are you always this honest?"

"Only since my coma. You know what you need?"

"More wine?"

"A plan," Emma said. "A plan to win him over with your smartassy, bitchy brilliance."

Alison was speechless for a full minute. Her throat actually felt tight.

"What?" Emma asked.

"That's the nicest thing anyone's ever said to me."

Emma blinked. "Are you saying I'm the nicest person in your life?"

"Who's not related to me, yeah. Terrifying, isn't it?"

"Very. But while you think I'm so nice, what's your getting-Ryan-back plan?"

"I'm working on it."

"I feel like that's code for 'I don't know,'" Emma said.

"I'm starting with being his friend." *By practicing . . . sometimes on you.* A fact she wisely kept to herself.

"How are you being his friend?"

Alison sighed. "It's still in the planning stage."

Emma snorted and grabbed her iPad. She opened up a blank note and began to type.

ALISON'S MASTER PLAN:

1. Be his friend—i.e., be there for him.
2. Pay attention to him and show interest—e.g., ask questions.

3. Respect him—e.g., care about the things he cares about, like his family and friends.
4. Flirt with him—e.g., smile.
5. Don't try to change him—i.e., accept him as he is, flaws and all.

"There," Emma said. "Complete with examples."

"Seems complicated," Alison said, also keeping to herself the fact that she already had a list going, mostly because her list wasn't working, and neither was practicing.

"It's called Being Human one-oh-one."

Alison's phone dinged an incoming email.

Emma was putting away her iPad. "It's in your in-box. You are welcome."

"It's not that easy."

"Look, think of it like this. The only way you can blow it is if you do nothing. What do you have to lose?"

Good question. And she had one for Emma as well. "So why are you only this honest since your coma?"

She shrugged. "Life's too short for bullshit."

Alison lifted her red Solo cup. "Amen to that."

Chapter 18

Step 18: It's the small things.

The next morning, Alison pulled up to Paw Pals, this time fully suited up, armor in place. She was juggling three coffees in a carrier, Killer, and her laptop, and she'd decided not to question why she felt the need to be here when she could've done the books from her office at Armstrong, or even her own place.

But the truth was . . . she'd fallen in love with Paw Pals. She loved the space, loved what Emma had done to it—though she'd definitely take that to her grave.

She and Killer entered the building and Killer went immediately on Yorkshire Terrier High Alert. "Behave," Alison said over her barking. "Or I'll put you in with the salties." She handed Miss Kitty one of the coffees.

"A bribe?" Miss Kitty asked.

"Yes."

Miss Kitty smiled and accepted the coffee.

Alison moved to the front desk, where Khloe stood. "How's things?" she asked the girl.

"Well, my boyfriend's a dick and my rent just got raised, so—"

"I meant here," Alison said. "How are things here?"

"Oh. Right." Khloe blushed. "Things here are good. We've got a full house today. Oh, and I just checked in our first turtle! Sammy's one hundred years old and he hits his pie tin when he wants you to fill it with lettuce. Cute, right?"

"Right," Alison said distractedly because . . . a turtle? How did one day-sit a turtle? She moved to the back. Marco was watching over the yards, playing with the dogs. He waved and she nodded and turned to Emma, who was sitting on the floor going through some boxes of what looked like cat food inventory. Emma said, "You might want to at least pretend to have interest in your employees."

"What do you mean? I'm perfectly friendly."

"Are you though?"

Alison sighed. "I'm working on it."

"Now that we're open again, you might want to work harder."

"You know, maybe *you* should hang out in the salty yard today."

"Ha ha," Emma said. Then her eyes locked on the two coffees. "Tell me one of those is for me."

"Yes. The one that's sugar and cream with a splash of coffee."

Emma hesitated. "Did you poison it?"

"Yeah, you caught me. I'm killing you off so I can handle all the customers on my own." She shivered in horror. "Trust me, you're not going anywhere until you earn us both some serious dough."

With a snort, Emma took the coffee and sipped. "Admit it, I'm growing on you."

"God forbid." Alison unhooked Killer from her leash and let her loose.

Killer barked and headed for a once-again snoozing Hog.

"Killer, sit," Emma said, and to Alison's shock, Killer skidded to a stop and sat.

Alison was reluctantly impressed.

"Be nice," Emma said, pointing at Killer. "Only *very* good boys and girls get to stay up front and be greeters."

Killer whined, lay down, and set her chin on her front two paws. Like an angel.

Alison was boggled. "Seriously. How do you do that? Magic?"

"You have to mean what you say."

"Can you teach me to do that?"

"Yes," Emma said. "Mean what you say."

Alison rolled her eyes.

An hour later, Khloe took a break and asked Alison to cover the register because Emma was busy with Marco manning the full yards.

Alison looked at Emma.

"Deal with it," her partner said.

Great. Fantastic. She'd deal with it.

A woman walked in, went directly to the cat aisle, picked out a small bag of food, and then came to check out.

"I'm also picking up my boy Kevin," the woman said. "He's a Pekingese." She set the food on the counter.

Alison tried to ring up the food, but it wouldn't scan.

"It's on sale," the woman said. "Nine ninety-nine."

Alison shook her head. "This food is the highest-quality food we have in the place. It isn't on sale."

"Yes, it is." The woman pointed to the sign over the basket of collars, adjacent to the food. "See? The sign says nine ninety-nine."

"For the collars," Alison said.

"But I'm not buying a collar. I'm buying gourmet cat food."

"Which is *nineteen* ninety-nine." Was she not speaking English?

Emma popped in from the back. She gave the customer a warm smile. "Mrs. McCreary, so nice to see you."

"You too, honey. How are you doing?"

"Wonderful, thank you. How can we help you today?"

"Well, your helper here is trying to overcharge me."

Emma glanced at Alison.

"The food's not on sale," Alison said.

Emma held up a finger to Mrs. McCreary and then pulled Alison aside. "Remember how we said we each have a lane?"

"Yes."

"Is this your lane? Because you're about to sideswipe us out of a customer."

Alison sighed. "Fine."

"And . . . ?" Emma asked.

Alison tossed up her hands. "And this *one* time you might be a little bit right."

"I'm going to need that in writing. Framed. I'll fix this while you first adjust the sign so it's obvious that it's for the collars. Then I need you to run to Costco

real quick before you leave for Armstrong Properties."
She moved back to Mrs. McCreary. "So sorry about
the mix-up."

"You'll honor your sign?" the woman asked.

"Of course."

Alison opened her mouth, but Mrs. McCreary spoke
first, beaming at Emma. "I love this place. My Kevin
is so happy here, I can't thank you enough. My favorite
part's being able to see him on the app when he's in
the play room. I'm going to my book club tonight and
bowling league tomorrow—I'll be sure to tell everyone
they need to use your services."

Emma glanced at Alison over her shoulder, her expression saying: *Now do you see why the customer is
always right?* "I'll have Marco bring out Kevin," she
said to Mrs. McCreary. "It will be just a few minutes."
She then gestured for Alison to follow her to the side.
"Okay, so at Costco, you'll—"

"Why aren't you sending Khloe or Marco?"

"Because both Khloe and Marco are willing to
scoop poop." Emma looked at Alison's expensive suit.
"Somehow I think you'd rather make the Costco run."

Alison grabbed her purse. "What do we need?"

"More cookies."

"We have a bazillion varieties of dog cookies. And
cat cookies. And bird cookies—"

"But we don't have any human cookies. If you hurry, the Girl Scouts will still be selling right out in front of the store. I need a minimum of five boxes."

Alison stared at her, then laughed. "I'm not your errand girl. And jeez, you're awfully grumpy today. Let me guess, you still haven't talked to Simon? Maybe you should make your own master plan."

"I think we're now officially in the avoiding-each-other phase, which actually takes talent considering we live in the same building."

"Huh," Alison said.

"Huh? *That's* all you've got?"

"What were you hoping for?"

"Advice?"

Alison laughed. "You already know I'm even worse with men and relationships than I am with checking out customers."

Again the bell above the front door jingled.

Killer began barking at decibels capable of piercing eardrums, sounding the alarm.

Alison and Emma moved back to the front. Alison drew a deep breath and channeled her inner Emma. "Killer, stop. Stop and sit."

Killer did not stop and sit.

Emma looked at the little heathen. "Killer, stop and sit."

Killer stopped. And sat.

"Ingrate," Alison uttered as she and Emma both looked toward the door to check out their next customer.

It was Simon. He looked at Emma, who was suddenly doing a great imitation of a frozen Popsicle.

Alison grinned. *Who said work was no fun?* "Yeah, so . . . I'm going to go to Costco now. Bye."

Emma defrosted enough to glance over at her. "No. Don't you dare—"

Alison swept up Killer and left, chortling to herself the whole way.

Chapter 19

Step 19: Ask questions.

When her traitorous partner shut the back door behind her, Emma gritted her teeth, then forced a smile because she had nothing to feel bad about. Then the smile became real when Dale came into the shop behind Simon, waving a cast on his arm, but otherwise looking good.

Relieved to see him, she waved back, pretending not to see Simon—though how could she not; he looked tall, leanly muscled, and like everything she'd ever wanted in jeans and dark sunglasses, and he had an easy confidence that was hard to resist.

Mrs. McCreary, still waiting for Marco to bring out Kevin, smiled at Simon and Dale. "Hello." She let her gaze linger on Dale. "While I'm waiting for Kevin, I'm just going to go browse through the dog training books on that shelf over there. I don't suppose you know anything about training dogs?"

Dale smiled. "I know everything about training dogs."

"Then maybe I'll see you over there." She walked toward the shelves.

Simon looked at his dad.

Dale shrugged. "Still got it. I can't help that."

"Dad, you have to stop lying."

"That wasn't lying. It was flirting." Dale winked, though because of the strokes, it looked more like he was having a seizure, and then followed after Mrs. McCreary.

Leaving Emma alone with Simon. They stared at each other for a long beat. She wanted to play it cool and mysterious, like she had her shit together, but she didn't. Couldn't. Not with the man she was falling for in spite of herself leaning against the counter.

Then Simon pulled off his sunglasses and gave her a small smile. Suddenly she could see past the mouthwatering exterior. The weary—and wary—gaze. The set of his broad shoulders. His hair was standing up from running his fingers through it. It all added up to unhappiness. If she wasn't so mad at him, her heart would ache. Okay, fine, her heart did ache. "Hey," she said quietly. "What's up?"

"I'm sorry about last night."

"You mean when you said things couldn't keep happening between us unless my life was back on track because I wasn't ready?"

His gaze was steady. "Yes."

"Then I'm confused. Because my life *is* on track. I've got a business partner. A job. A place to live. That September 5K. So there's a pretty big hole in your rationale for why we're not having mutually satisfying orgasms as the opportunities arise."

His eyes heated at the orgasm comment, but he didn't say anything. Yep, she was definitely missing a piece of the Simon Armstrong puzzle, but she thought maybe she was getting closer to locating it. "You didn't bail because of me not being ready," she said. "You bailed because *you're* not ready."

He wasn't exactly an open book, but she saw something flicker in Simon's eyes—regret?—before he turned his head and took in the organized chaos going on around them.

"I'm right, aren't I?" she asked.

His gaze came back to hers. More longing. More regret. "My life doesn't lend itself to relationships."

She didn't know which was worse, the frustration or the anger that he wasn't willing to even try. No, neither of those things. The worst part was the way her heart ached for what would never be just because he was stubborn. "Who said anything about a relationship?"

"You deserve one, Emma. You deserve everything."

"I told you from the very beginning that I wasn't looking for a relationship."

He looked at her, *into* her, it seemed, and she let him because she'd spoken the truth.

"What *do* you want?" he finally asked.

Emma spread her hands. "Look at me. I'm living day to day. Hell, sometimes moment to moment. That's where I live now, in the moment."

"And that's enough for you?"

"Yes."

"It shouldn't be."

She shrugged. "I'm focusing on healing—physically *and* emotionally," she said, letting Simon know she'd heard what he'd said on the roof, because he'd been right about that. "I don't think I can open up to another person while I'm doing that. It wouldn't be fair to them, plus why would anyone want to sign up for that kind of baggage?"

"You don't think that person can decide for themselves?"

"I think feelings cloud things," she said, letting the steel of her resolve come out clear in her voice.

"You deserve more, Emma. A lot more."

She leaned in close, like she was telling him a secret, when really she just wanted to feel him against her. "You know, for someone whose life doesn't *lend itself to relationships*, you sure talk about them a lot."

Simon leaned in too, until they were practically chest to chest, thigh to thigh. "I meant what I said, Emma. You deserve a real relationship, a good one. But—"

"I swear, if you say 'my life doesn't lend itself to relationships' one more time . . ."

"Listen to me. I ruined my last relationship because I'm either at one of two jobs, or taking care of my dad. I don't have time for anyone else in my life, and from experience, most women expect—"

"I'm not most women, Simon."

He stared at her and then let out a breath, a hint of a smile in his eyes. "No kidding."

Emma wanted to wrap her hands around his throat and squeeze . . . but she also wanted to have her merry way with him. If only she could do both, but she did neither. "I've gotta get going. What brought you here today?"

"Besides you?" he asked, and she had to ignore the way her heart skipped a beat. "I needed to talk to Alison. I've got a PT appointment and I can't miss this one. I'd take Dad with me, but the last time I did that, he walked off and ended up at the mall with my credit card. I'm still paying off the massage chair."

She snorted. "Gotta love him. So what was your plan? Drop him off here?"

Simon looked around, like that hadn't occurred to him. "I didn't think she'd be staying here all day." He noted Miss Kitty in her chair in the front corner, knitting away. "Do you take people too?"

"Just dogs and cats, and as of today, a turtle named Sammy."

As if on cue, there was suddenly an odd banging-on-tin sound.

Hog tipped his head back and gave a mournful howl.

Simon raised a brow.

"Meet Sammy," Emma said.

"The turtle?"

"He's banging on his pie tin. Wants his lettuce."

Simon stared at her for a beat and then smiled. "This place really does suit you."

Another skipped heartbeat. At this point, she was going to start needing beta-blockers to control the arrhythmia. "Alison won't be back for a few." Emma glanced over at Dale, who was now sitting on the floor with Mrs. McCreary, surrounded by books he'd pulled off the shelves, happily reading to her out loud. With one arm, of course, because the other was casted. "I'll take him," she said softly.

"What? No. I couldn't ask you to do that."

"You didn't."

They stared at each other.

"In fact," she said, "the only thing you've asked me to do is to walk away from you."

He drew a deep breath. "If you think that was an easy ask . . ."

"It doesn't matter."

"Emma—"

"Leave your dad with me. I'll keep him safe."

"Why? Why would you do this for me?"

"Because you've helped me in a way I can never repay. If it hadn't been for you, I don't know if I'd have ever gotten here."

Simon gave a slow head shake. "It was all you."

She shook her head. "You believed in me, even when I didn't. I'll never be able to pay you back for that. But I like your dad, and this is something I can do for you."

"Emma." He lifted her chin. "I never meant to hurt you."

Okay, so she could hold on to her hurt about how he'd backed off from a romantic entanglement—or she could toss it out as an experiment gone wrong and keep him in her life. The decision was actually surprisingly easy. "I know. And it's all good." Emma held out her pinkie. "Friends?"

He hooked his pinkie with hers, mouth curved but eyes very serious. "Friends."

She felt the muscles in his arm spasm, as if maybe he was fighting the urge to pull her into him. She hoped he was. She was evolved, but even she had some feminine pride.

"We okay?" he asked.

"We're okay. Go work, Simon. I've got your dad."

"I'll call Alison. She'll take him with her when she leaves here."

She nodded, watching his gaze land on her mouth. She wasn't the only one who missed having that mouth on hers. Even better . . . A small comfort, but she'd take it.

The rest of the day was a blur for Simon. He'd gone from the PT clinic to Armstrong Properties, where he spent just over eight straight hours putting out various fires all over the place. A remodel on an older building where a contract worker slipped and twisted his ankle. A broken pipe at another property that had flooded the bottom floor. And the list went on.

He'd called into Paw Pals and checked on Dale. Emma had assured him that his dad was good and staying out of trouble. He'd also called Alison, who'd told him the same thing and also that he was an idiot.

Like he didn't know.

At six thirty, he walked into his apartment with a good amount of trepidation. Alison was very good to Dale, but when she was the one in charge, the house tended to completely fall apart around them. Dale liked routine. Also he was still unsteady on his feet. If even a chair was out of place, he'd trip over it. So Simon often spent several hours cleaning up after his dad was in bed.

But when Simon entered his apartment, it was quiet and peaceful. The living room was spotless and there was music playing softly. No wait. Not music, but sounds of waves hitting a shore, an incredibly sooth-ing sound. And the scent. Something so delicious he walked like a zombie toward the kitchen, following his nose.

Emma was at the stove, stirring something. His dad was at the table, laughing.

Laughing.

And for the first time all day, Simon felt like he could breathe. But there was something else, something still tight in his chest, he realized, as Emma turned from the stove, her hair piled up on her head, her cheeks flushed, a ready smile on her face for his dad, looking so adorably sexy, his heart rolled over.

"Oh," she said, flustered to see him. "Hi."

Ten and a half hours since they'd pinkie promised to be friends no matter what and still his body hadn't gotten the memo. He wanted to blame it on the tight, faded-to-threadbare jeans she wore with a gauzy top that had tiny straps crisscrossing over her bare back. But it was the sandals that stopped his heart. Also strappy, they had a three-inch heel that put her at eye level to his mouth. Her toes were painted alternately in blue, purple, and green, and that made him smile.

"Present to myself for signing on the dotted line to buy Paw Pals," she said. "I haven't worn heels in a year and they were on sale."

"You look beautiful."

"Thanks, but . . ." She kicked off the heels and sighed in relief. "Going to have to work my way up to them. Maybe after the surgery."

"You got your approval?" he asked hopefully.

"Not yet."

Damn. "We're going to have to find another way."

The look she gave him reminded him that they weren't a "we" at all, and that it was his own doing.

Dale got to his feet. "Going to go wash up for dinner."

When he was gone, Emma turned to Simon. "Alison got called back to work. She had a showing, and before you say a word, I offered."

"You should've called me. It shouldn't have been your responsibility to take him home."

"It's not a big deal." She shrugged and turned back to the counter. "And it's kind of nice to have dinner with someone for a change."

She spoke casually, even lightly, but there was suddenly a new tension in her body. Her parents were gone, as were the two people who'd been closest to her, and they'd ripped themselves out of her life in a way that had left nothing but betrayal in their wake.

She was lonely, and he'd not thought of that. Feeling like a dick, he shrugged out of his jacket, wishing he could shrug as easily out of the asshat skin he'd been wearing. He'd been so caught up in his own shit that he hadn't even realized how isolated she'd become after moving in here.

Simon walked around the island to peer over her shoulder into the pot. His chest brushed her back and he felt her freeze for a beat and then kind of melt into him.

Her body hadn't gotten the memo either, and just like it always was with her, anticipatory tension danced in the air between them and stole his breath.

Emma turned to face him in the small space he'd left her, holding out a wooden spoon. "Spaghetti sauce," she said. "It's my only real kitchen talent."

Holding her gaze, he took a nibble just as she said, "Mostly my talents lie elsewhere," and made him choke.

She grinned at him while he nearly coughed up a lung.

"You're evil," he murmured, unable to hold back his smile. "I like that."

"And the sauce?"

"Best thing I've tasted in a few days."

He watched with erotic fascination as she did the math and color flared in her cheeks. Hard to believe he could react from just being near her, but that was exactly what was happening. To distance himself, Simon stepped up to the counter where she had salad makings spread on a cutting board. Grabbing a knife, he began to chop up the veggies. He finished a red pepper and offered a bite to Emma.

She took it with her teeth, making sure to nip his finger while she was at it. Not hard, but not soft either. When he sucked in a breath, she let go and laughed.

He turned back to the counter to finish chopping, then found himself pressed up against the granite when Emma had to reach around him to grab a few wine-glasses from the cabinet in front of him.

He stilled, his breath catching. Turning in place, he came face-to-face with her.

They looked at each other for a long beat before he reached up and pushed a lock of her hair behind her ear, his fingertips lightly stroking along her earlobe. "Why don't you go sit down," he said. "I'll finish this up."

"You've had a long day."

"And I can tell by how you're standing that yours was longer. Sit. I'll serve you. Dad?" he called out. "It's ready."

Dale came in and sat with Emma. Simon served Emma first, then began to load up a plate for his dad, who gestured for more. "Don't be stingy, son. I'm starving."

"Guess all that flirting today with Mrs. McCreary was hard work."

"I can't help it if the ladies love me." Dale pointed his fork at Simon. "If you need any tips, all you've gotta do is ask."

Emma laughed.

Simon slid her a look, unable to help the smile he felt curve his mouth. "You think I could use some tips?"

She playfully shrugged, making Dale grin.

"Is it his talking game that's off, or his kissing game?"

Emma bit her lower lip. "Well . . ."

Simon narrowed his eyes at her, and she laughed out loud, the sound utterly contagious.

"Okay," she said. "So it's not his kissing game."

Dale nodded. "It's his stubbornness, isn't it. He's not great about acknowledging relationship things like emotions."

"Sounds like it runs in the family."

Dale smiled. "Yes, but Alison doesn't like emotions. Simon doesn't have that problem. He likes 'em just fine, except for the deep ones. The deep ones scare the shit out of him."

"They do not," Simon said.

Dale rolled his eyes at Emma, who laughed again.

"So you agree," Dale said.

"Well, I'm not one to judge on such matters," she said diplomatically.

Simon snorted.

"Oh really. You have something to say on the matter?" she asked him, brow arched.

"Just wondering if you're the kettle or pot?"

She gave a wry smile. "Possibly both."

"Oh my God, this tastes delicious," Dale said of her food, shoveling in spaghetti and sauce, missing his mouth every third or fourth bite. "Tell me you bake too."

"I do make an amazing double-fudge cake that I save for special occasions, but it's just from a box mix."

His dad reached out and squeezed her hand. "*Never save anything for a special occasion. Being alive is the special occasion.*"

Emma smiled. "Cheers to that."

Dale ate some more. "I used to cook some, after my Jenny died." He pointed his fork at Simon. "This one hated everything I made."

"That's because you'd pan-fry some fatty ground beef, toss in a pot of overcooked macaroni and a soggy tomato, and call it health food."

"Hey. That was decent stuff. And you were an ingrate. Remember that time you showed up needing money?"

"You mean on my twenty-first birthday?" Simon looked at Emma. "I was at a bar with my college roommates. I took six shots of tequila in about two hours. Woke up on my dad's front lawn the next morning— and keep in mind that my college was three hundred miles away. Apparently the Uber driver asked for my address and I gave them Dad's."

"Hey, I paid the three-hundred-dollar fare," Dale said.

Simon nodded. "Yep. And then you left me in the yard all night. I didn't wake up until the sprinklers came on. At dawn."

Emma covered her mouth to hide her laugh. "Tequila is the worst."

"Agreed." Simon shuddered at the memory. "But I really was a pretty shitty teenager."

Dale shook his head. "That's not what I said."

"Ingrate then."

Dale sighed. "I shouldn't have said that. You'd lost your mom. Your world was hard then."

"That's not an excuse."

Dale's easy expression faded. "I could've been a better dad to you back then."

Simon sighed. "Dad, come on. You did good."

"No, I didn't. I was locked in my own grief and that meant you were often completely on your own. Sometimes I think it convinced you that sometimes you still are. But you're not. Alone. And you deserve the world."

"Wow. The whole world?"

"Son, I'm trying to have a moment with you. Don't ruin it."

Simon smiled. "All right, Dad, let's have a moment."

Dale toasted him and winked at Emma, and Simon just shook his head, but he wasn't irritated. He was something else entirely. He hadn't seen his dad like this with anyone but himself or Alison in a long time.

There was a carefree ease about him tonight, and sitting there laughing together felt . . . good. *Everything* about Emma felt good. Way too good to be true, in fact. What would happen if his dad got really bad again? Even though Simon and Emma were just friends now, would she walk away? Resent him for having no time for her?

She hasn't done either in spite of you being an asshole, a voice whispered in his head.

But he knew better than to bank on hopes and dreams.

"Thanks for having me tonight," Emma said.

"Are you kidding?" Dale smiled at her. "You're always welcome. I knew it'd take someone special to make my son give up the apartment he loved so much. Especially since 1B is also empty and available, although granted, not updated or as nice as 2A."

Emma turned and looked at Simon.

Shit. He'd not given her the option of the downstairs apartment on purpose, wanting her to have the steps to work on for her recovery. But if there was anything he now knew about Emma, it was that she liked to have choices. "Dad—"

"And," the man went on, "I knew that special someone would also have to be smart and warm and also willing to go toe to toe with this guy." He jabbed a thumb in Simon's direction, ignoring the daggers Simon was sending him. "He hit the jackpot with you, Emma." He smiled at Simon. "I approve, son."

Thanks, Dad . . .

"You gave up your apartment for me?"

Nope, not going to go well at all. He looked at her. "I wasn't using it. I haven't since my dad's first stroke."

"But there was another apartment I could've rented. Downstairs."

"Not renovated or as nice," Simon said, repeating his dad's words.

"Admit it, you *wanted* me to walk up and down the stairs every day."

"You needed to push yourself past the hump. Which you did. In less than a month, by the way. You're not even limping anymore and you're using your left arm and hand more and more every day."

She looked down and found her left hand holding her water glass; she hadn't even realized.

"Emma, I pushed you because I knew you could handle it."

"What would you have done if I *couldn't* handle it?"

"I've had a lot of patients over the years, but I've never had one as strong and determined as you."

"Or as pretty," Dale said. "But, son, you could learn a lot from me. Now, granted, most of my experience is from decades ago." He smiled. "The eighties. Great memories. No evidence."

"*Dad.*"

"Right. Okay, well, I'm going to go . . ." Dale hitched a thumb out the door. "Do stuff."

Simon waited until his dad was gone before looking at Emma again, thankfully still there, feet still bare, eyes narrowed. "For the record," he said quietly, "I pushed you because I care."

"Even back then?"

"From the second I first saw you."

She stared at him for a moment. "At the rehab facility?"

"No, at the hospital. You were still on heavy meds so you probably don't remember. When I came in, you were talking to your doctor."

"Wait." She frowned. "I do remember." Her voice was full of surprise. "I was wearing a stupid hospital gown and a bunch of tubes and wires, and I was a hot mess."

"You were beautiful and determined and said you'd do whatever it took to get better. I was bowled over by your tenacity and strength."

"And I wasn't talking to my doctor. I was yelling at him."

He smiled. "Actually, you tried to throw your water bottle at him, but you didn't have your arms back yet and it just hit the floor."

She grimaced.

"He deserved it. He was blunt and disconnected," Simon said. "You were understandably upset, as he'd just told you to prepare yourself for the hard fact that you might never walk again. I was there because they'd requested an initial PT report and plan. And then, when they moved you to the rehab center, I was called in again. I was actually hoping you'd be assigned to Kelly, or anyone other than me."

"Why?"

He shook his head, still surprised by it. "It was just a feeling. I couldn't explain it to myself back then. All I knew was that you were special, and that you'd become incredibly important to me."

She was looking stunned. "*Me?*"

"Yes, you."

"And now?"

"And now . . ." She'd been the first woman who saw his life and got it. Got him. She hadn't batted an eye when he'd said he and his dad were a package deal. His dad wasn't a burden to him, but he understood that it was a burden to any relationship he was in. Except

Emma had stepped right into their unit, easy as can be. "And I was right. You've become incredibly important to me."

"Because . . . ?" she whispered.

Simon didn't answer. Couldn't. Or they'd end up naked somewhere. For days. *Only you'd put a stop to that . . .*

Emma got up and moved to where he still sat. Standing between his spread-out legs, she looked down at him. "Because I'm not just a job to you."

"Because you've never been just a job to me." Simon let his hands go to her hips, pulling until she came in even closer.

She stared at his mouth, then into his eyes. And smiled. "Good," she said. And then she stepped back and walked out to the living room to play cards with his dad.

Chapter 20

Step 20: It's about the little things.

Emma couldn't remember the last time she'd enjoyed an evening as much as she had with Simon and his dad. It'd been since before her accident, certainly. But so many of the memories in the years before the accident were still fuzzy. The doctors kept saying it'd probably come back, maybe in pieces, maybe as dreams. The brain was a funny, fickle thing.

How well she knew that.

The body too. Just playing cards, an underlying current of energy bounced between her and Simon, back and forth, back and forth, every time their fingers brushed together reaching for a card, every laugh, every accidental meeting of their gazes. They all played for an hour before Simon helped his dad to bed.

Emma went into the kitchen to do the dishes, and a few minutes later, Simon came in eyeing his phone.

"I installed a security camera in the hallway outside his room so I can see if he leaves. It's also wired for motion and sound, so if he calls out for help, the app will alert me. No more accidents." He raised his head. "You don't have to do the dishes."

"Wanted to."

"No one *wants* to do dishes."

"My brain likes the mindlessness of it when it's too full of thoughts," she said.

"Yeah?" He gently nudged her aside and took over, looking very at home cleaning up. And dead sexy too. "What thoughts are making your brain too full?"

Emma shrugged, not wanting to say since they were all erotic, every one of them; thoughts of Simon's mouth back on hers, his hands on her body . . . "I like how you take care of your dad."

"Nice deflection."

She smiled. "My thoughts are feeling shy."

His eyes heated. "Maybe they'll come out to play later then."

"That's probably against our friend decree." Yes, she was baiting him.

Simon finished the dishes, dried his hands, and turned to her. "Did I ever mention I say stupid things when I'm feeling emotionally invested? It's fear."

"I believe your dad alluded to that for you."

"He's superhelpful."

She laughed, but then she was suddenly transported to a dream she'd had when in her coma. At least, she'd thought it'd been a dream. Two women in her room, probably going over her chart, talking.

"He's the hottest PT we've ever had here."

"Maggie actually dated him for a few months. She fell in love with him on the first date but he carries his dad with him everywhere."

Simon cupped her face, his warm hazel eyes filled with concern. "You went somewhere. You okay?"

"I just remembered something." She put her hand over his. "I've told you some of the things I heard when I was in the coma. I forgot one. The nurses or two techs, I'm not sure, they were talking about you."

"Me?"

"Called you hot."

He grimaced.

"One of them talked about someone dating you. Someone named Maggie."

"I thought Kelly told you that."

"Yes, but I didn't make the connection until now. She dumped you because you were carrying your dad around. At least that's what I thought I heard. But you weren't *carrying* your dad, you were *caring* for him."

He shook his head, looking marveled. "Yes. I can't believe you heard all that and retained it. You're a miracle, Em, you know that, right? A walking, talking, beautiful, amazing miracle."

She felt her heart swell up against her rib cage, and the words she'd been biting back escaped her. "I'm emotionally invested in you too, Simon."

He let out a rough breath, closed his eyes, then opened them again. "You should know, you could actually take me out at the knees if you wanted."

"I . . . wouldn't."

That got her a smile. "No?"

"No," she whispered.

"That makes me feel better."

She smiled.

"Actually," he said, "I feel better than I have in a long time."

"Yeah, spaghetti does that for me too. We should have ice cream for dessert. That always helps too."

He laughed low in his throat. "It's not the spaghetti." He shifted closer, his warm body at her front, the counter against her back. "It's not that I need ice cream either." Putting a hand on the granite on either side of her hips, he slowly leaned in and rubbed his jaw along hers. "It's you."

"Simon?"

"Yeah?"

"Are you scared right now?"

Giving her a hungry look, Simon replied, "No. I think you cured me."

Emma's heart was thundering now. She pressed up against him, letting out a low sound of pleasure that she couldn't hold in to save her life, and he answered with a slow, deliciously deep kiss.

"Your call, Em." His voice was husky with desire when he pulled back just enough to speak against her lips. "What do you want to do now?"

What did she want to do? Ride him like a pogo stick.

"How far does that security camera app allow you to go?"

"As far as I want."

She took him by the hand. "My place then," she said. Smiled. "Which is also *your* place, apparently." She tugged on his hand, but he resisted until she looked back at him.

"Bring the heels."

She laughed until she saw the heat in his eyes. Not a minute later, she had Simon's hand in one of hers, her pretty shoes dangling from her other as he tugged her up the stairs. "Normally you make me do this all on my own. Thanks for the assist."

He brought their joined hands up to his mouth and kissed her palm. "I don't want to wear you out. Yet." At her door, he pressed her up against the wood, brushing his lips against her earlobe, absorbing her full-body shiver. "Just to be clear, I'm staying fired."

"But . . . I like you."

"Good. I like you too."

She laughed. "I mean as a PT."

He shook his head. "Pick."

She stared up at him, making the decision without a question. "I pick you. Not as my PT, but as the giver of orgasms."

"Good choice." Laughing low in his throat, he kissed her. "But it's more than orgasms."

She knew that, but not quite ready to discuss it, she pulled his head back to hers. When they finally broke for air, she had her hands beneath his shirt, one north, one south. His eyes were hot, his hands tightening their grip on her. "Inside, Em."

She fumbled behind her and managed to open the door.

"It wasn't locked?" Simon asked.

"I forgot."

He held her back from entering and stepped into the apartment first, moving through it. She stepped inside, shut her door, and watched him.

"It's a safe neighborhood," he said, coming back to her. "But you can't bank on that. You need to be careful."

"I know. But after this past year, sometimes I feel . . . indestructible." She grimaced. "I know that sounds ridiculous, but it's true."

He came back and wrapped her up in his arms. Lowering his head, he kissed her softly. "I get it, I do, but you need to be careful with you. For me."

She nodded, suddenly feeling a little distracted by what she'd brought him up here to do. Was her bed made? Did she need to brush her teeth?

His warm hand slid to the nape of her neck, his thumb running along her jaw. She looked up at him, finding his gaze serious. "Is this too fast, Emma? I can go."

"You should." She smiled. "You should go straight to my bed. And if you could carry me while you're at it, that'd be great. I mean, I could walk, you literally taught me how, but at the moment, I can't concentrate on that *and* this."

"This?"

Tightening her grip in his hair, she kissed him, pouring all her need and hunger and desire into it, making him groan.

"I love the this." He lifted her up, helped her wrap her legs around his waist, and started toward her bedroom.

"Wait!"

He froze.

She pulled free and slipped her feet into her strappy high-heeled sandals one at a time, using his arm for balance, eyes locked on his. "Okay, now."

With a low, appreciative groan, he reached for her again, just as his phone buzzed a notification. He swore creatively and she knew it had to be the security app.

"Get it," she said.

He let her slowly slide down his body and pulled his phone from his pocket. When he brought up the security cam, he snorted and turned the screen so she could see it as well.

His dad was sitting on the side of his bed. He was holding the camera, staring into it. "Son? You there?" He shook the camera before bringing it up to his mouth like it was a phone. "I don't mean to interrupt you," the lips said. "I mean, I really hope you're getting some. But I kinda doubt you're lucky enough to catch that sweet, amazing girl. Anyway, just in case, I'm scout's honoring you. I won't leave this bed until daylight. You are welcome. Oh, and P.S. to cutie pie Coma Girl—he's pretty amazing too." Then he set the camera on the bookshelf in the hallway and went back to bed.

"He's kind of adorable," Emma said.

"I'm pretty sure no one in the history of ever has accused him of being *kind of adorable* before."

"Don't worry." She grinned at him. "You're even more adorable than he is."

Simon grimaced. "I think that just lowered my testosterone levels."

"As if." She pushed him into her room and onto her bed.

He fell back, giving her a sexy, half-lidded look and a smile as she knelt on the bed next to him.

Splaying her hands across his stomach, she let out a hum of pleasure when his ab muscles quivered. She tugged on his shirt until he shucked it, then continued to strip everything else she demanded, getting her mouth on everything he exposed. She was just settling in for some serious fun when he rolled her beneath him with a rough, "My turn."

He got her out of her jeans. He was good too. It'd taken her a good five minutes and almost a pair of pliers to get into them but he had her free in a matter of seconds—leaving her in nothing but the shoes.

Simon sat back on his heels, taking her in. "You're so beautiful, Emma."

So was he. Leanly muscled from head to toe, giving off pheromones and testosterone until she felt almost drunk. Emma came up on her elbows. "You could have a flaw, you know. It'd make your bed partner feel less inadequate."

"I've got plenty of flaws." He wrapped his big hands around her ankles and tugged. She fell back and he slowly climbed up her body, kissing every inch as he went. "One of them being so muleheaded that this almost didn't happen. But you, Emma, you're flawless."

"Those are some pretty great rose-colored glasses you've got on." She had scars. She hadn't been able to run in a year, so she'd lost muscle tone. And in recovery she'd found a love for chips. Oh so many chips . . .

"You're perfect, Emma." He kissed her then, kissed her until his mouth melted her into a puddle of sensations. Then he took that mouth on a tour south, lifting his head only to give her a directive. "Relax." He ran a hand down her left leg until she managed to unclench. "Good. Stay that way."

"But . . ." She bit her lower lip. "I have to tighten up to . . . you know, get there."

His fingers were being diabolical even as he held her gaze. "I don't want you to move. I'm going to do all the work, and you're going to get there. Trust me?"

When she nodded, he lowered his head and kissed first one inner thigh, and then the other.

And then in between . . .

She flew apart for him in shockingly little time. Rising up, he protected them both with a condom, then wrapped her legs around his waist and sank into her. With a mindless moan, she dug her fingers into the hard muscles at the small of his back, trying not to bite his shoulder and failing.

She felt his rough laugh and then his mouth found hers again. After that, everything was blinding white light.

Simon stirred, entangled in warm, sexy, sleeping woman. Emma had her face pressed into his throat, a hand low on his belly, and a leg thrown proprietarily over both of his.

Neither of them were wearing a stitch of clothing, although he was wearing a smile that wouldn't go away. She'd called him out on his bullshit, made him face his fears, and . . . nothing had blown itself up.

Just went to prove that she was smarter than he was. Because while he'd been focusing on holding her at arm's length, she'd broken down his defenses with one smile. The one that warmed his heart and slipped under his guard until he not only needed her, he also loved her.

She drew in a deep breath and opened her eyes. "Hey," she whispered. "You have to go."

"Yes." He kissed her softly, then not so softly, and the ever-present searing sexual attraction between them reared its head again. She put a hand to his chest. "It's okay, Simon."

Her words warmed him more than anything else could have. She understood his life, she got it.

And he felt something he hadn't felt in a long time. *Hope.*

Chapter 21

Step 21: Don't judge.

A week later, Alison was at Paw Pals. She stood behind the front counter, but off to the side, working on inventory on her laptop. Saturdays had never been her favorite day, at least not since she and Ryan had broken up. With no work to distract her, the weekend days had always stretched out in front of her, a yawning, lonely silence.

She liked to think of herself as a true introvert, but that wasn't actually accurate. She didn't really enjoy being alone. She wanted to be surrounded by people who loved her, she just didn't want them to talk to her.

She'd told Emma she would take the Saturday shifts. Normally they didn't take in as many clients on Saturdays, which Alison had made it her business to know. She'd made it her business to know everything, including the fact that Gabby had been overpaying herself while severely underpaying Emma.

She'd told herself she didn't care about Emma as a person, that this was a business arrangement only, but it'd bothered her a lot. Emma had been a huge asset to this place. She'd deserved better.

So she'd given them both raises.

Emma was also here, effortlessly playing nice with all who came into the shop, making instant friends for life like she'd been born to it. Which of course she had. Emma's parents had been beloved members of the community. Hell, Emma was practically Wildstone royalty.

"You keep frowning like that and it's going to stick," Emma said as she walked by.

"I'm not frowning."

Emma pulled out her phone, accessed the camera, and turned it to face Alison. Damn, frowning really wasn't a great look for her. "*Whatever.*"

"If you'd just try and fix things with Ryan, you could turn that frown upside down."

"Oh my God. Please stop talking. And 'turn that frown upside down'? Are you watching *Sesame Street?*"

"Have you called him? Enacted our plan?"

"You mean *your* plan?"

"I was trying to be inclusive," Emma said. "And stop trying to divert me. I can't be diverted."

"You know, people think you're so sweet."

"Step one," Emma said after whipping out her phone to review her notes. "You were going to try being his friend."

"I'm working on that," Alison said. In fact, she was practicing at this very moment, on Emma herself. Again, she decided it was best to keep that little detail to herself.

"Step two," Emma went on. "Pay attention, show interest, ask questions. Step three, care about the things he cares about, like his family and friends. Step four, flirt with him. Smile—" She slid a look to Alison.

Alison feigned a smile.

Emma rolled her eyes. "Step five, don't try to change him, accept him, flaws and all."

The problem with that was the flaws weren't Ryan's. They were hers.

"Did you do any of that?" Emma asked.

Alison had thought about it only every second of every single day, but no, she hadn't actually made a move yet.

Emma shook her head. "Wow. I didn't see that coming."

"What?"

"You're a coward."

Alison narrowed her eyes. She was a lot of things, but she refused to believe she was a coward. "You take that back."

"Live your damn life, Ali."

"*Alison.*"

"Whoever you want to be," Emma said with a wave of her hand. "Just live it like it was meant to be lived. Forgive yourself and move on."

"Forgive myself for what exactly, *Emmie*?"

Emma glared at her. "Whatever's eating at you."

Whelp, there happened to be a long list. Letting Ryan down. Pushing people away. Not letting herself fall because she feared getting hurt . . .

"While you're figuring all that out, I'll just—"

Alison looked over when Emma didn't finish that sentence and found her staring out the window at that same man they'd seen before. The man who'd hit Emma with his car. He was walking down the street, away from them. "Emma?"

Her partner didn't budge. Didn't blink.

"I thought you wanted to talk to him. Now's your chance."

Still nothing. Emma had become a statue.

Alison sighed and put her hand on Emma's arm. She was still as a statue. And chilled. "Hey, what was it you just told me? Live my life?" She leaned in closer. "So, live your life."

Emma drew in a deep breath and nodded. "Yes."

But she still didn't move.

"Do you want a push?"

Ignoring this, Emma fully galvanized and moved closer to the window. "He looks okay, right?"

"I mean . . . how do you tell?"

Emma swiveled her head, eyes wide. "Because I need him to be okay!"

"Right." Alison nodded at the crazy lady. "He looks *great*."

Emma shook her head and headed for the door. She stopped, hand on the handle. "Maybe I should just leave him alone?"

Dear God, they were both in trouble if Emma wanted advice from Alison. "Live your life," she said, repeating Emma's words, and gave her the shoo hands. "It seems like you can't do that until you talk to him, so go already."

Emma stepped outside.

Alison hurried to the window and watched Emma watch Jack Swanson turn the corner and vanish from view.

Emma came back inside, looking a little sick. Without making eye contact, she moved behind the counter and fiddled with the display next to the computer.

"What are you doing?"

"Working," Emma said. "You?"

"Watching my partner pretend she has her shit together."

"Oh, and you think *you* have your shit together?"

"I know I don't. But I might actually have it slightly more together than you." A terrifying thought. "Why didn't you chase him down?"

Emma didn't answer, just came around the counter as a woman entered the building, holding a carrier with two little Chihuahuas, both barking loudly. Luna and Rex were checked in and taken to the "salty" yard, where Dale sat. He said he related to the salts.

He was here because Simon had needed to take an emergency client for Kelly, who was out of town, and had he called Alison for help? No. He had not. He'd called Alison's business partner.

And, given the well-satisfied glow Emma was wearing, they weren't spending their nights staring at the TV like Alison was. She was happy for them. Sort of. No, dammit. She *was* happy for them. That was one of the rules she'd learned in this whole being in a relationship with someone. You had to be happy for them when good things occurred in their lives. Even if you tended to self-destruct your own happiness at every turn.

"We used to have a Chihuahua," Dale said. "She got out one day. Just ran across the street into the woods and was never seen again. Assumed she ran into a coyote."

Alison gaped at him. "You told us she'd gone to live on a farm upstate."

Dale grimaced. "Um. Yes?"

Alison shook her head. "Oh my God."

Emma gave her a sympathetic gaze.

"No," Alison said, pointing at her. "I don't want sympathy from the person sleeping with my cousin while pretending nothing's going on."

"I'm not . . ." Emma glanced at Dale, flushed, and lowered her voice. "*Sleeping* with your cousin."

"That's true," Dale said. "Simon's home by midnight just about every night. Well, there's been a few times when he's snuck in at dawn, but he's always home by breakfast."

Emma leaned forward and thunked her head on the counter a few times.

Alison couldn't say a word without being a hypocrite. Yes, Emma was pretending that she wasn't in a relationship with Simon for whatever reason, but Alison was doing the same to Emma, practicing to be a better woman in order to get Ryan back.

And as if she'd conjured him up, the bell above the door jingled and there he was.

"Finally," Emma whispered in triumph. "*Your* turn in the hot seat. Let's see how you like it."

Alison very carefully didn't look at her. She just kept her eyes on Ryan—which didn't help her suddenly racing pulse.

He looked . . . hot, and a little dirty, like he'd been working outside all day. He wore work clothes and held Killer against his chest; he should've looked ridiculous carrying a little froufrou dog with her pink bedazzled collar, but somehow he looked even more masculine.

It drove her crazy.

He drove her crazy.

"What are you doing here?" she managed.

Ryan pushed his dark sunglasses to the top of his head and held up a flyer.

20% OFF YOUR FIRST WEEK AT PAW PALS!

Alison stared at it and then whipped around to Emma.

"Hey, don't look at me like that. Coupons were *your* idea," her so-called partner said.

Alison took Killer, sucking in a breath because her fingers brushed against Ryan, and why oh why did he always smell so good? She wanted to press her nose to his throat and breathe him in. Instead, she kissed

Killer's adorable little face all over. Her baby allowed it for a minute, then squirmed to get down.

"Think I can leave Killer with you for a few hours?" Ryan asked. "I've got an appointment at a client's office, and the last time I brought her with me, she left a . . . *deposit* in the client's wife's Louboutins. A very stinky deposit that cost me a thousand bucks."

Killer was running around looking for Hog. She found him sleeping in the sun and immediately went nose to nose with him.

Hog woke from a dead sleep with a surprised howl and ran to hide behind Emma.

Ryan crouched low and studied Hog peeking out from Emma's legs. "Don't let her bully you, man." He held out a hand.

Hog studied it, and then he slowly came out from behind Emma.

Ryan waited patiently, and finally Hog bumped his head against Ryan's hand. Permission to touch. Ryan gave him a full-body rub—Hog's favorite. "You're way too sweet to be stuck with my little woman."

"Your *four-legged* woman too," Emma said.

Ryan laughed. "So you know them both well then."

"Oh yeah."

Then the two clowns laughed softly as if in commiseration with each other. "Hey!" Alison said. "Standing right here." She looked at Emma. "Did you give out flyers to the whole damn town?"

"Still working on it."

Great. Alison looked at Ryan. "Can we talk a moment?"

"Talk or fight?"

She grabbed him by the hand. "Just come on."

He let her drag him down the hallway. Let her, because he was a big guy with lots of yummy muscles that ensured he never went anywhere he didn't want to go.

She tried to take comfort in that.

Alison took him past the large, open yard room where Khloe was presiding over their guests with an assist from Dale and shut them in her small office. "So."

Ryan smiled. "So."

She took a deep breath. "I'm going to start out with the fact that I'm not exactly ready for this moment. I mean, I've been practicing being a good enough friend and a good enough person to make you want to be a friend back. *Practicing* being the key word, so I'm not *quite* ready for prime time yet, but—"

"You've been practicing . . . what now?"

She refused to blush. Absolutely refused. "You heard me."

"I'd like to hear it again."

Because he said this without glee or amusement of any sort, but what sounded like genuine interest, she repeated it. "I've been practicing being a good friend—"

"No." He shook his head. "That's not what you said. You said you've been practicing being a 'good enough' friend. No one better have told you that you weren't good enough for any damn thing, ever. That's not why we broke up. Tell me you know that."

She drew another deep breath. How was it that with so few words he could turn her upside down and inside out, not to mention melt all the bones in her entire body? Before she could respond, a sudden rustling sound came from beneath her desk. Ryan bent down and came face-to-face with Sammy the turtle, making his slow way out.

"Emma!" Alison yelled.

Emma came running. "Yeah?"

"Why is Sammy out of his crate?"

"He likes his freedom. Want me to take him?"

Sammy stopped in the sole sunny spot in the room thanks to the window and appeared to smile as his eyes slowly closed.

Alison sighed. "No. He's fine." She drew a deep breath when she was once again alone with Ryan.

And Sammy.

Past time. "I'm just going to say this fast," she said. "So I don't lose my nerve, but also before we get interrupted again." She sucked in some air. "When we broke up, you said some things to me. Things that were hard to hear, so it took a while for it all to sink in. But you're right. I shut people out. I shut people down. I don't give second chances. I wear a suit of armor so thick that nothing can penetrate. Although . . ." She looked up and found his gaze on her, serious, warm, curious, which gave her the courage to go on. "You were wrong about that last one, because when we broke up, *it* penetrated, believe me." It'd hurt like hell. "So I took a good long hard look in the mirror and came to some realizations. I'm . . . not a good friend, but I'm working on that."

His eyes softened, and though he'd started with his arms crossed, they were loose at his sides now. "Go on."

Khloe knocked on the open door with a small pie tin that held a cut-up strawberry. She set it in front of Sammy. "Lunchtime."

Sammy opened his eyes and dug in, looking ecstatic.

Alison sighed and shut and locked the door. "I know I wasn't a good friend, Ryan. And I know how important that is to you. I'm hoping for a second chance there."

Sammy began to bang on his empty tin. They looked down to find it already empty and his entire wrinkly face covered in strawberries.

"I think he wants more," Ryan said.

Dammit. "Hold, please." She rushed from the room, hit up the staff room fridge, grabbed another strawberry and a knife, and made her way back to the office. She crouched next to Sammy, cut up the strawberry in the tin, and met Ryan's amused eyes. "I'm sorry."

"Don't be. It's cute, you taking care of Sammy. And Killer. And your employees. And your business partner." He smiled. "It's a new look, watching you care. I like it."

Alison was speechless, a rare condition for her. "You like seeing me as a total mess, slimed by Hog slobber and covered in fur, running around like a chicken without a head?"

"I like seeing you invested. Unguarded."

All those dates they'd gone on, she'd spent so much time making sure her clothes and makeup and hair looked perfect. She'd been so careful to put forward her best-looking self. And yet Ryan liked how she looked right now, harried and swamped. "You're a strange man."

"True story." He studied her for a long beat. "I've got a couple of people coming over tomorrow night for a barbecue. Interested?"

She opened her mouth to ask which people, but managed to stop herself. "What can I bring?"

Before he could answer, someone banged on the door. "Hey, hate to interrupt," Emma said through the wood, "but we've got two new clients and I need help."

Oh my God. Alison whipped open the door to kill someone, but Emma was holding a black-and-white fuzzy dog in her arms.

"This is Bandit," Emma said. "I'm going to check her in. Can you handle the other one?"

"Yeah." Alison gave Ryan an apologetic smile. "I'll be quick!" She ran out front. There were two women at the front counter, one in her fifties, the other in her eighties. "Hi," she said breathlessly. "My partner said you wanted to check in a pet. Dog or cat?"

The woman in her fifties jerked a thumb at the older woman. "*Human.* This is my mom, Phyllis."

Phyllis crossed her bony arms. She was maybe five feet tall with gray corkscrew curls tight to her head, skin wrinkled and slack, and an unlit cigarette dangling out of her mouth that looked like it'd been there since 1960.

And that's when Alison recognized her. Phyllis had been the supervisor at the women's center where Alison had volunteered in high school for a scholarship she'd never received. Great. This was going to be just great.

"I should be back by five," Phyllis's daughter said, "but just in case, what's your late policy?"

Alison held up a finger. "Excuse me a moment, I'll be right back." She went through the door to the back again and found Emma in the "sweet" yard with the dogs. "What the actual fuck?"

Emma, on her knees next to Bandit, introducing him to Hog, choked out a laugh and covered Bandit's ears. "Watch the language in front of the impressionable ears."

"Oh, well, excuse me," Alison said. "*What the actual hell?*"

"Still a bad word. You owe the jar. Twice."

"Yeah, yeah, whatever. Since when do we take on geriatrics? Especially the mean-ass woman who was the supervisor at the women's center?"

"Oh, we're not charging for Phyllis. I don't think that would be cool, not to mention possibly illegal. She's just hanging out here today because her daughter, Cathy, has to work. She's a librarian, and apparently she tried bringing her mom to the library, but she yelled at everyone and Cathy was asked to not bring her anymore."

"And you thought Phyllis would be fine here?" Alison asked in disbelief. "You remember her, right? Mean as a snake? Evil?"

"Actually, she was always very kind to me," Emma said.

Of course. Because everyone loved Emma. Whatever.

"And anyway, we already have Miss Kitty, and I think she's making us all scarves. And there's Dale too. He loves hanging out with the animals, and the animals love him. I guess Cathy heard about it and—"

"Oh my God. Wildstone is worse than Mayberry when it comes to gossip."

"What's Mayberry?" Emma asked.

Alison shook her head. "Never mind. Please go on."

"Okay, so Cathy heard about Dale and thought it'd be great for her mom too. She asked us if we minded."

"Half of us mind. A lot."

"Look, *I'll* handle Phyllis," Emma said. "All you've got to worry about is the business side of things. Oh and hey, how did it go with Ryan—who, by the way, looks at you like you're lunch."

Shit. She'd left him in the office. She pointed at Emma. "This isn't over."

"Never is."

Shaking her head, Alison started to go back to Ryan, but stopped and turned back. "He looks at me like I'm lunch?"

"Yep. And dinner. And a midnight snack . . ."

Alison felt pleasure fill her, which she had to shake off because the office was empty. Ryan had left. Disappointment making her chest heavy, she walked to the front room and . . . found him talking with Cathy. It'd been like that when they'd dated too. Everywhere they went, he knew someone, and if he didn't, he'd make a friend in two seconds. The man could chitchat with the devil himself. It'd driven her crazy, but watching him handle her "client" with an effortless ease did something deep inside her.

It warmed her. "Thanks," she said to him meaningfully, putting her hand on his arm. His definitely solid arm. She ignored the inner quiver and smiled at Phyllis's daughter. "We'll see you after work."

Cathy nearly sagged in relief. "Thank you." She turned to Phyllis. "Mom? You behave, you hear me?"

"Bah humbug."

"*Mom.*"

Phyllis ignored her.

Her daughter sighed, mouthed *I'm sorry* to Alison, and left.

Phyllis moved to the end of the counter where Khloe was stocking shelves. "You. Call me a car right away."

Khloe blinked. "Uh . . ."

"*Now,* young lady."

Nope. Not happening. Alison walked over there. Her first inclination was to get firm and possibly mean right back. But she remembered how Emma handled situations like this. And Ryan too. So she drew a deep breath and worked at imitating their techniques. "I've got this, Khloe, thank you." She looked at Phyllis. "What's the problem?"

Phyllis looked at her, mouth tight. "I'm leaving now."

Alison looked into her blue rheumy eyes and realized Phyllis wasn't angry, she was . . . scared. Anxious. Unnerved, and probably feeling alone.

Dammit. Alison's chest squeezed hard enough to hurt, and she realized it was empathy. Phyllis was acting out because she didn't know how else to handle herself. "I get it, you know," Alison said quietly. "You're in a new place, and nothing feels familiar, and you don't know anyone."

Phyllis looked away. Swallowed hard. "I miss Angel."

"Angel?"

"My dog."

Alison realized the older woman was looking at Hog with . . . longing? "Was Angel a big dog?"

"Big and sweet. He'd sit at my feet and sleep while I crocheted." She patted the big shoulder bag she wore, like maybe she had her crocheting with her. "He's gone now. Been five years. My daughter said I couldn't replace him because he kept eating the furniture."

This woman had made Alison's life at the women's center a living hell. She'd been mean, cranky, and demanding. And yet suddenly, Alison understood her on a core level. "Come with me," she said and reached out her hand.

Phyllis slowly put her small, frail hand in Alison's, and again her heart squeezed. Good God, this place was going to kill her. She walked Phyllis over to a chair near Miss Kitty. "Sit here."

Phyllis sat. "Your music is too loud."

Actually, that was true. "I'll turn it down," she said. "Hog?"

Hog came close. He lifted his big old head and took in Phyllis. He seemed to smile, and then he lay down at the old woman's feet.

Phyllis gasped in delight, even as her eyes went misty. Very slowly, as if she ached from head to toe, she leaned down—she didn't have to lean far—and stroked a hand down Hog's back.

Hog made a sound that if he'd been a cat would've been a purr of contentment. Phyllis pulled out her crocheting.

Miss Kitty tsked and gestured with her knitting needles, clearly saying knitting was superior.

"What did she say?" Phyllis asked.

"That you have great taste in yarn," Alison said.

Miss Kitty rolled her eyes.

"You good?" Alison asked.

"I need tea. Hot. But not too hot."

Alison could feel a headache coming on. She rubbed the spot between her eyes but nodded. "Sure thing."

"From Starbucks. The peach kind."

Yep, definitely a headache. Alison pulled out her phone and brought up her Starbucks app.

"No added sugar. Gives me the runs."

"No added sugar," Alison said firmly, making the order.

"I know who you are, you know," Phyllis said when Alison was done.

Oh boy. "And I know who you are."

Phyllis eyed her warily. "You going to call my daughter to tell her I'm a menace and that she should come get me?"

Alison looked into the elderly woman's eyes and saw resigned expectation. And . . . sadness. She let out a long breath. "Is that what happened at the library?"

"And at my son-in-law's work. The old folks' home too, although to be honest, I tried to get kicked out of there. It didn't smell so good. Plus, everyone was dying." She paused. "I have a house only a mile or so from here. But my daughter and son-in-law came to live with me when they lost theirs. Now they want me out of the house every day. *My* house."

Damn. Another pinch on Alison's heart. She had no idea how many more she could take. "Is it maybe because you're grumpy?"

Phyllis shocked her by laughing. "You know, you remind me of someone."

"A saint?"

"Myself, when I was your age."

Sounded about right. "Look, no one's going to call you a menace or kick you out of here," Alison said.

"Of course not." This was from Dale, who'd moved close, dragging a chair over for himself. "Plus, they need us," he told Phyllis in a conspirator's voice. "The new owners are wonderful, but they don't know much."

"Hey," Alison said on principle.

Ignoring that, Dale smiled at Phyllis. "They think we're guests, but the truth is, we're working. We're soothing their animals. They need us."

Phyllis looked at Alison for confirmation, clearly knowing that she of all people wouldn't bullshit her.

Alison shrugged. "It's true."

Phyllis nodded and seemed to relax.

Alison turned to head to the front counter to ask Khloe to go pick up Phyllis's tea. Leaning against it, taking in every word, was Ryan. He was watching her with a new look in his eyes, one she couldn't quite place. She really hoped it was lust.

Reaching out, he gently tugged on a strand of her hair. Affection, she realized, her heart tripping. He was looking at her with respect, which was somehow even better. "Where were we?" she whispered.

"You asked what you could bring to the barbecue."

"Yes," she said. "Anything. Name it."

He smiled. "Just you."

Chapter 22

Step 22: Suspend your ego.

Emma marveled at how fast the time went. Starting her own business—well, half her own, anyway—had been exhausting, stressful, and . . . *exhilarating*. It was the end of the day and she and Hog were climbing the stairs to her apartment. As always, she counted, but she no longer had to stop to catch her breath.

She was probably almost ready to start running. Not that she'd tested the theory. In fact, she hadn't expanded her horizons by more than the three-quarters of a mile she'd been walking daily from Paw Pals to go by Jack's place, hoping for another chance at possibly talking to him, since she'd blown it the last two times by freezing.

She'd canceled the 5K.

Her entire life was different, down to how she looked, so why in the world had she thought she needed to do something that she'd wanted in her old life? It didn't make any sense.

This was what she told herself, but in the deep, dark of the night, she knew she was afraid to do the race, because if she did, it'd mean she'd be considered whole again, in spite of herself.

That's how she knew her secret truth. It wasn't fear of physical pain stopping her. She'd conquered that fear a long time ago. It was fear of moving on when she didn't believe she deserved to. Emma was also harboring another, even deeper fear. Fear of the relationships that she was forming. With Alison. With Simon. Of loving her new life while still feeling guilty about it.

She hadn't been able to talk to Jack, but she'd bet her life that *he* wasn't whole, wasn't anywhere close to whole, and she couldn't leave him behind. Stupid as it might seem, she just couldn't go forward until he could.

That was when she saw the note on her door, taped right at nose level.

Meet me on the roof.

She recognized Simon's scrawl, but even if she hadn't, she'd have known by the way her nipples got happy. Being with him was a thrill that never got old or boring. There was a raw power to his physicality, pure animal instinct just under the tender surface. Knowing each other's bodies so well only made the intimacy even better.

It was addicting.

He was addicting.

Which was why, even though nothing good could come of continuing their relationship—and that's what it was, dammit, a relationship—she rushed inside to strip out of her clothes that were covered in slobber and other questionable things. She grabbed a quick shower, then stood naked in her room, pawing through her underwear drawer for the sexiest thing she could find. Catching sight of herself in the mirror above the dresser, she stilled because something was different. It took a moment to hit her.

She felt comfortable in her own skin again.

When had that happened?

And it was more than skin deep, she realized. Maybe she had set aside her old hopes and dreams. Okay, so she'd canceled her race. That was okay because she had new hopes and dreams now. Better ones. And knowing it was like a weight coming off her chest.

She couldn't wait to tell Simon.

She pulled on a sundress and turned to Hog. "Coming?"

He closed his eyes and started snoring.

"Fine, hold down the fort here. I've filled your bowl, don't eat anything not in it, okay?"

On the roof, she stopped short in wonder.

There were strings of white twinkle lights hung, candles on the coffee table, and a gorgeous night sky, scented by the ocean air.

And Simon, looking good enough to eat.

"I came," she said inanely.

"Not yet," he said softly. "But you will."

Her entire body quivered with anticipation as his eyes soaked her in like she was the best thing he'd ever seen. She might say the same thing about him. He wore jeans and an untucked button-down, the sleeves shoved up to his elbows, looking more delectable than whatever was smelling so good in a takeout bag on the table in front of the couch.

That, coupled with her revelation that her life was good as it was, great even, and that she couldn't wait to tell him, had Emma smiling a ridiculously cheesy smile she couldn't hold back. Simon was going to be happy for her, maybe even proud of her. "It's beautiful," she said. "I feel so lucky."

"Every moment I'm with you feels lucky," he said.

Nope, her smile wasn't going anywhere. "I thought you were hanging out with your dad tonight."

"He's at Alison's. I wanted tonight with you." He took her hand and drew her down beside him on the love seat. "No pressure, no games. That's what I promised you. Do you remember?"

She met his gaze, a little wary. "Yes."

"We haven't talked about us in a while."

"No," she agreed. "Not since I had to talk you into sleeping with me."

"You didn't have to talk me into anything. I wanted you too. Emma, I understand your reservations about us."

"After all we've done, I think you know I no longer have a lot of reservations when it comes to you."

That got her an almost smile. "Being with you has been the best time of my life," he said, pulling her into him until she was straddling him, his hands at her hips. "You mean a lot to me, Emma. I want to be heading somewhere with you."

If he hadn't been holding on to her, she'd have fallen right off the love seat. Verbal emotions were new for her. Her parents loved her, she knew that, but they weren't a demonstrative family. Yes, they'd sat by her side for months, making sure she could function on her own, but that was how they loved. By action. Few words. Ned had also been a man of few words. So having someone look her in the eyes and say she meant something to them was humbling. And scary. "Are you sure?"

With a rough laugh, he tightened his grip on her. "Very. Do you need to hear it again?"

"I think so."

Simon pushed Emma's hair back from her face. "You mean everything to me."

Her heart felt all squishy, like it was melting. "You amended."

"I corrected. You're one of my very favorite people, Emma."

Her throat felt thick with emotion as she wrapped her arms around his shoulders and touched the tip of her nose to his. "You've got a lot of favorite people."

"My dad and Alison are important to me," he agreed. "Ryan too. But to be clear, I don't think about them night and day and I certainly don't ache to nibble every inch of any of them."

She nipped his finger. "Good to know."

He gave her the full two-hundred-watt smile. "I'm falling in love with you, Emma."

The words raced through her veins, shocking her system. "*Are you sure?*"

He laughed. "Are you going to keep asking me that?"

Her heart was pounding. "Possibly."

He cupped her face. "One hundred percent."

She let out a breath. "That's . . . very sure."

He nodded and she bit her lip. "Um . . ."

"You're looking panicked." He ran his thumb gently over her lower lip, rescuing it from her teeth. "I don't expect anything in return."

That couldn't be true. Nobody put themself out there without expecting something back. She stared at his chest, but she was seeing Ned walk away from her. Cindy walk away from her. Her entire life turn upside down. She was doing the best she could, but she felt like she was walking through a schoolyard without clothes. Did she feel like she was falling for Simon? Yes. Did it scare her? Yes. Could she admit either of those things out loud? She could not . . .

"Emma."

"Yeah?"

"Look at me?"

She hesitated, knowing this was it. If she didn't step up, he'd walk away too.

With a finger beneath her chin, he tipped her face to his so that her eyes met his warm but curious ones. "Breathe."

"If this is you putting on your Hard-Ass PT hat, then let me tell you where you can shove—"

"You're holding your body so tight you're trembling. I just don't want you to cramp."

Oh. Right. Emma let out a shaky breath. And then another.

"Better," Simon murmured, his hands on her thighs, lightly stroking up and down. "You've been walking a lot, your muscle tone is good."

She stared into his eyes and knew she had to tell him the truth. "Yes to the walking, but not as much as you might think."

"I thought you were adding distance every day for the 5K."

She started to nod, then shook her head in the negative. "I'm up to three-quarters of a mile, and that's because I'm spying on Jack Swanson, who lives pretty close to Paw Pals. Or at least I'm *trying* to spy on him."

He didn't say anything for a moment. "Why?"

"I need to know if he's okay."

"Emma—"

She slid off his lap. "You should know, I canceled my registration for the 5K."

"You . . . canceled?"

"Yes."

Simon sat up a little. "I thought you were excited about getting that part of your life back."

She stood up and turned to watch the water.

"Emma. You promised you were okay."

"I am. More than. I've decided I like this new life of mine, just the way it is."

She heard him stand up, and then he was at her side. "As recently as a week ago you wanted to do this, what changed?"

"Maybe I've just peaked."

"No, you quit. And I took advantage of you," he said quietly, sounding unhappy.

Well, that made both of them unhappy. No, wait. She wasn't unhappy. She was mad. "I have my own brain, you know, and I use it. I can change my goals when and however I want to." Emma shook her head, realizing her anger was getting the best of her. "My life's just different now. And I'm okay with that. I was hoping you would be too."

Simon looked at her, his eyes intense and focused. "I don't want you to settle for less than what you had."

"Maybe settling isn't a bad idea."

He drew a deep breath, looking unhappy. "Settling wasn't an option before. That you feel it now is why I shouldn't have allowed us to happen. I knew better."

"You're not listening to me," she said, heart thundering.

"I always listen. I just don't always agree." Simon's voice was flat, impassive. His annoyed Hard-Ass PT voice. Well, good. No use being in a full-blown temper all by herself. After all she'd gone through and done to get better, after finding new hopes and dreams that worked for her in the here and now, who was he to tell her what she should want? Emma said defiantly, "This is my life, not yours."

"I'm well aware," he said evenly, which only made her more mad. "You've made your stance on relationships clear from the beginning. But this isn't about me, or even about us. You're still not willing to be all in with your new life."

"You don't know what you're talking about."

He shook his head. "When are you going to stop punishing yourself for surviving?"

Embarrassed that he'd called it exactly how it was, she tossed up her hands. "Look, waking up from a coma . . . sometimes people feel different. Maybe I don't care about the same stuff that I used to. Maybe I don't care about anything!"

Simon looked at her for a long moment. "Since when did you stop telling either of us the truth?"

Oh hell no. Emma turned to go, but he caught her hand. "At least let me help you run off this time." And he opened the roof door for her.

Her heart begged her brain to give it a moment, to think it through. Actually, her brain wanted that too. But nope, her feet couldn't be stopped. She walked away, and he let her go.

Chapter 23

Step 23: Forgive.

The next evening, Alison stopped at Paw Pals after getting away from Armstrong Properties. To be honest, she wasn't sure why. Guess she needed a little bit of mac-and-cheese-level comfort without the calories.

Emma had just shut down the computer for the close of shift and looked surprised to see her. "Hey, didn't expect you. You were here early this morning working. What's up?"

"Nothing." *Everything.* She was about to go to Ryan's barbecue and had nerves the size of Texas bouncing around in her gut. She stood there in the center of their reception area, surrounded by the warm, welcoming space, and took a deep breath.

It's going to be okay . . .

But was it? She'd been studying up and sort of practicing for weeks now. She was working on being more open, but was it enough?

Something warm brushed against her thighs. She looked down and found Hog leaning against her, staring up at her with those sweet milk chocolate eyes, worry etched in every line of his massive face.

Alison smiled at him and started to look up again to Emma, but Hog nudged the top of his head into her palm. *Pet me.*

Accepting the gentle demand, she patted him on his head. But he just nudged her again, and this time when she looked at him, he seemed terribly sad. If this had been Killer, she'd have picked the sweet thing up in an instant. But Hog was too big for that. So without thinking, she dropped to her knees and wrapped her arms around him, and when he set his heavy head on her shoulder with a soft sigh, she completely melted. "You were right, Hog's one of the best doggos out there."

Emma was walking through the place, woodenly turning off lights.

"What's wrong?" Alison asked.

"Nothing."

"Yes, there is. I just said you were *right* and you didn't even react."

Emma stopped in the middle of the room. "I accidentally broke up with your cousin." She shook her head. "No, that's not true. I did it on purpose, but I hate it."

"Oh my God," Alison said, stunned. "What happened? No, let me guess. He's a guy, so . . . he did something stupid."

Emma sagged. "I think I have a problem with being all the way happy."

"Well, that's dumb."

"Gee," Emma said dryly, "I'm so glad I'm sharing this with you, you're being so sweet and understanding."

Alison laughed. "You've got the wrong person if you think I've got any sweet or understanding in me."

"I signed up for a 5K."

Alison blinked in confusion. "You were going to run? On purpose?"

Emma snorted. "I used to love to run." She paused, her eyes reflective. "Things are different now."

"What does this have to do with the breakup?"

"Canceling the 5K made Simon think that I've settled with my recovery, rather than pushing for more, and because of that he thinks he took advantage of me before I was ready to be with someone."

"Men." Alison shook her head. "Look, just tell Simon you're different now, and so are your goals."

Emma stared at her.

"What?"

"I've been struggling with this whole thing for what seems like forever, unable to put it all together in my head, and you just figured it all out in less than a minute?"

Even though she knew Emma wasn't necessarily complimenting her, Alison still felt a warm fuzzy. "It's because I'm brilliant. Just go to Simon's, tell him about your epiphany, and then jump his bones. He'll forgive you."

"Yeah? And how's it working for you and Ryan?"

"Hmph." Alison was hoping tonight was the turning of the tide. "Are you going to talk to Simon, try to work things out? Tell him my brilliant thought on the matter?"

Emma looked away, but not before Alison saw a sheen of tears. "I don't think it's that simple," she whispered.

"Is that why Hog's sad, because you are?" Alison asked.

They both looked at Hog, asleep on the floor.

"Huh," Alison said. "He's okay now, I guess."

"He was never not okay. He was emotionally supporting *you*. It's what he does."

Alison felt something in her chest sort of roll over. Damn. What was it with all the feels today? "For a drooler and a guy who poops literal mountains, he's not so bad, is he?"

"He's tied for the best dog on the planet."

"Tied?"

"With Killer," Emma said, like *duh, wasn't that obvious?*

This shocked Alison almost as much as Hog had. It shocked her into feeling bad about the whole pretend-friendship thing. "You love my dog?"

"Of course I do."

She was flummoxed. And speechless, which almost never happened. "But . . . you're not a big fan of mine. And Killer and I, we're two peas in a pod."

"Yes, but *your* personality in a six-pound fur baby is a lot easier to handle."

"Ha ha." Alison's phone buzzed. Her calendar alert, and the warm fuzzies vanished, replaced by anxiety. "Whelp. Fun as this is, I've gotta go."

"Where to?"

Alison hesitated. She'd really like to talk to Emma about the barbecue to get her take, but if she failed tonight, and let's face it, odds were not in her favor, then she'd have to admit that.

"Spill," Emma said. "It's your turn. I know you came here for a reason."

Alison warred with herself, but apparently her need to get Emma's opinion won. "I'm going to Ryan's. He's having a barbecue."

"You're finally working the plan to get him back in your life. Nice. What've you accomplished so far?"

"I'm bringing my famous seven-layer dip to the party."

Emma laughed.

Alison didn't.

"You're serious?" Emma asked. "You made him a dip? That's it?"

Alison pulled out her phone and looked at it. No notifications. Why didn't it ever buzz when she needed it to?

"Nothing from our list?" Emma asked. "Nothing at all?"

"Well, I *am* learning to be nice even when people are insinuating I'm a dumbass."

"You're a *brilliant* dumbass," Emma said. "If that helps."

Alison shook her head. "I'm going to be fine at this thing, right? Lie to me. Tell me I'm going to be fine."

Emma smiled, wrapped her fingers around Alison's wrist, and tilted it up so they could both see her *I'm fine* tat.

"And if all else fails," Emma said, "take your own advice and jump his bones."

Alison laughed. "Yeah, you're right. Thanks."

Half an hour later, Alison pulled onto Ryan's street and gulped at the number of cars parked . . . everywhere. In his driveway, on his grass, lining the entire street.

Don't panic. Probably there's another party on the street somewhere, which would mean all these people milling around weren't here for Ryan's barbecue.

Of course he did know everyone in the whole damn town. And . . . oh boy. His front door was wide open, and music and laughter and talking spilled out into the night. There were people on the porch, people on the grass.

People everywhere.

Alison had to park two blocks down. Heart pounding, sweating in some very uncomfortable places, she pulled out her phone and texted Simon.

Alison: Where are you?

Simon: Got delayed. Be there in thirty.

Alison: You said you'd be here when I got here.

Simon: Dale called 911. He wanted to thank the first responders for being so nice when he fell. Only he didn't tell that to the dispatcher, and the first responders who showed up aren't the same ones as last time, and now he's invited them inside for brownies. We don't have brownies. Wrapping up now.

Alison: YOU SAID YOU'D BE HERE WHEN I GOT HERE.

Simon: Gee, I'm sensing panic.

Alison: Yes, join me won't you? I'm going to blow this without you.

Simon: Stop texting and get your ass in there. Smile. Maybe refrain from speaking until I arrive.

Alison: Omg. Bring your dad and the first responders. Just hurry.

Alison: Hey!

Simon:

Alison: I hate you . . .

Simon:

Alison: Okay, I don't hate you, but you'd better be driving!

Shoving her phone away, she rolled down her windows to help with the sweating-in-uncomfortable-places thing. "You want this," she told herself in the rearview mirror. "You want Ryan back in your life. All you've got to do is smile. That's it. And it'll be because you like him. In fact, you're *pretty* sure you love him and have since that very first night when you were stuck in a cabin with no power and he produced a battery-operated lantern and a deck of cards, and you entertained each other without a single awkward moment. So suck it up and remind him how good you can be together." With a nod at her reflection, she got out of the car and came face-to-face with Bill.

Ryan's friend was carrying a case of beer and looking at her with an odd expression on his face.

Oh, God. It was pity. He'd heard her pep talk.

"Alison," he said.

She swallowed hard. "Bill."

He stood there, shifting on his feet, while she struggled for something to say. And then realized there was only one thing she could say. "I'm sorry about the last time I saw you, at the game. I'm sorry about your boat. And the divorce."

"Did you mean it?"

"Yes. I really am sorry that you had to go through all that—"

"I meant about what you were just saying to yourself in the car. Did you mean it?"

A bead of sweat trickled between her breasts. "Every word."

He nodded. "You'll do then." And with that, he began walking to the house. After a few steps, he turned back for her. "Coming?"

"My feet haven't decided yet."

He let out a small chuckle. "Would it help to know that your presence will make his whole night?"

"You sure about that?"

"*Very.* Come on."

"I'll be right behind you."

He nodded and hesitated. "So, uh, that little pep talk thing. Does it work? Cuz I'm working on winning my ex back and I'm a little low on self-esteem at the moment."

She wasn't sure why her chest felt all tight and fluttery, but she knew one thing. This man was important to Ryan and that meant he was important to her. "Yes. It helps." She found a smile. "It got me out of the car, anyway."

He nodded. "Thanks."

When he was gone, Alison grabbed the seven-layer dip she'd made. Ryan's favorite. He used to tease her that he'd do *anything* for it. It'd been a running joke between them, her making him prove it with return favors. One memorable night skinny-dipping beneath a no-moon sky came to mind . . .

She walked a block and a half toward Ryan's house, but at the last minute, chickened out and cut into the alley, where she came out at the fence leading to his backyard.

The fence was lined with ivy and a fragrant flower that she had no idea the name of, but she sucked in a full lungful of it. And then gave herself the pep talk all over again, adding in a bonus promise—if she made it out alive without screwing anything up, maybe she'd get to sleep with Ryan tonight.

And there was nothing, not seven-layer dip, not romantic evenings on the beach, not a new pair of shoes . . . *nothing* better than sleeping with Ryan.

Juggling the casserole dish, she reached out to open the gate when from the other side of the fence she heard a voice she recognized.

Ryan's mom.

"You're waiting for her," the woman said.

"She said she'd come," Ryan said, sounding so sure of Alison that her belly quivered in the very best of ways.

His mom sighed. "Honey, why are you letting her back into your life? You're too old to be wasting time on relationships that aren't going anywhere."

"Mom," he said with a low laugh, "since when is thirty-two old?"

"She isn't the one, Ry," chimed in Nicole, Ryan's overbearing, nosy, incredibly perfect sister.

Alison's face burned with humiliation and embarrassment. She wasn't the one. She was wasting his time . . .

"Listen," Ryan said kindly but firmly. "I love you guys. But me and Alison together, or me and Alison *not* together, is none of your business."

"It is my business when someone's standing between my son and his happiness," his mom said. "Honey, we're not trying to pick a fight, we're just looking out for you. You deserve better. You yourself said you couldn't see having a family with her."

Actually shaking, and feeling like an arrow had just slammed through her heart, Alison pressed a hand to the spot that ached like a bitch.

"You said your friends don't like her," Nicole said. "And that she doesn't try to fit into your life. She's . . . distant."

"Not with me," Ryan said. "Never with me."

"But shouldn't the people you care about mean something to her too?"

Alison was frozen, rooted to the ground because they were right. She'd been nuts to think that a few weeks of studying up on how to make friends and bringing a seven-layer dip would be enough. It was nowhere close. But also . . . she was suddenly realizing this wasn't 100% her fault. Ryan had a hand in this too, they both did. But she had to at least address her part.

Snapping her backbone ramrod straight, she stepped into the yard. Visible now, she stopped and soaked up the sight of Ryan, tall and handsome, a surprised smile curving his mouth, his eyes lighting up at the sight of her, like his whole world had just gotten better.

Which made this so so so much harder. But eating crow when she was wrong was one thing. Turning the other cheek when she'd just realized that she *wasn't* all to blame for their failing was another. So Alison drew a deep breath and looked past Ryan to his mom and sister, both looking a little uncomfortable.

Good. They were finally even. "You're right," she said. "About me. At least the old me, the introvert who'd rather sit home with a book than ever go to a party. My mistake was in not seeing that Ryan isn't like me. He's the opposite, in fact. And I need to learn to meet him at least halfway. That's why I'm here tonight. But now I know that no matter what I do, it won't be enough for you."

And with that, she turned and walked away. Still holding her seven-layer dip. She was going to go home and eat all of it. Every single bite.

She got just outside the gate when a gentle but firm hand settled on her arm and turned her.

Ryan. He was holding Killer.

"I'm sorry," he said very quietly, very seriously. "I would never have wanted you to overhear that."

"Don't." She stepped back from him. "Please don't."

"Ali—"

"Look, I know you can't control what your family says or thinks. That's not what got me. What did were the things they said, the things that had to have come from your mouth; the not being able to see having a family with me, that your friends think I'm cold and distant."

Ryan closed his eyes briefly. "I know, and those things shouldn't have ever been voiced."

"Of course you should have voiced them, they were your feelings. But I did try. I was with you, in the only way I know how to be—and you broke up with me instead of helping me fix what was wrong. And yeah, I've got issues, but you do too. You don't just end things because there are issues. Not if you really love someone." She felt her eyes burn. "You gave up on me," she whispered. "Threw me away."

"You're right," he said quietly, staring into her eyes, his own filled with regret. "After that week we spent together and we clicked into place like we were meant to be, I didn't think about how things might change in the real world. I took your hand and jumped with you into the deep end with my life and expected you to be able to swim in the shark-infested waters."

She choked on a laugh.

He didn't smile. "It was wrong of me. You're not me. You're more thoughtful, more internal, a beautiful soul that deserved better. I never wanted you to think you weren't enough just as you are. I'd never ask you to change for me."

"But I would have tried," she said quietly. "In a heartbeat. Not just for you. But because it was the right thing to do. I was immature. Insecure. And far too needy to even consider how much you were hurting too. I'm sorrier for that than I can ever say."

"And I'm sorry I wasn't more open with you." Ryan moved in closer. "You were going through your own things, and I wasn't there for you. This is on me, Alison. And I can only hope you'll give me the chance to fix it. I want to be the right guy for you."

She'd never been the right girl, not once in her life. "I need you to be *really* sure," she whispered. "Because I don't ever want to go through losing you again."

He tipped up her face to give her a soft, warm kiss filled with promise that was no less intimate for being sweet. "I've never been more sure."

Alison's chest filled with warmth. It spread outward to all her hard spots and she fisted her hand in his shirt. "How can we make sure it'll work this time?"

"We start over. From the beginning." Shifting Killer to tuck her under an arm, he held out his free hand to Alison. "Hi, I'm Ryan Dennison. I'm an engineer. I've got a close but *annoyingly* nosy posse." This caused a ripple of whispers behind them, which they both firmly ignored. "I love all sports, all food—"

"Except for tomatoes," she whispered. "You hate tomatoes."

"I really do." Ryan smiled and tugged Alison a little closer. "I make a good show of being easygoing and laid-back and open, but the truth is, I've recently had my heart broken, so I can actually be quite guarded and hold my emotions inside. I'm working on that, by the way. Also working on *showing*, not telling, people how I feel." He paused. "I hurt someone, someone very important to me, and I'm going to learn from my mistakes so that never happens again."

Throat tight, she squeezed his hand. "I'm Alison Pratt. I'm a numbers girl. Things have to add up for me, which means I can miss the nuances and the little things. I'm obsessively organized and anal, and sometimes when I get defensive or someone hurts my feelings, I say stupid stuff and then retreat. I'm working on that. I've not let many into my life, and I'm working on that too."

Alison caught sight of Bill on the other side of the yard, giving her a thumbs-up and an encouraging smile, which helped. "I'm never going to be perfect," she said, "but I'm loyal and honest and will step in front of a train for those I care about. Oh, and I can do ten cartwheels in a row before falling over."

Ryan laughed. "Impressive." He brought her hand to his chest and pressed it over his heart. "I'm not perfect either, Alison. I've let you down. I promise to do better at letting you know what's on my mind *and* protecting you from my well-meaning but overbearing family."

This brought more whispers from the sidelines.

Alison didn't care. Her heart felt so full it hurt. "I'll get better at trying to fit in with your family and friends, who obviously love and adore you, which is an amazing thing to have. I'm new to that, I've never had more family in my life than my cousin and uncle, and they're both guys, so . . ." She shrugged a little self-consciously, extremely aware that the whispers had abruptly stopped.

Ryan touched Alison's jaw, then let his fingers slide into her hair. "Alison," he said, voice low and hoarse with regret. "I love you—"

She kissed him, just as he'd kissed her a moment before, soft and sweet, full of her own promises. She lifted her head and glanced over at his mom and sister. "Should I repeat any of that or did you catch it all?"

Both his mom and sister grimaced, but Alison smiled. "I'm actually asking sincerely."

"Can you really do ten cartwheels in a row?" his sister asked.

"Do you really love him?" his mom asked.

"Yes and yes—more than you'll ever know," she said.

Ryan smiled, his gaze holding hers as he spoke. "Mom, Nicole, everyone . . . meet Alison. She's going to be a big part of my life, the best part, and I hope you can get on board with that."

There was no hesitation from his mom or sister; they both nodded yes like two bobbleheads.

"Maybe we can even be friends," Nicole said.

Touched, Alison swallowed hard. "I'd like that. But fair warning, I'm really new at this. I mean, I've been practicing, but apparently I'm the type of person who has to make a lot of mistakes before figuring her shit out."

"Some of the best people I know make mistakes," his mom said softly, smiling at her son. "And I've certainly also made my share. One of them with you, Alison. I'm glad you're here. I hope you'll stay."

Alison took in the backyard and the house, with all the windows and doors open, letting in the warm summer air while letting out a lot of yummy food scents and love and laughter. "I'd love to."

Ryan's smile was slow, affectionate, and sexy. "What can I get you to drink? We have a bar set up on the patio. I could make your fave—a martini?"

When she nodded, he led her over there. "How about a *dirty* martini?"

"What makes a martini dirty?" she asked.

He gave her another smile and leaned in, putting his mouth to her ear. "Anything you and I do later, after your second or third one."

Chapter 24

Step 24: No judgment.

The next morning, Emma was sitting in the middle of the salty yard. Given her mood, it was right where she belonged.

Phyllis, of all people, was sitting in the sweet yard, petting Hog.

Oh the irony.

Marco had needed a break to take a phone call, and Emma was holding Luna and Rex, the two sassy Chihuahuas, while reminiscing to herself about her recent failures. Her most recent being Simon, of course.

Actually, no. She refused to think of that as her failure alone. He'd hurt her with his single-minded expectations for her recovery and life. She understood where he was coming from given his role in her recovery, but it was *her* life, and if he couldn't close off the physical therapist part of him to see the human side of her and her needs, then screw it.

But damn. She missed him. She missed his smile. Missed his laugh. Missed him in her bed—*so much*—but she missed him even more as a friend, the closest she had. The loss felt . . .

Catastrophic.

At this point, the intense anger had worn off, leaving her feeling a little bruised. And with some hindsight, Emma understood that Simon had only wanted the best for her, didn't want to be the thing holding her back.

As if he could . . .

"Arf!" This was Rex.

"Arf, arf!" his sister, Luna, answered. They were fourteen years old and hugely resented any dog bigger than they were. Which was *every* dog, including Hog, who was currently standing on the other side of the picket fencing, torn between his loyalty to Emma and his self-preservation and utter fear of all things Chihuahua.

Emma lifted Rex and Luna up to nose level and stared them down. "Can you guys please tell Hog you won't beat him up if he comes in? He really wants to come in."

Hog whined in agreement.

Rex bared his full set of teeth. Actually, it wasn't a full set. He'd lost a bunch in his older years, but he still sounded fierce.

Hog took a few steps back and sat with what sounded like a long-suffering sigh. Just then someone ran into the yard, dropped to her knees in front of Emma, and hugged her so hard they both toppled over.

"*Alison?*" she gasped in shock.

Alison just kept hugging her, even though they were both on the ground now.

Phyllis was watching, looking fascinated. "Maybe you two should date each other. Men aren't worth a woman's time anyway."

"Can't. Breathe." Emma tapped on Alison's arm. "*Uncle!*"

Alison pulled back and grinned. *Grinned.*

"I'm scared," Emma said. "Are you . . . okay?"

"Better than okay."

Emma eyed her suspiciously. "Are you . . . drunk?"

Alison laughed. "At nine in the morning?"

Emma sat up and studied her partner closely. "Are you under some sort of mind control or something? Quick, blink twice for yes if you need help."

"Funny." Alison sat up too. "*Guess what happened last night?*"

"You were possessed by aliens."

"Oh my God, you're no fun." Alison stood up and ran a hand down the front of her to smooth out her wrinkles before holding out a hand to help Emma up. "I went to Ryan's barbecue."

"And . . . ? Given your glow, which I suppose could be from your ridiculously costly BB cream, but which I suspect is really from a bunch of orgasms since you're still wearing yesterday's clothes, it went well."

"Actually, it was a complete disaster. His mom and sister said some crappy things about me. I mean, they were all true, but still . . ."

Emma's smile faded. "I'm so sorry. But I'm confused. Why are you smiling? Oh my God, did you kill them? Do you need help burying the bodies?"

"Nope, I don't need help."

Emma paused. "Because . . . you already buried the bodies?"

"No!" Alison hooted with laughter, looking lighter and happier than Emma had ever seen her. "I stood up for myself. And Ryan stood up for me too. He told his family he loved me, that I was a *part* of his life, a big part. He told them to get on board and accept it, and they did!"

"Wow, that's great. I'm so happy for you."

"Right? It worked! All the reading, studying, and practicing with you worked! Ryan and I are really friends. And more." She smiled again. "I can't believe it."

"Wait," Emma said. "What?"

"I said *it worked*!"

"No, the other thing," Emma said with what she thought was remarkable calm given the sudden dread in her gut. "Before that. You were practicing with me. What does that mean?" She carefully set Rex down and stared at Alison, never resenting her ridiculously gorgeous and perfect high heels more. "You being nice to me over the past few weeks . . . it was *practice* for you?"

"No." Alison grimaced. "I mean, okay, yeah, a little bit. But you *know* why. We had history, bad history—"

"Oh my God." Emma left the salty yard, but didn't get one step past the gate before Hog was at her side, giving her a low whine as he pressed against her, love in his eyes. Phyllis had let him out and nodded at Emma with what looked like sympathy.

"Look, I know it sounds bad," Alison said, trailing her. "But I needed to learn to make friends. And you'd already told me we weren't ever going to be friends. So I decided if I could befriend you anyway, I could befriend anybody. Even Ryan."

Emma found herself speechless. And angry. And hurt. And damn . . . *so* hurt. It seemed like an Armstrong specialty, to be able to get under her skin. "I get that I said we weren't going to be friends, but you know why I said that, and where I was coming from."

"Hey, it's not like I cheated on you with your best friend."

Wow. Emma actually staggered back a step as though she'd been physically pushed. "No," she managed. "It's worse. Because the no-friendship thing went out the door weeks ago and you knew it, because we became friends in spite of ourselves."

"And I was supposed to know that how?"

Emma tossed up her hands. "*Anyone* who's ever had a good friend would know that!" Nope. Not doing this. She headed to the door, which opened just as she reached for it, knocking her off balance into . . . fabulous . . . Ned.

He steadied her and smiled. "Well, hello."

Emma pushed free. "What are you doing here?"

His smile faded. "I need to talk to you."

"Get in line," Alison said from behind them.

Emma pointed at her. "You and I have nothing left to say to each other." She stabbed a finger at Ned next. "And neither do we."

He caught her hand. "I broke up with Cindy."

Emma yanked free of the man she'd once thought she loved, the man she'd planned to say "I do" to, the man she hadn't even thought about since the last time she'd seen him.

"Actually," he said, "she broke up with me. Tomayto/tomahto, right?"

She stared at him. "And?"

"And I thought we should talk. I realize I've got apologies to make, and I was hoping you'd let me make some things up to you."

Carefully not looking at Alison, because just looking at her felt like a sharp arrow piercing her heart, Emma slowly shook her head. "No."

"No, I don't need to make things up to you?"

"No, I don't want to hear your apology." *What is it with men thinking they know what someone else wants?* She narrowed her eyes at Ned. "Go away."

Phyllis helpfully opened the door, but Ned reached for Emma. Suddenly Hog was there, inserting himself between Emma and Ned, teeth bared, growl ferocious.

"Holy shit," Ned yelped and jumped back.

Hog leapt up, planting his two front paws on the guy's chest and he went down on his ass.

"Hog, sit," Emma said.

Like a total sweetheart, Hog sat, smiling up at Emma, clearly proud of himself.

"What a good, sweet boy," Phyllis said. Patting Hog on the head.

Ned scrambled to his feet. "I told you that dog was a menace and not good for your well-being."

"There's only one menace here who's bad for my well-being," Emma said. "Well, maybe two. Get out."

"Emma—"

"Get out and don't ever come back, Ned."

He straightened his shirt, gave her a long look during which he apparently accurately assessed her feelings for once, and walked to the door. "For what it's worth," he said quietly, "I'm sorry I hurt you." And then he was gone.

Emma nodded to herself, swallowed the lump in her throat, and reminded herself that even if she had no real friends, she still had Hog.

"Emma," Alison said.

Emma buried her face in Hog's thick, furry neck. He smelled like bacon. And faintly of his last fart. "I should've known. Never settle for a man who'd dump you when someone better comes along. Same should go for friends." She dusted herself off. "I'm going to put an 'Out of Order' sticker on my forehead and call it a day. I'm out."

"Hey," Alison said, in front of her now, hands on her hips. "Don't you lump me in with your asshole ex-fiancé and BFF. I'd never hurt you like that."

Emma laughed ironically. "You've been hurting me since high school."

"Okay." Alison nodded. "So we're going there. Fine." She crossed her arms. "Do tell. How did I ever hurt you?"

"For starters, you accused me of cheating."

"And lying," Alison said. "And I stand by that one."

"Funny. That didn't sound like an apology."

"Because it wasn't one." Alison laughed without mirth. "You had everything I didn't, yet you took the college scholarship that should've been mine. And even worse, you, *Miss Goody-Two-Shoes, lied* to get it."

Emma just stared at her in shock. "I did not."

"You had me picked up by the cops and taken to the station for questioning!"

"Because you and your evil mean girl posse scratched BITCH into the side of the car I was driving. *And* popped two tires!"

Alison winced. "That was mob mentality. My so-called friends back then weren't exactly good people. I did try to stop it, but I mean, you owned a BMW, so you were sort of asking for trouble."

"It wasn't my car! It wasn't even my mom's car. It was her boss's car. She was borrowing it because our car had been repo'd."

Alison blinked. "Did not know that."

"My mom had no choice but to call the cops. It got her fired, by the way."

The air seemed to leave Alison's lungs in a rush. "I thought *you* called the cops on me. I got picked up from an assembly in front of the whole school, frog-marched up the center aisle of the auditorium while everyone watched. I hated you for that. I hated you for that for years."

Emma felt her eyes fill with tears, though she had zero idea why. No, that wasn't true. She was sad because she thought she and Alison had been real friends, past forgotten. "Oh, grow up," she said. "You weren't formally charged. I even apologized to my mom's boss so he wouldn't press charges."

Alison's shoulders lowered slightly from where they'd been up at her ears. "*That's* why they let me go? Because you tried to help me after trying to destroy me?"

"I had to talk my parents into it, letting me go talk to her boss to get you off. They were really upset with me. My mom lost her job. The year before, my dad lost his business. It put us in a terrible position."

Alison looked a little sick. "I . . . didn't know about your parents' jobs."

No one had. Emma had been too embarrassed to tell anyone. "How did you think we lost the house?"

"I just thought your parents chose to move off to Florida while you went to college."

"It was more of a necessity than a choice thing." Shit. Emma felt the telltale tingle in her toes. An impending freight train was barreling down on her in the form of a vicious cramp. She sat on the floor.

Alison came closer. "Are you going to cramp?"

"No." Probably, but pride—the current bane of her existence—had her pretending otherwise. "So you've hated me all these years because we were going after the same scholarship?"

"No, I hated you all these years because I got stuck here in Wildstone."

Emma shook her head. Alison. Jealous of her. She never would've believed it. "I don't know what you mean. I didn't steal a scholarship."

"Come on." Alison gave her a get-real look. "You know what you did. When the scholarship committee called the women's center and asked if I worked there, they were told no."

Emma stared at her. "It wasn't me."

"Except it was. You were the one working the front desk. They were told Alison Pratt doesn't work here, period. Not she did work here, got her required hours in, and now is no longer working here. None of that. They were just told nope, no Alison working here."

"I didn't do that!" Emma said.

"She's right." Phyllis stood up from her seat in the sweet yard and cleared her throat. "Because I did it."

Emma and Alison turned to her in shocked unison.

Phyllis grimaced. "I took the call. And technically I didn't lie because you hadn't worked there in over a month when the call came in. And oh yes, I should have clarified."

Both Alison and Emma stared at her.

"That wasn't a very nice thing to do," Emma said quietly, actually feeling sorry for Alison.

"Agreed," Phyllis said. "But to be fair, the woman didn't identify herself as being from the scholarship board until after I said you were gone." She took a deep breath. "But what *was* a shitty thing to do was what I did next. Because even after the woman identified herself, I didn't change my answer or let her know that you *had* worked there." She met Alison's gaze. "You were . . . not a nice girl. You constantly sassed me, talked back, and didn't always show up on time. Frankly, I never gave it another thought, not your family, or what it cost you."

"I *needed* that scholarship," Alison said, voice shaking. "When I lost it, I had to go to a city college at night while working full-time during the day."

Phyllis's eyes went suspiciously shiny. "I'm sorry. I'm so sorry. I know I've been terrible to people. I'm working on that."

Alison looked stricken. "Oh my God. I'm you."

"Well, if that's true, at least you figured out how to change while you're still young. You're nice now. It's taken me a lot longer." Phyllis looked away. "As in until this week."

Alison let out a breath. "I can't blame you for what you did. You were right. I was a terrible teenager." She shook her head. "It wasn't about what anyone did to me. I brought that all on myself. I was standoffish and bitchy and harsh, because that was my defense mechanism. I'm my own worst enemy. Which is no excuse for how I behaved."

"I'm confused," Emma said. "Why didn't you just go to your family for help?"

"Uncle Dale was still dealing with the fallout from Aunt Jenny's death. Simon was in college, and I refused to call him about it because he'd have come back, and at that time, he and Dale weren't okay. They had a lot of baggage and issues. Dale was a bit of a workaholic." Alison paused. "And also a bit of an asshole. Simon didn't come back until his dad's stroke, and that was only because his mom's dying wish had been that he promise to always take care of his dad. Which he's *still* doing, by the way. Luckily, Uncle Dale's mellowed, a lot. Not that it matters. Simon would be taking care of him regardless, because to him, a promise is a promise, never to be taken lightly. He's good like that," Alison said. "Once you're in his life, you stay. He's loyal as hell. He'd never cheat on anyone, but . . ."

"But what?"

"But he won't commit either. He feels he let his mom down, so he's set aside the job he loves more than anything to take on Armstrong Properties and to be Dale's caretaker. I don't see any of that going away anytime soon to clear up room in his life. And I can tell by looking at him that he doesn't either, no matter how much he feels for you."

Emma nodded, feeling suddenly, overwhelmingly sad. "I know."

"You love him."

Emma nodded again. "I do."

Alison looked to be warring with her conscience for a moment. "I'm really sorry I was so mean to you in high school."

"I'm sorry I took your scholarship."

Alison looked down at her tightly clasped fingers. "I'm even more sorry that I called you a practice friend."

Emma lifted a shoulder. "I worked myself up over that, but I just realized something."

"What?"

"It's much more about actions than words with you. And your actions told me you weren't practicing." She met Alison's gaze. "You like me."

Alison rolled her eyes.

"See?" Emma pointed at her. "You do. You like me. *Say* it."

"Seriously?" Alison asked.

"Seriously."

"I'll say it if you acknowledge that I had the higher GPA in high school and should've gotten that scholarship."

"By one-tenth of a point!"

"Still higher than yours," Alison said.

Shit. *True.* "They don't even measure to the one-tenth of a point! In their eyes, we were equal."

Alison shrugged. "Not *exactly* equal."

Emma had to laugh as she yanked Alison into her for a big hug. "Don't freak out; real friends do this too. They also say they like each other. I like you, Ali." She pulled back and waited expectantly.

Alison huffed out a breath. "Fine. I like you, all right? Jeez! But if you tell anyone or make me say it again, the rent on this building is going up."

"Not a chance. You're too cheap to let our rent go up. You—" Emma broke off at the sight of a man outside the large picture window. Jack Swanson. Finally.

"You going to go talk to him this time?" Alison asked. Emma could hear her heartbeat in her ears. "I will." "Today?"

Emma bit her lower lip. "I'm just going to bring up bad memories for him. He lost his wife, Alison."

"I know. And it's awful and tragic, and I wish it hadn't happened. But taking on all the blame? That's just emotion getting the better of you."

Emma was sweating again. And her heart was pounding, echoing in her head. "You can't just discount emotions, no matter how much you resent and try to ignore them."

"Okay, first of all, *ouch*," Alison said. "And second, fine then, so you can't discount emotions. But you can't discount actual facts either. Fact numero uno: you were *not* responsible for everything that happened that night. It was ruled a no-fault. Fact numero dos: you need to go out there and make peace with what happened. Who knows, maybe he needs you to forgive him every bit as much as you need him to forgive you, have you ever thought of that? What if you're *both* scared and only half living?"

"He's *less* than half living," Emma said. Whispered actually, as if Jack could hear her. He couldn't, but he'd stopped walking and they were staring at each other. She couldn't look away. "He's alone and looks . . . sad."

"So you *have* to go out there then." Alison jabbed a finger at the door. "If you won't do it for yourself so that you can fully get over what happened, then do it for him."

Emma bit her lower lip.

"You know I'm right," Alison said. "I'm brilliant, remember? It's street smarts. I had to hone those skills instead of getting book smart."

"Oh my God," Emma said. "I didn't steal the scholarship on purpose!"

"Right. I've been mad about it for so long I forgot. Now hurry before he gets away." Then she gave Emma a nudge that was a whole lot more like a shove.

Emma stepped outside and went stock-still.

Jack wasn't alone this time. A woman had caught up to him, putting her phone in her pocket like she'd just stepped away to take a call. She slipped her hand in Jack's and went up on tiptoes to kiss his jaw.

Swallowing hard, Emma approached them, but stopped a good ten feet away, not sure of her welcome, or what she even thought she was doing. "Jack."

He met her gaze with the same trepidation she knew she wore, but . . . no surprise.

He knew she'd be here.

"Emma," he said. "Hi."

The woman at his side gently let loose of his hand. "I'm going to be right over here so you two can talk." She stepped back while Jack stood there uncertainly.

Emma was going to have to go first. She drew a deep breath. "I've seen you walking by here a few times. I didn't come out because . . . well, I didn't want to . . . intrude."

Jack was shaking his head. "You're not. At all. I'm happy to see you."

"You are?"

"Ever since I realized you were working here, I changed my walking route so that I could try to catch sight of you. I wasn't trying to be a stalker, just wanted to see if you were doing okay."

That was a sweet shock. But something was different about him. It took Emma a moment to realize he was smiling. She said, "You look good."

"I am." Some of his smile dimmed then. "I was hoping the same for you. You're up on your feet, not even a cane or crutch. I hope that means . . . things are back to the way they were? Before that day?" Jack asked this breathlessly, as if he was holding his breath, on pins and needles waiting for her answer.

"Not exactly back to the way they were," she said, then, when he looked tormented, she quickly added,

"No, I mean I don't want them to go back to the way they were. I'm . . . better. I'm good, Jack."

The relief that poured off him was like a balm to her soul. He reached out and grasped Emma's hands in his. "You've lost so much. I've been so worried about you."

"Same." Her throat was almost too thick to speak. "But you lost more, so much more."

Jack shook his head. "That sort of thing . . . it can't be measured or compared." He waited until she looked him in the eyes. "Do you know the hardest part about losing someone? It's not having to say goodbye. It's learning how to live without them, always trying to fill the hole they left in your world, the emptiness where your heart used to be." He paused. Shook his head. "But much as I didn't want it to, life goes on, for everyone. It did for me. I'm okay, Emma. . . ." He gave a small smile. "I'd really like you to be too."

She thought of her physical recovery. How she'd held back, even now. She thought of Simon, and how she'd also held back from him.

Because she hadn't wanted to be all okay until Jack was.

But Jack was okay . . .

"I played a game with myself," Emma admitted. "I couldn't get all the way better until you did. And knowing how much you lost . . ." Her eyes filled. "I couldn't imagine you being all better, no matter how badly I wanted it for you. So I really thought my best days were long behind me."

"Your best days aren't behind you. They're right in front of you. Maria?"

The woman with Jack came up to his side, slipping her arm around his waist, smiling sweetly at Emma. "Maria," he said, "this is Emma. She's the jogger from that day." His breath hitched. "She nearly didn't make it, and now look at her, back on her own two feet."

Maria let out an emotional, happy sound and hugged Emma. "He prays for you every night," she whispered. "He didn't want to be okay until he knew you were."

Emma tried to block her tears, but lost the battle, and nodded. "*Same.*"

Jack's eyes were sparkling with unshed tears too. "We lost a lot, but we survived. And it's okay to live your life." He looked at Maria, brought her hand to his mouth where he brushed a kiss to her palm. "We're engaged."

Emma gasped in sheer happiness. "That's amazing. I'm so happy for you both."

"So now you know. I'm okay, I'm better than okay— which means it's your turn now. No matter what it takes."

"Jack—"

"Do it for me. Do it for *you*. Our lives have been forever changed, but I found closure and so can you. Promise me, Emma," he whispered.

Your best days aren't behind you. They're right in front of you. "I promise." Life was short, so damn short, and Emma suddenly felt so blessed for her second chance. And she wasn't the only one who deserved a second chance. The people in her life . . . Alison, Simon . . . they deserved a second chance too.

She and Jack hugged goodbye, then she turned to go back inside. To her surprise, she found Alison was on the stoop, tears running down her face, making Emma stop short. "Are you . . . crying?"

"No." Alison swiped away her tears. "I've just got something in my eyes."

"You're crying. You *are* a real girl, Pinocchio!"

"Shut up." Alison hooked an arm around Emma's neck and hugged her tight. Emma found herself hugging her back just as tight. Which meant hell had frozen over and also that maybe . . . *maybe* it really was a day for new beginnings.

Chapter 25

Step 25: Reach out.

Simon spent the morning in meetings at Armstrong Properties. It wasn't his favorite thing, managing people. He could do it, he was doing it, but Alison had once told him it was slowly squeezing every last bit of his soul from his body, and he was starting to see that she was right. He'd promised his dad he'd personally handle things, but there had to be another way to do that without losing himself entirely.

He was coming to some other uncomfortable realizations as well. He'd told Emma she wasn't ready for a relationship because she'd stalled her life by holding back on her recovery. The truth was that it was *him* who'd stalled his life.

That made him a complete asshole. He was working on that too.

At two o'clock, he left the offices to meet Ryan on the jobsite of one of Armstrong Properties' newest acquisitions—a building on Commercial Row that had been built in the early 1900s, renovated a few times, but not since the 1980s. It needed a lot of love.

Ryan was the engineer on the project, and a smart choice. He was good, performed timely, never padded his bids, and was always professional.

Today though, he showed up wearing a lazy grin and was looking so chill and laid-back, Simon was tempted to check him for a pulse. "What's with you?"

Ryan grinned. "Life's good again, man."

Simon shook his head. He'd gotten to the barbecue late and Ryan and Alison had already vanished. Together. "I'm happy for you guys. Is it going to work out this time?"

"Yeah, it is. Second time's the charm. You ought to try it. With Emma."

Simon turned and looked at the building's rough interior, not seeing any of it. Instead he saw Emma standing on his roof, looking at him with her entire heart in her eyes . . . right before *he'd* destroyed them both. "Sometimes you don't get a second chance."

"Only if you're a dumbass."

"Gee, thanks."

"Truth hurts. You Armstrongs are so over-the-top stubborn you can't get out of your own way. You look for love to be easy, or forsake it entirely. Love isn't easy, nowhere even close. But it's worth the work."

"It's not about the work."

"No?" Ryan asked. "So you didn't look for the easy out and take it by walking away?"

Simon's temper stirred. "Are you kidding me? That was the hardest thing I've ever done."

"Yeah? So how's living without her going for you?" Ryan waited a beat. "Look, go to her. Apologize straight-out, and not the kind of apology where you dress up your mistake with a rationalization to make it look like you were not really wrong, just misunderstood. Women see right through that shit."

"Okay, you know what? We're going to work now." He unrolled the plans and they went over the job. An hour later, Simon left to take his dad for a checkup on his wrist. The doctor had wanted a new X-ray to see if there was healing happening. Should've been easy, but like everything with his dad, easy never came into it.

First Dale refused to sit in the waiting room while Simon checked him in. Wanted to do it himself. It wasn't worth the argument, so Simon stood back a few feet pretending to look at the magazine rack on the wall while his dad checked in.

"I'm here to get my cast off," Dale told the receptionist.

Simon bit his tongue rather than move in and correct his dad, which would only start a disagreement.

"Name?" the receptionist asked.

"Simon Armstrong."

Simon leaned in. "He means Dale Armstrong."

His dad frowned. "That's what I said."

"You said Simon Armstrong," the receptionist said.

"Why would I say my son's name?" Dale asked in a grumble. "I'm Dale. I'm here to get my cast off."

"She's got it, Dad."

"I do," the receptionist said, eyes on her screen. "I show this as a wellness check."

"No, I want the cast off," Dale said.

"Dad, let's wait and see what the doc says, okay?"

"No, it's not okay. I want the cast off. And you're not the boss of me." Then he huffed his way over to a seat and plopped into it.

Simon drew a deep breath and headed over there. They sat in silence for five minutes before Dale spoke. "I just don't like when my mouth and my brain don't connect."

"I know."

"You'll see for yourself soon enough. Terrible horrible death is coming for all of us."

Simon sighed. "How about we concentrate on the fact it hasn't come yet. Can we do that?"

Dale shrugged. "Maybe, if there's pizza after this. And then I need to go to Paw Pals. I promised Alison and Emma I'd work today."

"Work" being that Alison and Emma would watch over Dale while pretending not to, and Dale would hang out and greet people or sit in the sweet or salty yard and play with the dogs. It'd been the highlight of his days.

"Son, you know I love you, right?"

Simon sighed. "Yeah, Dad. I know."

"Good. Do you know you also deserve to be happy? Your mom wouldn't want the promise she extracted from you to mean you don't get your happy."

"Dad—"

"How long are you going to be stupid about Emma?"

Simon looked over at his dad. "Excuse me?"

"Yeah, I heard you dumped her. Which actually makes you an asshole on top of stupid."

The receptionist slid her head out her glass window and gave Dale a hard look. "Mr. Armstrong, please watch your language."

"Yes, ma'am," he said politely, then looked at Simon. "You do know that girl is your better half, right?"

"Thanks, Dad."

"I mean it, son. She puts up with your shit, she puts up with my shit, she puts up with Alison's shit, and on top of all that, she's the magic behind your smile. Son, you don't get rid of your magic. You keep it. You treasure it, for always."

The receptionist glared at Dale, who lifted his hands in apology. He turned to Simon. "You deserve a lot too. Look, son, different angle. You know how my life is different now. You see it, right? That I'm different because of it."

Simon nodded. "And?"

"And . . . it would be stupid for me to choose to try and do things I could do before the strokes. Not only would I fail, I don't want to do those same things anymore. You get me?"

Yeah. Simon did. He'd asked Emma to become the same person as before the accident. Not only couldn't she do that, she didn't want to.

"Mr. Armstrong?" the receptionist called. "The doctor will see you now."

An hour later, Simon walked his dad into Paw Pals, still thinking about what his dad had said. "Is Emma here?" he asked Marco.

"No, she's out. But Alison's here."

Simon put Dale in the chair by the big picture window. He was balancing his personal-size pizza and Killer on his lap. "Don't feed any of that to her."

"Killer loves pizza."

"But pizza doesn't love her."

Dale smiled. "True. She gets pepperoni farts." He looked at Killer. "Same, dude. Same."

Miss Kitty helped herself to a piece of pizza just as Alison peeked out from the back, wearing the exact same glow Ryan had been wearing.

"Where's Emma?" Simon asked her.

"Don't you mean 'hi, cuz, how great to see you'?"

"Yes," he said. "That. Now where's Emma?"

"PT with Kelly. And also, you're stupid."

"No doubt, but is there any reason in particular?"

"Because you broke things off with Emma under false pretenses. You said she wasn't ready for a relationship, simply because she wasn't trying to get her old life back."

"I know."

"Simon, she doesn't want her *old* life back! Why are us Armstrongs so damn slow? She wants *this* life, her new life. And you don't get to decide if that's good enough."

"I said I know."

But Alison was all wound up and still talking. "People change, Simon. And sometimes what looks good to you in the moment won't look good a year later. You wronged her, and you want to know how I know? Because *I* did the same thing. I used her as a practice friend. Who does that? Me. I did that to her. I was an asshole. Don't be me. Emma's not a practice anything. She's the real deal, and you know what else? *You* deserve the real deal too, Simon."

She was right. Not about him deserving the real deal. That was still up for debate. Nope, she was right that Emma wasn't a practice anything and she deserved more. And he wanted to be the man to give her that more. "I know, Alison. I know all of it, especially where and how I screwed up."

"Oh." She took a breath. "Okay, then. As long as you know."

"What time was her appointment?"

She glanced at the clock. "She's probably almost done at PT. I told her to go home after, that I'd close up today. Leave Dale here with me."

"You sure?"

Alison softened, then hugged him. "Just go fix things with her." She put a finger in his face. "And don't screw it up."

"I won't." Or so he hoped.

Simon drove home, went straight to the second floor, and knocked at Emma's door. He felt himself being watched through the peephole and did his best to look like the one thing she couldn't live without.

She finally opened the door to him, though he had no illusions the battle was won. "Hey," he said, smiling at just the sight of her. Hog was at her side, his tail going a mile a minute.

Emma was showing nothing, but she also didn't shut the door on his nose.

He'd take that. "Can we talk?"

She shrugged. "As long as it's not about your opinion on my life and how I live it."

He looked her straight in the eyes. "I shouldn't have said what I did. I shouldn't have said a lot of things. I'm sorry, Emma."

She stared at him for a long beat, then shifted aside and gestured him in. She wore his wool throw, the one that always was on the back of the couch. He'd never used it, not once, but it'd been in his mom's cedar chest at the foot of her bed, and he'd kept it. It was one of the few things he had of hers that he'd known she'd loved.

It looked good on Emma, and he wondered what was beneath it. All he could see were her bare feet.

She looked like the rest of his life.

When Simon didn't move, Emma cocked her head. "You okay?"

"Better now." And he'd never meant anything more. She was standing close enough to him that he could see the light reflected in her eyes. Her hair was unruly and defiant around her face. She was beautiful, from her vibrant stare to her sexy mouth. Reaching out, he traced her waist to pull her closer.

At his touch, she softened and drew a deep breath. "Damn," she whispered.

"Yeah." He knew exactly what she meant, and he groaned when she stepped into his arms. The hug was something he hadn't known he needed, even more so when she curled close to him, offering comfort. He hadn't realized he even needed that in his life, but he did. He needed her. Until this moment, he could never have imagined such an intimate embrace that had nothing to do with lust, and yet somehow was *everything*.

Emma took him by the hand and drew him down onto the couch. "Before you say whatever it is you wanted to talk to me about, I missed your friendship."

Simon took his first deep breath since he'd seen her last. "Me too."

Her eyes never left his. "So we can go back to that?"

It killed him that she thought they were no longer friends—which was all on him. "Yes, please." He also wanted a whole lot more than that.

She nodded. "Is your dad okay?"

Even now, she was thinking of him first . . . He did not deserve her, but he was going to give it everything he had to make it up to her and prove that he could change and be the right man for her. "He's good. Though today's doctor visit was a complete shit show. He told his doctor that she needed to take his cast off because he had a hot date and he's right-handed in the sack."

Emma laughed. It was the sweetest sound he'd heard in days.

"He also asked if they gave out free condoms." He gave a wry smile. "I might never recover."

She was still laughing. "What did you do?"

"What could I do? After the doc, I took him to buy condoms and pizza."

"That explains the phone call I got from Alison just before you arrived. She said your dad was making animal balloons to hang around the entryway. From condoms."

Simon grimaced. "Sorry."

"Don't be. It all worked out. Mrs. Bessler had come by, and according to Marco, she convinced your dad that *she* needed the condoms. She said she had her eye on one of her neighbors."

Jesus. "Is that neighbor named Dale Armstrong?"

"Pretty sure."

"God help me." He took her hand in his. Met her still slightly wary gaze. "I hope you know you're the best thing that's happened to me all week. Hell, all year."

"You really *did* miss me," she said, her dark eyes warming up.

"More than I can say, although I'd like to try. Is that okay, Em? Can we talk? Like really talk?"

No hesitation this time. She nodded just as a tea-kettle began to whistle from the kitchen.

"I'll get it." Simon moved into the kitchen and turned off the flame, pouring the hot water over the tea bag in the waiting mug. As he did, his eyes caught on the stacks of paperwork spread out over the table. Bills.

"Pour yourself some tea too," Emma called out. "It's a de-stressor."

He doubted a tea could ever de-stress him. In fact, his stress rose a notch when he realized that all the bills she had in this particular stack were marked either

Past Due or Final Notice. He drew a deep breath and flipped through them. X-rays, radiology, blood work, labs, doctors . . . "Have you heard back from your insurance company on your surgery?"

"No. Will you add sugar too?"

He stared down at her insurance policy payment, also past due. "You mean will I add tea to your sugar? Yes." Hating how underwater she was, he racked his brain for a way to help her, knowing she'd never accept financial help. "One of our tenants is an attorney," he said. "I could ask him to—"

"Thanks, but no. I've already spoken to two different lawyers. I don't have the money right now to hear the same verdict. I'm fine, Simon. It's not that bad."

He had no idea what her barometer was for "not that bad," but it was a far different barometer than his. He knew she'd used her settlement to buy her half of Paw Pals. He also knew Paw Pals was in the black, but she wasn't going to get rich anytime soon. He eyed the bills again, and suddenly he knew how he could help. The solution was right in front of him and had been all along. Just thinking about it had a peace settling over him. And, he could admit, excitement. Smiling, he poured the hot water over the tea bag, added her sugar, and walked out to the living room.

———

Emma watched Simon come toward her. With his build, he filled any space he was in, and she sucked in a breath because just looking at him did things to her. She'd missed him, so much. Not enough to let him off the hook though. Nope, Emma 2.0 didn't beg for love. Still, she couldn't look away from him. He seemed to have the same problem, which was gratifying. The throw had fallen to her hips, but in spite of the fact that she was wearing only a white tank and a pair of teeny boy-shorts panties, his eyes stayed locked on hers. Until she smiled at him.

Once she did that, his gaze warmed and he let it drift slowly over her, taking in the sight of her, turning his hazel eyes from warm to scorching.

Good. If she couldn't have him, she was damn glad he at least knew what he was missing.

"Cute pj's." He set the mug on the coffee table, pointing at Hog to mind his own business when the dog lifted his big head, seeming interested in sampling the tea. Hog sighed and went back to sleep.

Simon sat on the coffee table in front of Emma. "I know you don't want help."

Still feeling the surge of heat from the pj's comment, not to mention his close proximity, her brain wasn't working at full capacity. "What?"

He took one of her hands. "I was a jerk the other night on the roof. I'm sorry."

"You were actually right. I couldn't let myself heal all the way." She met his gaze. "I talked to Jack. He was able to move on from the accident and has gotten himself a really nice life. It's like knowing that gave me permission to do the same."

"You deserve that," he said softly, gently squeezing her hand. "So much."

"I guess I've been a little slow on the uptake."

He gave a shake of his head. "Actually, I'm the slow one here. Emma, can you ever forgive me for being so stupid when it comes to you?"

"You weren't. You were . . ."

"*Stupid*," he repeated.

"Okay, maybe a little bit." She smiled, liking this vulnerable side of him, aching in the very best of ways that he was sharing it with her. "Scared too."

He let out a rough laugh. "Yeah."

"So . . ." Her smile faded and she voiced *her* fear. "You're not those things anymore?"

"Oh, I'm still scared. Scared that you won't believe me when I say I want you to be happy, whatever you decide to do with your life. I told you once you were in the driver's seat." He flashed a self-deprecating smile. "I'm going to learn to stop backseat driving. I hope you can forgive me."

Unable to access her words for the emotion swamping her, Emma took their joined hands and pressed them to her heart. "Already done," she whispered.

Simon's eyes were solemn. Fiercely intense. "Don't let me off the hook too easily, Emma. You deserve—"

"Already done," she repeated softly.

They reached for each other, hands grappling, not stopping until she was on his lap and straddling him. The first touch of their lips was almost a query, as if they needed to make sure they were both on the same page. Good news—they were. Their second kiss went nuclear, but Simon stopped them before they lost any clothes, which was a huge bummer.

"I got distracted," he said, not breathing all that steadily, which gave her a rush. "We were talking about your medical coverage. I could—"

"We weren't talking, we were kissing."

"But I can help—"

Emma put a finger over his mouth. And still breathing hard from the kiss, she managed, "I'm going to stop you right there." She pulled away. "I saw my doctor yesterday, and my PT today. Also talked to my health care advocate and my parents—who, by the way, *only* talk about this. Nothing else, *ever.* So while it's very sweet of you to try and help, I just want to have a night off from all that with someone who cares about me. Can you be that person or not?"

"Yes, of course, but—"

Done with this line of talk, Emma let the blanket fall to the floor. Taking in the view, Simon groaned and reached for her, running his big, warm hands over her body, making her feel things she'd forgotten she could.

"Emma." He buried his face in her hair. "God, I missed you. So fucking much."

She opened her mouth to say she'd missed him too, but once again her brain disconnected and acted independently, and what came out was, "I love you, Simon."

She froze. And so did he. She closed her eyes but it was the damn truth. She loved him. But she hadn't intended to put it out there, and certainly hadn't meant to say it first, before she knew his feelings.

In the space between her heartbeats, she could hear Hog snoring, the TV soft in the background, the cadence of Simon's heart. All so normal, when what she felt was anything but.

Simon slid out from beneath her and dropped to his knees, cupping her face as he looked into her eyes, his own brimming with emotion. "Marry me, Emma."

Her eyes flew open. She stared at him. "Did you really just . . . ?"

"Yes. Which is what I hope you're about to say."

"Oh my God." *Marry him.* The idea took hold and she felt her eyes well up, but she was also laughing. "You know my last engagement didn't work out so well for me."

"So let's skip the engagement. Let's just do it. I don't have a ring yet, but we can do that tomorrow and be married by the weekend."

She laughed.

He didn't, and a sense of unease began to spread through her. "That sounds . . . great, but I'd really want my parents to be here, and they'd have to fly in. And I'd need time to get a dress . . . A few months at least." She smiled. "Besides, what's the rush? A piece of paper doesn't matter to me, just knowing we're together is the good part."

"But if we got married now, before the end of the second quarter, then I'd be able to get you on my insurance in the third quarter, and you could get your procedure back on the books. And with my coverage, there's almost no copay."

She shook her head, confused. "Why are we talking about my procedure in the same sentence as marriage?"

"Because the marriage will allow my insurance to cover your procedure."

Emma's world stopped turning on its axis and she felt herself tremble because she was suddenly cold to the bone. Standing, she wrapped the blanket around her tightly, feeling like her heart had just been sliced in half. Right. She loved Simon. But he hadn't said it. He was just trying to take care of her, which, okay, was sweet, but entirely misguided.

Hog padded over to her, watching her face carefully before pushing up against her legs with a soft whine.

Simon stood up too and held the blanket closed for her. "This is something that's easy for me to do, and it protects you."

She held up a hand. "Just to be clear," she said, not giving away any of her sudden urge to beat him over the head with a couch cushion. "You're proposing to me so I'll be covered by your insurance."

"It's the solution to all your problems," Simon said.

Look at him with all the answers. "Yeah," she said tightly, holding on to her composure by a thread. "Except one—*you proposing to me for insurance reasons.*"

"It'd get you the surgery—"

"Oh my God." The man had lost his mind. "I'm not marrying you for insurance coverage, Simon! I'd rather stay exactly as I am."

"But—"

"No." Damn, she never knew she could be so hurt and mad at the same time. No, that wasn't actually true, was it? She just never thought she'd be here in this state again. She'd learned nothing. "The last guy I was engaged to, the *second* things got difficult, he bailed. And now you're offering to marry me for the insurance. So tell me, Simon, how's that going to last, if love couldn't?"

"We love each other," he said.

There it was, but somehow it no longer mattered. Hog was licking her toes. Apparently he loved her too. She nodded, her throat so tight it hurt to talk. "The answer's still no." She went to storm out before remembering she was in her own apartment. So she yanked open the front door. "Please go."

Simon moved toward her. "Emma—"

"I want to be alone."

He opened his mouth, but she was done. She gave him a nudge over the doorsill and shut the door on his sexy, handsome, confused face.

Chapter 26

Step 26: Trust.

Emma took an Uber to Alison's place. By the time the driver pulled to the curb, she was crying so hard she could hardly see.

Alison opened the door before she knocked. "He's such an idiot. Come in."

"You know?"

"Yeah. He called to tell me what he did and I hung up on him for you."

Emma choked out a laugh as she followed Alison inside, where they went straight to the kitchen. Alison pulled a bottle of vodka from the freezer and grabbed two shot glasses.

They each tossed back a shot and Emma let out a pained breath as it burned all the way down, matching the fire already in her chest. "Okay, I feel a little better."

"Liar."

"Yeah." What Simon had done had hurt her worse than everything she'd been through: the last year of recovery and physical therapy, losing the two people closest to her, having to change careers . . . *everything*. "I'm fine."

"Then why are you still crying?"

"Dammit." Emma covered her face. "I'm afraid I'll never be able to stop. I thought it was real."

"It *was* real. It *is* real. His intentions are good, Emma, even if his timing and delivery sucked. He loves you."

Emma shook her head. "A person who loves you doesn't propose for monetary reasons. They propose because they love you so much they can't imagine living another moment without you being theirs."

Alison sat down next to her. "Okay, far be it from me to pretend to be an expert here, but play along with me. Maybe he really does love you, and he did what he did because he's terrified of people walking out on him. If he told himself he was proposing to help you out with your surgery and it didn't work out . . . well, that wouldn't hurt as bad as proposing for love alone, only to find out you don't love him enough to say yes."

"I *do* love him enough. I love him more than I've ever loved anyone."

"Ouch," Alison said in a teasing tone, hand to her heart.

"I'm serious."

"I know. And this is serious. But some people"—Alison coughed and said "Armstrongs" at the same time—"need to hear 'I love you' more than once for it to sink in and really believe it."

Emma just stared at her. "If I say something, I mean it."

"Yes, but not *everyone* means it. Simon's heard it before and then still been walked away from."

Emma had known this, but she'd compartmentalized it. She'd taken the time to think about how her past relationships affected her, but she hadn't thought about how *Simon*'s past relationships might've affected him.

"Emma—"

She held up her hand. "Processing. Hold, please."

Alison gave her a minute, but apparently that was her limit. "In my family, we show our love by taking care of people. Think about all Simon's done for the people in his life. For *you*, including giving up his apartment, trying to marry you so you'd be protected by his insurance . . . He's a guy of action, Emma, not words."

"And I love the actions. But I need the words too. Ned was all actions: romantic dinners, flowers, picnics . . .

plenty of actions. But he never gave me any words at all. He didn't even have the words to say 'oh, by the way, our bed is now the bed I'm in with your former best friend.'" Emma shook her head. "I don't want to be taken care of, I want to be loved."

"I'm a dumbass," Simon said, voice husky with emotion.

Emma whipped around to stare at him.

"A complete dumbass," he said again, coming closer, until he stood before her, more serious than she'd ever seen him. "Regardless of the stupid way I went about it, I wasn't proposing so I could take care of you, or because it was the right thing to do. I *wasn't* trying to save you. Seriously, Emma, you're the strongest woman I know. You've inspired me with your grace, your fire, your spirit. You don't need me to save you, you don't need anyone. I just want to be with you, at your side. Not as your crutch, but as the guy who's lucky enough to be loved by you. Because nothing's ever felt so right as being with you. I realize I did this backward, so let me fix that right now. I love you, Emma, to my soul and back. Period. I want to spend the rest of my life with you because I can't imagine it without you in it."

"Now see, *that's* the way to propose," Alison said. "Good to know us Armstrongs can eventually figure our shit out."

Simon took his cousin by the hand and then pushed her out of the room.

"Hey, it's my kitchen!"

Ignoring this, Simon shut the door and walked back to Emma.

"I'm going to be listening!" Alison said through the door.

"And that's something else I should have mentioned," Simon said, never taking his gaze off Emma. "My family, they're a lot."

"Oh my God," Alison said. "I feel like I suddenly understand Ryan's family on a core level. Who knew?"

Simon lifted a hand to the door, like *See? A lot.*

Emma snorted, and Simon smiled. "God, I love when you look at me like that, like you're trying to crawl into my head. That's always been thrilling." He cupped her face. "And also, if I'm being honest, unnerving. No one's ever done that before. It's probably what made it easy for me to hold back. But with you . . ." He shook his head like he was a little awestruck. "Have you ever loved someone so much that when they smile at you, your heart stops? Because that's how it is with you, Emma, from the first day I met you. You look at me like no one else ever has. You see the real me. You call me out on my bullshit. Even now, your beautiful eyes are holding me accountable, analyzing me without even trying to hide your own thoughts. Do you know how amazing that is?"

She slowly shook her head. "I didn't know I was doing all that. I don't know how to be any different."

"I'm glad." Simon paused, and his smile faded. "My life isn't my own. There's my dad. Armstrong Properties. And both those things are pretty demanding of my time. You'd have to be okay with that, which is something I can't ask of you."

Emma could see Simon really was expecting her to turn and walk out the door. Her heart squeezed hard because she couldn't blame him. It'd happened to him before. "Okay," she said.

He was very, very still. "Okay?"

"Okay, I'm in. Dale's your family, and you're mine. Family looks after family."

He caught her hand and a second later she was plastered against his warm, hard body. His kiss burned with a gentle intensity, sending a trickle of molten lava into her belly and straight down. When he pulled back, he brushed a kiss to her temple. "I need you to be sure."

"I am. I want you in my life, Simon. At my back, at my side, stand wherever you want, just as long as you're mine."

Simon smiled. "That's already done. I'm yours."

"Seems fair, since I'm yours too." Her eyes went all misty again. "Simon?"

"Anything, Emma. Name it."

"Will you marry me?"

"Wait, I get to be maid of honor, right?" Alison yelled through the door. "I've always wanted one of those stupid overpriced bridesmaids' dresses!"

Ignoring his cousin, Simon hauled Emma in close. "Yes, I'll marry you. Tomorrow, next week, next year. Whenever you want."

They were kissing when Alison spoke again. "What am I supposed to do now?"

"Go away," Simon said.

"How long do you need?"

Simon smiled down into Emma's face. "The rest of my life . . ."

Emma's heart caught but she nodded. "That sounds like just the right amount of time . . ."

Epilogue

One year later

Emma's heart was pounding through her ears. She could feel sweat dripping between her breasts. Her lungs, taxed beyond endurance, refused to draw in another breath. So she stopped short, bent over, and put her hands on her thighs to gasp for air.

This was silly. She had only a quarter of a mile left. In fact, she could see the finish line on the beach ahead, flags blowing in the breeze, and a crowd gathered to cheer on the winner.

Except the winner had crossed the finish line a long time ago.

In fact, she was the very last one left in the 5K.

Trying not to care about that, she sucked in another breath. She'd insisted on doing this race alone, refusing to let anyone do it with her. Simon had understood, but she knew he'd been bummed. Not Alison. She'd pumped her fist with relieved victory.

But now the big day had finally arrived and she'd gotten through two-thirds of the race. The muscles in her legs were quaking like Jell-O, and suddenly she wasn't sure she could do this. But then a set of running shoes appeared on either side of hers, one male, one female.

"Hey, babe. Whatcha doing?"

Emma turned her head and, still bent over, looked up at Simon. "Oh, you know, just hanging out."

He grinned. "Looking good."

"Which is *really* annoying, bee-tee-dub." This from Alison, on her other side. "I've taken, what, maybe fifty steps, and my hair's already flat to my head and my mascara's running. The least you could do is look like you were in a coma two years ago."

Emma laughed wryly and straightened. "Why would you wear makeup to a 5K?"

"Why wouldn't you?"

Emma started walking. Maybe she couldn't run the rest of the way, but now that she wasn't alone, she'd crawl over the finish line if she had to.

Simon took her hand in his, gently squeezed, and when she looked up at him, his smile dazzled. "Proud of you, Em."

Yeah. She was kind of proud of herself too.

"Damn, this is hard work," Alison said. "Hey, Si, give me a piggyback ride like you used to do when we were kids."

"Maybe if you still weighed sixty-five pounds."

"Rude." Alison tossed her hair. "And anyway, technically, I'm your boss now, so you should have to do what I say."

A year ago, the same week Emma and Simon had gotten engaged, he'd promoted Alison to CEO of Armstrong Properties. Thrilled, she'd taken the job, but still kept up with Paw Pals, which thankfully was doing better than expected. Emma was so proud of its success.

"Actually," Simon said, "since I'm no longer working at Armstrong, you're not my boss at all."

"Oh yeah," Alison said. "That sucks. Do you have any idea how much I wanted to be the boss of you for a change? But no, you had to be your own boss by buying half of Kelly's PT clinic when she got overwhelmed and went looking for a partner."

"And now he's getting to do what he loves," Emma said, not nearly as breathless now. She smiled at Simon, who leaned in and brushed a kiss to her damp temple.

"I'm most definitely doing what I love, and *who* I love," he said, which made Emma laugh.

"Disgusting," Alison said and rolled her eyes, but she couldn't hide the fact that she was clearly pleased for them. It didn't hurt that she was wearing a big, fat diamond ring on *that* finger from Ryan. No date had been set yet. According to Alison, the date might never be set. They were happy and content to be engaged. All Alison had ever wanted was to feel loved, and there was no doubt Ryan made her feel very loved.

Emma looked down at her own ring.

"How you doing, Mrs. Armstrong?" Simon asked her.

"She's doing great," Alison said. "Just look at her. It's been a year and she's still wearing the newlywed glow."

"It's sweat." But Emma smiled. It'd been a year exactly. In fact, today was her and Simon's anniversary. There were certainly more romantic things to do than this, but after her hopefully final surgery six months ago, this felt right. She'd gotten the notion that by trying this race on her own, it would prove something to herself, like her life hadn't really changed at all, and she could still do whatever she wanted.

And she supposed that was still true. She *could* do whatever she wanted. Just not in the way she'd expected. It wasn't about winning, she'd realized. It was about finishing.

That was all she had to do. Finish.

The sound of cheers had her lifting up her head. While lost in reflection, she'd crossed the finish line.

She turned around and found Simon and Alison going around the flags, not through.

Through was only for the participants.

Simon reached her first and scooped her up, laughing as he kissed her. "You did it. Do you know what this means?"

"That I need you to give me a three-hour massage?"

"Gladly, but it also means you can do anything. *Anything*, Emma."

"Good." She slid her hands into his hair and tugged his face back to hers. "Because I know what I want to do now."

"Ew," Alison said, coming up to their side.

"I meant food." Emma cupped Simon's face. "Food, please," she begged. "I'm so starving my stomach is eating itself."

"What kind of food?" Alison asked. "There are a lot of choices."

Simon smiled into Emma's eyes. "Choices are always good."

"Yes." Emma kissed him, pouring her emotions into it. Surprise that she'd found this precious thing she hadn't been looking for. Joy that it was real, that he felt it too. Hunger for more. "And you're the best choice I ever made, Simon."

"Right back at you, babe."